CLAIMING TUESDAY

THE NEXT GENERATION
BOOK 4

RILEY EDWARDS

Claiming Tuesday
The Next Generation

This is a work of fiction. Names, characters, businesses, places, events, and incidents are either the products of the author's imagination or used in a fictitious manner. Any resemblance to actual persons, living or dead, or actual events is purely coincidental.

Copyright © 2022 by Riley Edwards

All rights reserved. This book or any portion thereof may not be reproduced or used in any manner whatsoever without the express written permission of the publisher except for the use of brief quotations in a book review.

Cover design: Lori Jackson Designs

Written by: Riley Edwards

Published by: Riley Edwards/Rebels Romance

Edited by: Eve Arroyo

Proofreader: Julie Deaton, Kendall Barnett

Book Name: Claiming Tuesday

Paperback ISBN: 978-1-7339667-3-3

First edition: **April 30, 2019**

Copyright © 2022 Riley Edwards

To my family - my team – my tribe.
This is for you.

CONTENTS

CLAIMING TUESDAY AUDIO

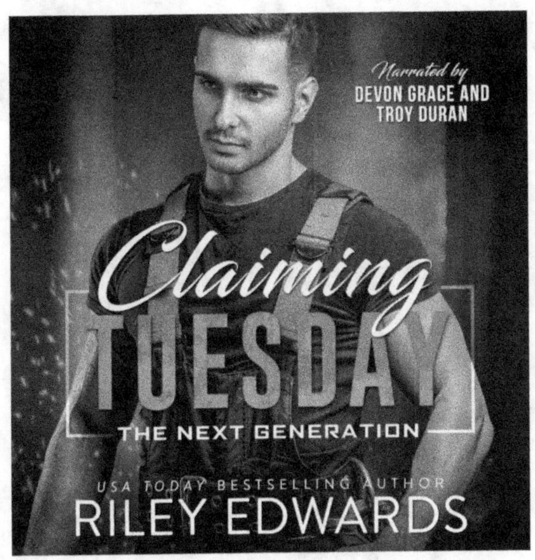

Performed By: Troy Duran & Devon Grace

PROLOGUE

"Tuesday! Put that down," my mother snapped.

I looked down at the donut in my hand and wondered what Mother would do if I quickly shoved the chocolate frosted goodness into my mouth. I bet she'd run across the room and tackle me before the delectable cream filled pastry passed my lips. The thought made me smile, and I didn't have much to smile about those days. Nothing would give me more pleasure than a wrestling match with my mother, all in the name of milk-chocolate-covered-fried-dough-confection treats.

Gladys Knowls did not run and she certainly didn't tackle.

That would be unladylike.

Beneath her.

Classless.

"What will one treat hurt?" my dad asked her.

"She has a fitting this afternoon before we leave. The five extra pounds she has on now is enough."

My dad's face got red, though he wouldn't argue further. He never did. My mother's word was law. The only person she couldn't boss around was my grandmother. Gladys was no match for my dad's mom, Patty. My grandmother had politely put her in her place for years. She was also one of the two people in this world that loved me, her and Pop, that was it.

I put the donut down, knowing there was no use trying to sneak it. My mom had already counted the delicious looking pastries. She counted everything in the house. I had to be weighed first thing in the morning and again before I went to bed. If the scale moved, Gladys would check my food journal and adjust it accordingly. At some point, all I'd be left with was a handful of nuts.

"Tuesday. Finish gathering your belongings. We're leaving in ten minutes."

Always barking orders. Giving commands. Would it kill her to say please?

"Are you sure this is necessary, darling? She's already missed a month of school."

"What else would you have her do, George? She's not very smart, average grades are not going to get her into a good university. Where will she go? Embarrass the family name and attend a community college? Unless you want her living off us or your parents' money for the rest of her life, this is all she has."

"But—"

"Don't argue with me, George. Modeling is the only thing she's good at. Agents take one look at her and fall over themselves to book her. She pulls in top dollar."

My mother was right. I was an average student and casting directors *would* pay top dollar.

That was the sum of my worth.

A golden ticket for my mother.

Nothing else.

1

Shiiit!

I gripped my steering wheel and slammed on the brakes. Rubber was burning, and I waited for the sound of crunching metal but, thankfully, I barely kissed the bumper of the canary yellow Porsche 911 in front of me.

Thank God.

Incidentally, the car had braked to avoid hitting a goddamned squirrel. Normally I would have applauded the driver's efforts, even admire saving the furry, little rodent's life. But, hello, you didn't go from sixty to zero in three point five seconds, *in* traffic, on a busy road.

I'd been too busy rolling my eyes at the Porsche's "all-mine" vanity plates, which had now disappeared from my sight considering our bumpers were touching.

His very expensive one to my not so expensive one, I'd completely missed the car behind until the sound of squealing tires had my eyes going to my rearview mirror and . . . bam! There went my back bumper. *Well, fuck me running.* Metal crunched, my body jerked, and I was really unhappy I was now paying for more than a scratch on the luxury sports car. The bumpers were no longer kissing, they were making-the-fuck-out.

Dammit.

I hoped the furry, little fucker that had scampered away unscathed had a nest full of baby squirrels because this was not how I pictured my Monday. The banging on my window pulled me from thoughts of nests and really bad Monday mornings, and I found Mr. 911 standing outside of my car with his arms crossed over his suit jacket looking pissed.

Pissed? At me? Um. No.

He yanked my door open, I jerked back in surprise, and he immediately laid into me, "I hope you have insurance." He pointed to his Porsche. "Do you have any idea how much that's going to cost?"

Yes, douchebag, I know you drive an expensive car.

"You better have fucking insurance," he snapped.

Maybe I'd bumped my head really hard and was hallucinating.

"Are you listening to me?"

Was he for real?

He was standing on a busy road yelling at me for scratching—okay, it was more than a scratch—his precious Porsche, as cars were trying to maneuver around the accident that he'd caused. It was morning rush hour and there were a lot of damn cars, not that he cared. All this asshole was worried about was a hunk of yellow metal.

It was then I took the man in. Really looked at him, from top to toe, and I understood his need for a flashy sports car. If a man was ever trying to compensate for a small penis, it was Mr. 911. He was short, had a gut, and was balding. Yeah, he needed the Porsche to get laid. Asshole.

I stepped out of my car and my anger got the best of me. "Listen, you jerkwad. You slammed on your brakes. You caused all of this. You should be asking me if I'm all right. But you're more concerned about your metal manhood over there than to have a little human decency." I stabbed my finger in the direction of his car.

Undeterred, he carried on, his face getting redder by the second. "I'm gonna sue you if you don't have insurance."

Was it too late for me to close my eyes and throw my hands in the air while I sang, "Jesus Take the Wheel"? I was right in the middle of praying for some patience when I heard sirens wailing, the sound unfortunately, wasn't loud enough to drown out the man, who was yelling at me again.

"Answer me," he demanded.

"You caused this three-car pileup, not me. The question is, do you have insurance?"

Deciding it was best to ignore the idiot flailing his arms as the buttons on his suit jacket were being tested to the max as his movements and his gut threatened to pop them off. Maybe one would break free and hit me in the eye, then I could sue *him* for damages and mental distress.

I surveyed the smashed vehicles and decided I needed a new car. My old VW Jetta had seen better days. Even before it'd been smooshed between the Porsche and Honda Civic. The car was a decade old and it was beyond time to put my old girl out to pasture. I'd been procrastinating. I hated car shopping and I loved my little Jetta. It had been the first thing I'd purchased with my own money. Now, she was a wrinkled mess, and I had no choice.

Damn! Why do Mondays suck?

I glanced at the Honda and saw a teenage boy in the driver's seat, eyes closed, and head resting back. I walked over and gently tapped on the glass. The boy slowly opened his eyes and looked over at me.

"You all right?" I asked as I opened the kid's door.

He nodded. Damn, the boy looked like he had tears welling in his baby blues. Poor guy.

"Are you hurt?"

"No. Not yet anyway. But my dad's gonna kill me."

The teenager started to unbuckle but I stopped him. "Whoa there, cowboy. You sure you're not hurt? Maybe you should wait in your car." As if on cue the first responders swarmed en masse, stopping not far from the accident.

What a clusterfuck. Cars were still trying to swerve around the mangled mess in their pursuit to get to work on time. Unfortunately, we were in the middle of the three-lane highway, making their quest difficult. This totally sucked, but, thankfully, no one had been injured.

"My dad's gonna kill me," the boy repeated.

"He should. You weren't paying attention. This is your fault."

My head whipped in Mr. 911's direction and I snapped. "Oh, shut the hell up. First it was my fault, now it's his?" I pointed to the kid still in his car. "When the truth is, it's yours. You slammed on your goddamn brakes to let a fuckin' squirrel cross the road. I'm all for wildlife rescue, friend. But when you're traveling sixty, you don't decide now is the time to take up a save the critters crusade, you stupid fuck. You're more concerned about your damn car than you are the people you could've hurt. You do not get to yell at this kid, he did nothing wrong. And when I talk to his dad, I'm gonna make sure he knows why his son is sitting on the side of the road, instead of on his way to school. And that's because some small-penis prick, with vanity plates on his Porsche, was too much of a pansy ass to run over a goddamn *squirrel!*"

"Tuesday?" The sexy drawl from behind me had me closing my eyes on a slow blink.

Damn, but I loved the sound of Jackson Clark's voice. Each time he said my name it never failed to send sparks to all the right places.

But seriously? Why, of all the people in the world, did he have to make an appearance just as I'd lost my shit on Captain Save the Animals? I'd been avoiding Jackson like the plague since the day I met him at his family's barbeque. He was *boy next door hot* and had the body of a full-time fitness model. But he wasn't, he was a firefighter, and damn if that wasn't hot, too. He was also way too young for me. The afternoon I'd spent with him, he hadn't tried to hide he was interested. The shit of it was, on top of his good looks, he was also hilariously funny and a genuinely kind person.

"Hey, Jackson," I muttered but didn't turn around.

"You all right, babe?" I could hear the humor in his voice and when I looked over my shoulder at him, it was confirmed. He was smiling.

Damn, he had a great smile.

"Just dandy." I feigned happiness.

I wasn't going to gawk. I really, *really* wasn't going to check him out in his uniform. *Who the hell am I kidding? Yes, I am.* My eyes roamed from his face to his yellow and black turnout gear, and just as I'd thought the first time I'd seen him at Autumn Lakes, he looked damn sexy in his uniform. Just to note, he looked hot out of it, too. Not that I'd seen him *out of it*, out of it, only in normal street clothes. And, let's just say, he'd filled out his tee nicely. The material had stretched tight across his chest, and his biceps had bulged at the cuff of his sleeves. He'd been so ridiculously hot, it had been difficult to turn down his offer to take me to dinner.

"Earth to Tuesday."

"Huh?"

"She probably hit her head when she slammed into me," Mr. 911 said.

Jackson was no longer smiling, we both looked over to the loud-mouthed prick.

"Sir. Please go wait by your car," a new voice instructed.

I looked to my right and Jackson's cousin, Officer Ethan Lenox, was on the scene, too.

Perfect. Awesome. What a great impression I was

making on Mercy's new family; she was now engaged to Jason, Ethan and Jackson's other cousin.

A family reunion—roadside. I'd met him, his wife Honor, and his daughter Carson at the same barbeque I'd met Jackson.

"Hey, Ethan. Fancy meeting you here." I tried to inject humor to cover my embarrassment. With a shake of his head, he smiled at me.

"That woman ran into me," the man interrupted.

"Sir. I asked you once, please go wait by your car. Someone will be right over to take your statement."

Thankfully a second officer had joined our huddle and escorted the man back to his Porsche before I did something to really embarrass myself—like take off my heel and beat him over the head with it.

"Let's go get you checked out," Jackson suggested.

"I'm fine. Really, nothing hurts. I'm more annoyed than anything. I'll sign an AMA form if you need me to." I turned back to the teenager, who looked a little scared and a whole lot shocked and asked, "Want me to call your dad, darlin'?"

"No. I texted him, he's on his way," he grumbled.

"Good. I'll be here when you talk to him. You should let the EMTs check you out."

"I'm fine. The airbag didn't even deploy."

"Right. Let me tell you a little secret. And I'm only telling you this, 'cause you did nothing wrong. It's gonna be hard for your dad to be upset about a dinged-up car while his boy's sittin' in the back of an ambulance. Not to mention, you hit me pretty hard. You should get checked. Bet you get a day outta school, too."

The teenager perked up and smiled. "Yeah, bet you're right."

I turned back to Ethan and Jackson, both were smiling and shaking their heads. "What?"

"Nothing," Ethan muttered. "Remind me to keep you away from Carson when she gets older. I have a feeling you know all sorts of secrets to manipulate would-be angry parents." I would've been offended he'd called me manipulative, but he was still smiling. "Come on, kid, let's get you to the ambulance before your dad gets here."

Jackson stepped close, cocky grin firmly in place, and said, "You didn't call."

It took all of my willpower not to lean closer and breathe him in. Even over the burnt rubber and exhaust fumes surrounding us, I could still smell his musky cologne. It was the same one he'd worn the day I'd met him. The whole day I'd secretly been trying to get close enough to catch a whiff. It smelled like sex and man. Which was a weird way to describe it, maybe the smell just made me want to *have* sex with the man who was wearing it. I needed to put more space between us, not less. I was weak and he was a yummy temptation of manly goodness. Hence, why I'd been avoiding him.

"Nope. Told ya I wouldn't."

And I had, before, during, and after he'd programmed his number into my phone. I thought back to the barbeque and there'd been a moment of weakness when I'd considered taking him up on his offer. He'd flirted, I'd flirted, but when Mercy had strolled over to us, I was reminded of all the reasons a romp with Jackson was not a good idea. My best friend was with his cousin. Jackson would be a mistake. A fun, really great, pleasurable mistake, but one I couldn't afford.

Now that the Porsche driver wasn't in my face, annoying the hell out of me, everything hit me. I needed a rental, to contact my insurance company, and I had to get to work. I didn't have time for Jackson's shenanigans.

"I should go call my insurance company."

"Right."

He smirked. Serious to God, he smiled at me. Just like he did every time I'd blown him off before.

"Jackson!"

"What? I'm not stoppin' you, Sweetness. Go make your call."

"I'm not going to call you."

Was I telling him, or reminding myself?

"Didn't think you would. I'll check back with you before we roll out."

Then he walked away. That was it. Conversation over. With his back to me I took in my fill, he couldn't see me so there was no harm. Too bad the fire-retardant suit left everything to the imagination. I couldn't even catch a hint of his ass. He looked over his shoulder with his signature smile on his lips and winked.

I continued to stare.

Jackson Clark was going to be a mistake. I could feel it deep in my bones. But, goddamn, he was going to be fun.

2

Five hours later, my ass was planted on a stool at a local hole-in-the-wall bar. I'd been seriously late to work. It had taken forever to get my car sorted and the rental picked up.

The last thing I wanted to do was strip bare for an uppity fashion designer so she could point out every new ounce of weight I'd put on since the last time she'd sewed me into her newest avant-garde creation. I'd thought about canceling my day altogether but it wasn't Olga's fault I was irritated and wanted to smack the hell out of Lawrence Piper. That was the squirrel saving prick's name.

When I first started modeling, I'd been excited. I liked it. However, that had lasted all of a few months. Then my mother had made my life a living hell. At fifteen I'd been tall for my age, and my mom had taken me to a casting call for a department store print ad on a whim.

I hadn't thought there was a snowball's chance I'd get the gig, but the owner of the agency had taken one look at me, being five foot nine as a teenager, and had deemed me perfect. Dad had deemed it a crock of shit industry that preyed on young girls. He wasn't wrong. He'd also caved when my mother told him his input was unwanted.

Everything had gone downhill after that until I'd learned to use the situation to my advantage and build my name. Eventually, I'd been able to start a side business, as a branding consultant. I loved it. Working with designers and helping them find their market was perfect for me. I was out of the spotlight, but was still able to use what I'd learned over the years. I wouldn't have to model for much longer.

Over the years plenty of photographers had commented on my weight and had suggested I lose some. Considering I'd fallen into the modeling world by accident, and it hadn't been some lifelong goal, and that my mother had bitched about my weight throughout my teenage years, I had no issue telling them to fuck off.

If they didn't like the way I looked they could go with someone else. That didn't mean that, before a show, I didn't watch what I ate, I did, because, hello, I was going to be strutting down a catwalk in next to nothing. But I didn't starve myself. And I didn't count calories or food.

Uh-uh, no way.

I liked pizza and cheeseburgers way too much for that shit.

Olga had been kind enough to fly to Georgia from New York for the fitting, not showing up would've been a bitch thing to do. The fashion designer was pleasant enough, a little on the strange side, but, as far as designers went, she was the nicest one I'd worked with. And being a model, I'd worked with a lot over the last fifteen years.

My mood was no better than it had been before Olga had strapped me into her latest design. Two shots of tequila and a beer later, I could still feel the bite of all the buckles she'd cinched too tight around my hips, stomach, and boobs. Not that I had much in the latter department. The sadist had a perfectly placed strip of fabric that barely covered my nipples but compelled my breasts to push together for maximum cleavage. She'd bitched all day that if I'd had the boob job she'd suggested years ago, she wouldn't have to fight with my *titties*, her words not mine.

I wasn't doing that either.

"Can I buy you a drink?" Was asked from beside me.

"No, thank you." I tried my best to keep my voice pleasant, even though I was mentally rolling my eyes. I didn't bother to look over. Partly because I didn't care who was asking and partly because I didn't want to encourage any further conversation.

"You sure? You look like you could use another."

Asshole. Nothing like pointing out how terrible a woman looked while trying to pick her up.

"Thanks, but, no." This time I didn't keep the bite out of my tone.

"Come on, Tuesday," the man cajoled.

What the hell? How did he know my name?

My head snapped in his direction, and I had no idea who this man was and it was a little disconcerting he seemed to know me, or at least my name. He wasn't horrible looking. My age. Full beard, which could be hot, but on him it just looked unkept.

Someone needed to teach him about manscaping. If his face looked like Grizzly Adams, God knew what his pubes looked like. It was probably a thicket patch down his drawers. No woman liked to have to hunt through bush to find the penis. And do not get me started on ball hair. I mean, why the hell does the sack need hair anyway? It's gross. The least a man could do was trim the area if he wanted BJ action. Not that I actually remembered what a penis looked like, it had been so long.

"Tuesday?" he called again.

"Do I know you?"

"I work at Autumn Lakes Nursing Home," the man said.

I still had no idea who he was.

"I'm sorry, I'm really bad with names," I told him.

"Randolph," he helpfully supplied.

Of course, his name was Randolph, he totally looked like a Randolph. I absentmindedly wondered if his buddies called him Dolph. Too bad the man standing in front of me didn't look like the pro wrestler Dolph Ziggler. That man had a body to die for until you got to his face. It wasn't nice of me to think that, but I did anyway.

"Well, Randolph, I appreciate the offer but I prefer to drink alone."

"A beautiful woman such as yourself should never drink alone."

Gag. If I had a dime for every time I've heard that I'd be retired on a beach somewhere.

Dolphy-Boy really needed to work on his game. His pick-up lines sucked ass.

"'Preciate it. But, seriously—"

"Come on, baby—" he tried again.

"Hey, Sweetness. Sorry I'm late."

Jackson!

He stepped closer. I knew this, not because I'd

turned to look. No, I knew because his hand was now around my waist and he was cozied up next to me. The first thing I noticed was my skin was tingling, and I was really sorry there was fabric preventing him from touching my bare flesh. The next was his deep voice, it was different than the fun, flirty tone he used on me when he was trying to get me to agree to go to dinner with him. And last, but certainly not least, was his musky male scent that drove me wild.

Serious as shit, it was a good thing more men hadn't found whatever cologne Jackson wore. Women around the world would be dropping their panties in the streets.

I should've asked him to step back and not touch me, but I didn't. I told myself it was because I'd rather have Jackson's arm around me than Dolph hitting on me, but, in actuality, I liked how his strong, warm hand felt when he'd lowered it to my hip and gave me a squeeze.

"Looks like you started without me," Jackson continued, ignoring Randolph completely.

"Randolph, it was really nice of you to check on me. See you around."

Randolph didn't look all that pleased with Jackson's intrusion. But, finally, he cut his eyes to me and answered, "Yeah, Tuesday, maybe next time."

With Dolph's departure I was now alone with

Jackson. I didn't know which was worse and was considering calling the other man back. I may've been mildly annoyed by his lame attempt to pick me up, but he was far safer than Jackson.

"Wanna 'nother?" the bartender asked, and I silently nodded. "Anything for you?" That was aimed at Jackson.

"A shot of what she's having and a Miller, bottle."

Perfect. Great. Fabulous. Jackson was settling in and didn't look like he'd be moving anytime soon.

"What are you doing?" I asked.

"Same thing you're doing."

That was highly doubtful. I was sitting in a bar, alone, contemplating my career and trying to figure out exactly when I'd become so miserable. He looked anything but miserable.

"Please don't do this, Jackson. I've had a shit day. I really wanna be alone to think."

"Worse time to be alone, Tuesday. Besides, I wanted to check on you. How are you feeling? Neck hurt? Sore muscles?"

"I'm fine. Nothing hurts. Just like the other fifty-two times I told you, the kid didn't hit me that hard. I was pissed at Mr. 911 and him blathering on about how expensive his sports car was. I mean, damn, dude, we get it. You drive a Porsche and have a small penis, so your car is super important to you in your quest to find companionship. I wasn't hurt, but my car's fucked. But I have a super cute rental, so there is that."

"Small penis?" He smiled.

"An assumption based on years of experience. Dude was compensating."

The bartender placed our drinks on the bar in front of us. He picked up his shot of tequila and motioned for me to do the same.

"Here's to lobster tail and beer. Three of my favorite things."

His toast was a little funny but mostly corny.

"Seriously?" I was trying my best not to smile. "Lobster, tail, and beer? Those are your favorites?"

"All right, fine. What about this one? To the kisses we've snatched, and vice versa."

"No. Just no. That one was worse," I told him.

"Um. Let me think . . ." His gorgeous, chocolate eyes sparkled, and he wasn't hiding his amusement.

This was the side of Jackson that scared me. Years and years of working with male models had made me immune to a man's good looks. I knew a guy could be hot as hell but a total tool. I'd spent the majority of my life being judged by my appearance, I knew better than most that all the superficial shit meant nothing. Sure, Jackson was an attractive guy, great hair, he was tall, broad shoulders and built, but that was not what had me wanting to take him home and end my self-imposed dry spell.

Part of it may've been how funny he was, but mostly it was because when he looked at me, he didn't see Tuesday Knowls the billboard model. He just saw me. Plain-'ol-nothing-special me. I liked that a whole lot. Too much. And because he looked at me like I was nothing special, I'd never felt more special in my life.

Seeing Jackson twice in one day was too much. I hadn't had enough time in between sightings to build up my defenses.

3

Tuesday's smile never failed to stir something deep inside of me. It was like the dawn of a new day, full of hope and the promise of good things to come. But when the spark hit her eyes that promise became wicked. Crumpled sheets and satisfaction came to mind.

I'd thought about her hundreds of times since I'd first seen her through the crush of people, and there were a lot. My eyes had landed on her instantly, and not because she was a newcomer, I would've noticed her light straight away in a crowd of outsiders.

She was beautiful, sure. But it was the way she'd held herself. She was confident in her own skin, comfortable being in a room full of strangers. When I'd gotten close, and her gaze had swung my way, I'd felt like I'd been socked in the gut. Everything about her lit my body on fire. And her smile? I couldn't get enough, it had even plagued my dreams.

I was thrilled when I'd walked in tonight and noticed Tuesday sitting at the bar. I'd heard my friend Brice chuckling from behind me when I'd peeled away from him and headed in her direction. He wasn't stupid, he knew I wouldn't be back. Not that he cared, the man never had any issue finding company, even if the company he found was questionable and mostly badge bunnies.

"I'm coming up blank," I told her. "You got any toasts you wanna share?"

"Here's to drinkin' single, seeing double, and sleepin' triple?" She chuckled and a pretty pink blush tinged her cheeks.

"Huh. You do that a lot, babe?"

"Which part?"

"Ahem. The sleepin' triple."

"Wouldn't you like to know."

Goddamn right I would. Though, unlike some men, the thought of sharing my woman did nothing for me. And thinking about Tuesday being intimate with any man had jealousy frothing near the surface. Two men? That had it bubbling over.

"Want another shot?"

"Sure."

It didn't take much to get the bartender's attention,

with a lift of my chin he turned and grabbed the bottle and refilled our glasses.

"So, what had you thinking so hard before I saddled up next to you?"

"Saddled?" Her lips curved up and she snorted a laugh. "Who says that?"

I ignored her question, mainly because she looked so fucking hot smiling over at me, I'd lost my train of thought. I shot the tequila, set the glass back on the bar, and savored the scorch as the liquid slid down.

She kept smiling, only now she was doing it while shaking her head.

I vaguely wondered if there would ever be a time her smile didn't take my breath. *God, I hoped not.* I continued to stare, her smile got bigger and the pounding in my chest intensified.

I was at a complete loss for words. Which hadn't happened since I was fifteen and Molly Blackburn had introduced me to the marvels of a hand job. Since then, I'd never had an issue talking to girls, then, as I got older, women. When I was a teenager that was a necessity if I wanted to get me some. As a man, I learned to listen more than I talked.

Though this was not one of those times. Sitting here next to Tuesday I was simply speechless. I didn't have the first clue what to say to her. She wasn't the type of woman who'd follow me home with a wink and a smile. She definitely wasn't the type you tried to run plays on. Mainly, because I wasn't playing a game with Tuesday Knowls.

It had taken me one afternoon laughing with her at a family barbeque to realize she was different. How different, I didn't know because every time I'd asked her out, she'd turned me down. Flat out. The woman hadn't let me down gently either. She'd basically patted me on the head and called me a boy.

The seven-year age difference didn't bother me. That was, she's seven years my senior. She'd told me she liked her men experienced, which was not an issue. I'd told her as much, but she didn't believe me.

The way I saw it, I only needed her undressed and under me for exactly five minutes. That was all the time it would take for me to have her screaming and prove I had the experience she desired, not only that, but I had it in spades. It wasn't because I had a bedpost full of notches. It was more quality than quantity. As I'd said, I'd learned to listen. And part of listening was paying attention.

"Well?" I prompted, going back to my question, ignoring hers.

"Nothing exciting. Work shit. Can we talk about something a little more fun? How was your day? Did you rescue anymore damsels in distress?"

"Is that what I did, rescue you?"

"Actually, the only person you rescued today was Larry the sports car driver from a Tuesday-style beat down."

"Oh, yeah? What does a Tuesday-style beat down include?"

"Well, first I was thinking about taking off my shoes and hitting him over the head with one but I didn't want my feet to touch the dirty asphalt. Then I was worried about breaking the heel off."

I didn't even have to close my eyes to draw the memory of her standing in the middle of the street in those heels. She was tall, nearly looking me in the eye with those sexy shoes on. It had taken an act of God for me to wrestle my dick into submission and not get hard while at an accident scene.

"It would be a damn shame to break a heel of one of those shoes."

At least until I had her in my bed, wearing those stilettos with the point of the heel digging into my back.

"Is that right?" She smiled, not missing a beat.

"Oh, yeah."

"You have a shoe fetish, Jack?" Her head tilted to the side, and all I could think about was it was the perfect angle to kiss her.

"Didn't before I saw you in those strappy sandals. Your ass, your legs, would look great with a pair of

Chucks on your feet. But those heels? Fucking phenomenal, Sweetness. What else did I save Larry from?"

"I'd already given him a verbal tongue-lashing for almost making the boy in the Honda cry. But I was contemplating strangling him. However, I refrained, only because I didn't want Mercy's soon-to-be cousin Ethan having to arrest me."

I skipped right over the Mercy comment. That was one of her excuses for not wanting to go out on a date with me.

"A tongue-lashing? Is that what you call a full-on bitch fit?"

"A bitch fit?" Her adorable nose scrunched, and she looked totally put off.

"Because, Sweetness, I gotta tell you. You and me? We have a totally different idea of what a tongue-lashing is."

"What exactly is your idea?"

"Come closer." I gestured with a nod for her to lean in. "And I'll tell you."

I enjoyed the flirty banter a fuckton, but I wasn't making a move to touch her in any way until she gave me the go-ahead. I was a patient man and I had every intention of waiting her out for as long as it took. Luckily, she tilted her body toward me.

"Well?" she whispered close to my ear. Her hot

breath puffed against my neck and I had to force myself to remember what I was going to say.

"Goddamn, you smell good," I noted. "I think maybe my explanation of all the ways my tongue can lash is better shown than told."

"Is that right?" she whispered. And even if I hadn't been paying attention to how close her body was to mine, I wouldn't have been able to miss her shiver.

"Oh, yeah. And, babe, when my tongue is lashing over all your sensitive parts you *will* be verbal. However, you'll be calling out my name begging, not bitchin' at some squirrel loving jackass."

"You seem awfully confident about your skills. Maybe I'd be calling out your name begging you to stop."

"Sweetness, the only time you'll be begging me to stop fucking you with my tongue is when you're ready to take my cock. And that is not confidence, that's fact."

"Hmm," she hummed and the vibration against my neck made me wonder what that sound would feel like if she had my dick in her mouth. "A fact is something proven to be true with evidence. As of yet, nothing has been proven. I'd say it's nothing but speculation on your part."

"How about we take this conversation back to my house? You give me five minutes, and I'll give you all the evidence you need."

"Five minutes? I'd call that a disappointment."

Holy shit, I loved her wit. I also noticed she hadn't said no.

"I said five minutes is what you'd need. Not what I had to give."

I kissed the soft skin below her ear and straightened.

"How about another shot?" I asked, changing the subject.

"You trying to get me drunk, Jack?" Damn, she was cute. The stupid nickname didn't even bother me coming from her. She'd taken to calling me Jack after my cousin and best friend, Quinn Walker, told her how much I hated it. I was finding I didn't mind it all that much falling from her lips. Though, if I had it my way, she'd be panting it as an orgasm tore through her. "Before you waste your money, trying to get me drunk to—"

"The fuck?" Her statement was like a cold, hard slap in the face.

I'd given her no indication I was some douchebag who would try and get her drunk and take advantage of her—or anyone for that matter. I'd also told her flat out I didn't want her drunk. We'd gone from playful banter to her forehead wrinkling in seriousness.

Tuesday's back went straight, and she flinched.

"Well, isn't that why most men try to get a woman drunk?" She went on, undeterred by my outburst.

What the fuck?

"That's jacked. I don't know what kind of men you've been hangin' around but, I'll tell you, I am not that kind of man. When you end up in my bed, and straight up, Tuesday, that's where this is headed, you're gonna be stone-cold-sober. You're gonna remember every part of the festivities. You're gonna be an active participant. And you're gonna wake up the next morning, exhausted and satisfied, having not one single regret you'd said or done something you didn't want to do because you were drunk."

"Sorry. That was shitty of me to say."

"Apology accepted. Another drink?"

She sat there quietly staring at me. Something was working behind her eyes, I gave her the time she needed and finally she answered. "Yeah."

I motioned for the bartender and ordered us another round. By the time the drinks were set in front of us she was smiling.

"Maybe I was wrong about you." My brow went up in a wordless question and she answered. "Here I thought you only had one thing on your mind when you asked me out."

"I have more than one thing on my mind when it

comes to you, Tuesday. But you will not be drunk when we explore the possibilities."

"Maybe I shouldn't have another drink then." Her sexy, full lips curved up into a smile.

"Bartender?" I called out and waited for the man to turn. "A water, please?"

Her smile turned into a chuckle. I noticed her thumb was tapping on the bar to the rhythm of the song filling the room.

"You like this song?"

"Oh, yeah. I love Genesis. I've walked the runway to this song a bunch of times. It has the perfect beat to strut to."

Phil Collins crooned on about not being able to dance and I could vividly imagine Tuesday's fine ass prancing down the catwalk in a pair of sky-high heels with her body swaying to the tempo. Phil was singing about a woman with the perfect body and perfect face, the song could've been written about her.

"I'd love to see that."

"What, me walk?"

"Hell, yeah. I bet it's sexy as all hell."

"You're crazy."

"Babe." I shook my head. "Your legs, your ass, your attitude. Shit."

Her body shook with laughter, complete with the snort. Damn, I loved that sound.

Her soulful brown eyes came to mine and, even in the dull light of the dingy bar and her shit day notwithstanding, they were flashing bright with humor. They were so striking I couldn't tear my gaze away.

"You ready to get out of here?" she asked.

"Absolutely."

I couldn't wait to see her bourbon orbs burn with something else.

4

"Jackson!" I panted.

"One more," he growled against my inner thigh right before his teeth sank in.

My hands tangled in his thick, brown hair trying to stop him from honing in on where his mouth was headed. Jackson had not lied. He hadn't even exaggerated a little. Brilliant. All of it.

I was flat on my back in my bed and I was going to beg. This was because his mouth was between my legs and his tongue was doing more than lashing. He'd also added his fingers. And they were working their magic. He'd already brought me off once to a screaming orgasm. Now he wanted to wring another out of me, but I wanted other things.

I was ready.

More than ready.

He'd spent a goodly amount of time exploring. He'd licked, sucked, and nipped from my neck to my thighs. I'd barely had a chance to touch him. So, yeah, I was ready for my turn. More than.

"Ohmygod."

Jackson soothed the sting of his bite, flattening his tongue, he left a wet trail as he moved toward my center. Every muscle tensed as he nibbled his way around my slit before he pierced his tongue inside.

"Please," I begged.

His thumb moved faster, rolling over my clit, and there was no way I could hold back.

With both hands fisting his hair, I held his mouth where I needed and rocked my hips, desperate for the orgasm that was just out of my reach.

"You taste so fucking sweet, Tuesday. Come on, baby, give me one more."

His mouth latched onto my over-sensitive nub and his fingers slid inside. That was all it took for me to fall into bliss.

It took a moment for my orgasm to move from me and to come back to myself, and when I did all of my senses were edlert. The room was filled with the smell of excitement, my skin was hot and tingling, and I could hear every labored inhale as I tried to draw in oxygen.

"Sweetness?" I opened my eyes to see Jackson's face hovering over mine.

"Kiss me," he whispered. His breath puffed against my mouth.

I didn't move the mere inches it would take for our lips to touch. I was too overwhelmed by the feel of his body pressed against mine. My legs wrapped around his hips, and I locked my ankles, pulling him closer.

One of his elbows rested near my head, propping him up. His other hand was on my neck, but he was moving it up to cup my cheek.

"Kiss me," he demanded.

His brown eyes held mine, and suddenly this didn't feel like the lust fueled romp it had been when we'd gotten back to my house and he'd torn my clothes off and tossed me on the bed. This was very different than the hot and heavy flirtatious exchange as he'd spread my legs and told me exactly how he was going to eat me out until I screamed.

This was soft and gentle. It was too much, it would be too easy for sweet Jackson to slip past the barriers I'd built. I needed him to be the rough and dirty man he'd been when he teased his tongue between my legs.

"What are you waiting for, Jack?" I lifted my hips and moaned when the head of his dick pressed against my clit.

"Kiss me, Tuesday, and I'll give you what you want."

"Why?" I whispered.

The tip of his dick nudged my opening. "Stop asking questions and kiss me," he demanded.

"Jackson."

"Babe, as soon as you kiss me, I'll fuck you until you see stars."

His promise spurred me on, I lifted my head the small distance, stopping with our mouths a hair's breadth away. I waited, testing him, but he didn't move, not a millimeter. He was serious.

My tongue darted out and licked his bottom lip. "I can taste myself," I murmured against his mouth, my legs tightened around his hips, and I let my hands roam his back. I lightly pecked one corner of his mouth, then the other.

His control was impressive, but mine was slipping. With another swipe of my tongue along the seam of his lips he groaned and started to press inside. "Please," I begged and gently bit his bottom lip. His mouth opened for me and in one thrust he filled me completely.

My back arched, my breath fled, and all attempts of kissing him were gone. He'd taken over. Completely. Our bodies were his to command and our kiss his to control.

My nails scraped down his back, settling on his ass, and I held on. One of his hands went to my hair and he fisted a hank, tilting my head where he wanted it. I couldn't keep up with his thrusts, my hips moved but I was a bystander, lost in the moment.

"Goddamn," he groaned as he surged in. "Fuck, baby."

His strangled voice sent an electrical spark to my core and my insides started to flutter.

"Jackson!"

"Take it, Tuesday." His hand went under my ass and he yanked me up as he thrust forward. My hands were still roaming the smooth skin of his back, and his mouth was exploring my throat and neck.

I couldn't take it, I was so close, but I couldn't reach it.

Almost.

His mouth moved lower and he pulled my nipple into his mouth, flicking his tongue, once, twice, then he bit down. Pain mixed with a rush of pleasure, and I was toppling over, screaming my pleasure. His lips loosened and he kissed around the sore nub.

He lifted his head and stared down at me, sweat dotted his forehead, and his eyes were wild. They drank me in, and I was afraid in that moment he could see everything I didn't want him to. Every insecurity I had, but pretended I didn't.

"Flip over." His roughened voice ripped through my sexual haze.

"Huh? I thought—"

"Not even close, Sweetness. I want you on your hands and knees so I can hold on to that fine ass while I get you off."

His words sparked aftershocks and my inner muscles clenched.

"Fuck, yeah," he groaned. "On your stomach, Tuesday."

He didn't wait for me to agree. He pulled out, flipped me over, then his hands were everywhere. Touching, gliding, kneading. He kissed one of my ass cheeks before he yanked me up to my knees, pressing his hand on my shoulder keeping my upper body flat against the bed, and slammed home.

"Holy . . . fuck!" I screamed.

He was a hell of a lot deeper this way, he felt thicker, bigger. "Fuck, yes. Spread your legs wider, Sweetness." I did as he asked. "Yeah, baby, just like that."

"Jackson," I panted. "Holy hell. Hurry."

"So goddamn good." He pounded into me. "I'm gonna fuck you, baby, you ready?"

Ready? Wasn't that what he was doing?

"Oh, God," I cried out.

"You're so slick and hot, and your pussy feels so good." One hand moved between us and zeroed in on my poor abused clit. The moment he touched it I jolted. "You're gonna come with me."

"No way. There's no way."

Jackson pinched and tweaked my clit, while his hips rolled. The onslaught of sensation was too much. My body was hot all over, and then his other hand snuck between the bed and my chest and, in some magical move, he found my nipple and pinched it between two fingers. My body bucked and my vision blurred.

"Please," I moaned, thrashing my head.

"Tuesday," he roared.

Our grunts and groans filled the room. There was so much heavy breathing it was surprising we hadn't sucked all of the oxygen out of the room.

"Fuck, Sweetness." He slammed in, rubbed my clit, and I was gone.

I wrenched my eyes closed and the last thing I remembered was the flash of bright lights dancing behind my lids.

Pure magic.

5

Tuesday started to stir in my arms, and I was enjoying the last minutes I had holding her while she slept. Her pliant body pressed to my side, one arm thrown over my stomach, and her hand was resting on my side. Last night she'd passed out seconds after I'd pulled the fourth orgasm from her. She was so exhausted she hadn't even fought me when I'd gathered her into my arms and tucked her close. Now that she wasn't lust drunk, I knew she was going to pull away.

It was going to piss me off.

I knew it; therefore, I was prepared.

So, I was enjoying this, the last moments of soft, sleepy woman. Memorizing. I needed to remember what this felt like as I went about the herculean task of talking Tuesday around to giving us a chance.

Before last night, I'd thought I'd been sure I

wanted to explore a relationship with her. I was infatuated with her smile and the way she let loose and laughed. She'd done it in a way that told me she lived life to its fullest.

But I was wrong.

So wrong. Now that I'd had her under me, wrapped around me, felt her let loose it in a whole different way, I knew how wrong. Her smile—breathtaking. Her moaning her pleasure down my throat—incendiary. Never have I had a woman so into me, and me into her. We didn't fuck last night, we detonated.

The second we'd walked into her bedroom we were tearing at each other's clothes. Wild abandon and desperation. There were no other words for it. Tuesday looked good, tasted good, and felt fucking great. But as rough as I'd been, there was an underlying softness to her touch. If I had to guess, she didn't do one-night stands. Though she was going to lie to me and say that's all this was. There was no way the woman I fucked last night had random sex. When I'd slowed things down and demanded she kiss me, I saw it. And after she flew apart for me, it was confirmed. We may've fucked, it may've been wild, but it meant something to her, even if all it meant was she was giving me something she doesn't often share. And it meant a fuck of a lot to me.

So I was waiting for it. The lie, that all we were

was a one-time thing fueled by alcohol and lust and it was going to piss me off.

Again, I knew it, so I was prepared.

I was also going to push because I wanted more.

Tuesday shifted, and her body turned to steel.

Here we go.

"Morning." I tightened my arm, kissed the top of her head, and braced.

"Shit," she muttered.

If I hadn't been ready, I would've been offended. But I'd known.

Tuesday was gearing up to shore her defenses.

I allowed my hand to continue to glide up and down her back. I decided it was best to focus on how soft her skin was. So damn soft and silky I could touch her all day.

But she was getting ready to kick me out so I was taking my fill.

"Jackson," she started. And in three . . . two . . . one . . . "We need to talk."

"No, Tuesday, the last thing we need to do is talk."

"We do. This was a—"

"Do not finish that, Tuesday."

"It can't—"

"Yes, it can."

The steel she'd infused turned to titanium.

"Jackson. Seriously. Stop cuttin' me off and listen. Last night was great. But come on, you know what it was."

"And what was last night?" I asked, though I didn't need to. I knew what last night was, and knew she was going to poison it.

"Fun. A one-time thing. That's all it can be."

One second, she was cuddled to my side, the next, I rolled her to her back. Big, expressive, brown eyes wide with shock stared up at me. I brushed the tangled, mess of blonde hair away from her face and looked down at her. One of her legs was pinned under me, and there was no way she could miss my hard-on digging into her thigh.

"I'll give you the fun part. Though, there are better ways to describe last night." I hooked her free leg around my hip and my hand moved to her ass and I hefted her closer. "But, you're straight up crazy if you think that after what you gave me last night, I'm not gonna want seconds, and thirds."

"Jackson."

"My name's not an answer, Sweetness."

"You may want seconds, but it's not gonna happen."

"Let me take you out."

"No way."

"Lunch? Dinner? Late night snack?"

She shook her head, I smiled, then lowered my mouth to hers. She did not open to kiss me. She did, however, press her lips together into two thin lines in an attempt to keep me out. I brushed my mouth against hers, and licked the seam of her lips. I lingered a beat, and she softened.

"We'll see," I said against her lips, then pushed up, rolled to the side, and out of bed.

"No, we won't. This is done. No more flirting. No more asking me out. And absolutely no more sex."

"We'll see," I repeated.

"Don't make this awkward. We had a few drinks, we laughed, and we fucked. Nothing more."

"Whatever you say."

"Jackson," she snapped.

"Yeah, babe?"

I turned, completely comfortable in my nudity. Her eyes dropped to my dick and I know what she saw. It was pointing straight at her. So damn hard, you could've used it as a towel rack. I gave zero fucks and certainly didn't mind her slow perusal.

"Put some clothes on for Christ's sakes."

She was now sitting up, holding a sheet against her chest. That was unfortunate. She had great tits. Medium sized, perky, with pretty pink tips that I knew, when played with, set her off. Next time I'm going to spend a great deal of time paying homage, seeing if she can come just from me talking to her while I played with her nipples.

I didn't answer her, just tagged my jeans off her bedroom floor, yanked them up, and buttoned my fly. Next were my shirt, socks, and boots. I wordlessly dressed but hadn't stopped looking at her. I was memorizing that moment, too. How she looked sitting in the middle of her bed, sheets tangled, comforter askew, sex hair, and thoroughly fucked. So damn pretty, a disheveled mess.

It was even better knowing it was me that had made her look that way.

I slipped on my boots, walked to the bed, both hands planted on either side of her, I leaned in and kissed her.

She opened for me immediately, my tongue swept in and it took a great amount of self-control for me not to go for it. My already hard dick throbbed in my jeans and I had to fist the sheet to stop myself from touching her. With one last, slow glide of my tongue against hers, I pulled back and kissed her forehead.

"See ya around."

I stood and turned to walk out, but I didn't miss the want in her eyes or the shock on her face.

She didn't move.

Not that I'd expected her to.

Nor did she say a word.

That was far easier than I'd thought. Not me walking away, that took a good amount of effort. But I hadn't given her the chance to kick me out and I'd figured that would've been the first thing she'd do.

6

It had been two weeks since I'd seen Jackson and I was seriously contemplating electroshock therapy or a lobotomy. I needed to find a way to purge all memories of Jackson Clark from my brain. If I'd thought he was a bad idea before I'd taken him home with me and invited him to my bed, I now knew, with undeniable certainty, he was a *really* bad idea.

He'd jumped over tempting when he whispered in my ear and told me I smelled good and I'd felt his breath on my neck. And that was before he'd explained what he could do with his tongue and sent a wakeup call to my girly parts. No, he'd gone straight to dangerous.

It had been weeks, and I was still pissed at myself about the whole interlude. Vacillating between kicking my own ass for being so weak and giving in, then for being all kinds of stupid and not taking him up on round two. I'd already broken my years-long dry spell, what would it have hurt?

I wished he'd been lying about his skills in the bedroom. But more than that, I really wished I could stop thinking about him. It was bad enough my libido had decided now would be a good time to have a resurrection, but I couldn't get his smile out of my head. And don't get me started on his laugh. It was deep and rumbly and it came quick. There was nothing selfish about Jackson. Not with his humor and not with dispensing orgasms.

"This shit is ridiculous," I mumbled and yanked my makeup bag out of my suitcase and flung it on my bed.

This had to end.

My phone rang, I checked the display and slid the red decline icon across the screen. I was too tired to talk to Mercy. I had to finish unpacking from my trip up to New York and it was nearing ten o'clock. I still hadn't eaten dinner and all I wanted to do was veg out and forget what a crappy few weeks I'd had. I knew it was a bitch thing to do, but I also knew she'd understand, which made me an even bigger bitch for totally taking advantage of my best friend's understanding. But I was too mentally exhausted to talk to anyone.

I also wanted to forget the new designer I'd been

forced to work with. She had found a little success, now she was a total diva, barking orders, complaining, and being generally bitchy. It was the show from hell, and her designs were uncomfortable. Not only that, but she'd insisted on all of us walking the runway to rap music. Not any old rap music either, the shitty stuff that you couldn't understand. There was nothing sexy about the beat or the words. It made for a really crap-tastic walk.

I tossed the last pair of shoes from my suitcase into my closet and beelined it to the kitchen. I was going to pig out big time now that I didn't have to prance around a stage in next to nothing.

I was vowing never to eat another salad, yogurt, or vegetable again while scrolling through my music on my phone. I finally found a 70s rock list that would hopefully erase all the shitty rap I'd had to endure over the last few days and fired it up through my Bluetooth speakers.

The second the electric guitar intro of "Owner of a Lonely Heart" filled the room I felt my mood lift. Yes, that was what I needed, loud music and real honest to God junk food. I rooted through my pantry, gathering all the items I needed to make a late-night dinner, which would consist of popcorn, a bag of chips, and boxed mac and cheese.

Popcorn in the microwave popping, my hips

swaying to quite possibly one of Yes's best songs ever recorded, water boiling for my mac and cheese, I opened the bag of chips. I was still belting out the lyrics when my hand dove in the bag to grab a greasy handful of yummy goodness. Then I saw a reflection from my kitchen window and movement out of the corner of my eye.

I was no longer singing, my hips weren't moving to the beat, and the bag of chips was no longer in my hands. They were flying up in the air, and I was screaming down my house.

The bag landed on the floor, chips flew everywhere, the microwave was pinging, announcing my popcorn had popped, and I was still screaming, Only, now, I was screaming words. "What the hell?"

"I knocked," Jackson announced, smiling.

I'd never before contemplated murder, however, seeing him standing in my kitchen, amused, I wasn't only contemplating it, I was plotting it. I picked up the box of mac and cheese from the counter and threw it at his head. Which, much to my annoyance, he easily caught before it smashed him in the face.

"You're such an asshole. I had a fucking heart attack," I was yelling partly so he'd hear me over the music but mostly because I was angry as fuck he was in my house. "What are you doing here?"

"Do you mind?" He motioned around the room in

what I assumed was his dickhead way of asking me to turn down the music.

"Owner of a Lonely Heart" had turned into the Beatles' "Blackbird," and I didn't want to miss one of my favorite songs. But I grabbed my phone off the counter and reluctantly turned the music down but not off. If for no other reason than for him to be able to hear me clearly when I threw him out.

"Now, why the hell are you here?"

"I left my watch here the other night." His lips were twitching in the sexy way they'd done the other night, and that pissed me off, too. He was definitely fighting a smile. Ass!

"Watch? You came to my house after ten at night to get a damn watch?"

"Yep."

What the hell was wrong with him? If it was at all possible for my ire to get any higher, hearing his smug one-word answer did it.

"Did you think maybe you should've called first? Send a text asking if you could stop by?"

"Don't have your number, Sweetness."

"A smoke signal?"

"Mercy said she'd call and tell you I was on my way over. I just left her house."

Shit, she had called, and I'd sent it to voicemail. Damn.

"When I didn't answer her call did it ever cross your mind it was because I was perhaps sleeping or otherwise occupied and didn't want to be disturbed?"

My heart rate was finally under control from having the shit scared out of me. Now that the fear had dissipated all that was left was white-hot rage that Jackson was again in my home. But more than that he looked good. Even him smirking looked hot, which was irritating as shit. I wished he'd grown a few moles on his face, got a bad case of acne, and gained five-trillion pounds since the last time I'd seen him so he would cease to look better than most of the male models I worked with.

"It had, actually. But Mercy told me not to worry about that, she said after you get back from a trip you crank up your tunes and eat junk food until you fall into a food-coma. Which, I gotta tell you, the way you look, knowing what those long, sexy legs feel like wrapped around me, I didn't believe her. Seeing as you were ripping into a bag of Lay's while getting ready to eat processed cheese sprinkled on pasta, I'm astonished." Why the hell was I so predictable? Of course, Mercy would know what I was doing, I had the same routine every time I came home.

I tried, *really* tried, not to think about my legs wrapped around him. Heat hit my cheeks, and I knew I was losing, but when my core gave a spasm, I knew I'd failed, miserably.

"I can't believe you just said that."

"Yes, you can."

Ass!

Moving on.

"Did she also tell you just to walk into my house and put me into cardiac arrest?"

"She did, yeah. And you're not having a heart attack. You may've peed your pants a little, but you'll live."

Ohmygod. All I could see was red when I picked up an orange from the fruit basket and chucked it at him. He easily caught my efforts. Again, pissing me off.

"I didn't piss my pants, you asshole."

"I didn't say you *did*. I said you may've."

Sweet baby Jesus, please give me the strength to not kill Jackson Clark.

"Where's your watch?"

"In your room on the nightstand."

For once he wasn't being smug, the way he casually mentioned he'd been in my room made my stomach stupidly whoosh. I wish I'd already eaten so I had buttery, processed, fried junk food to blame the flutter on.

"You can wait here. I'll go get it."

I scurried, yes scurried, down the hall to my

bedroom. I checked the nightstand on the side of the bed I slept on and it wasn't there. I walked to the other side and there it was, his freaking, dumb watch that was the cause of my latest run-in with Jackson. It being there reminded me why he'd been in my bedroom in the first place. That thought made my panties dampen.

Shit.

I had to get him out of my house, pronto.

7

The scent of gardenias lingered around the room. A smell I'd forever associate with Tuesday. I'd dreamt of the sweet-smelling flower since the night I'd spent with her. I couldn't get how she'd cuddled close and rested her head on my chest out of my head. Couldn't stop thinking about how good she'd felt pressed against me. The memories never failed to make me hard and make my heart pound.

I was checking out her living room when I heard the pan rattling on the stove and quickly decided on tonight's course of action. I wasn't going anywhere until she talked to me. And even after that, I was staying awhile.

I grabbed the box she'd thrown at me, ripped open the cardboard, and spilled the noodles into the boiling water. Her kitchen was just as nice as her living room.

Top of the line appliances, just like the electronics in her living room. Her furniture was expensive, too. Everything was in its place. No clutter, no mess, no character. This surprised me. Tuesday was full of life, funny, always smiling, and had a big personality. But not her pad. The space she lived in was boring and lonely.

I was picking up the bag of chips off the floor when Tuesday came into the kitchen.

"What are you doing?"

"Do you know how much salt are in these things?" I held up the half empty bag of Lay's. Tuesday stopped a few feet from me and a hand went to her hip and her pert little nose scrunched.

So damn cute.

"Good to know. Here." She was holding my watch out, letting it dangle on one finger trying to keep her distance.

The reasons why she needed that distance made me grin. She'd like me to believe she was unaffected, may even have been trying to convince herself she was. But it was a lie, and we both knew it.

"Thanks." I took my watch and made sure our hands touched. I heard it and saw it, the quick inhale she'd tried to cover up by yanking her hand back like I'd stung her.

"What are you doing?" she asked again.

"Cleaning up," I said, laying my watch on the counter.

"Why?"

"Well, it's kinda my fault there's a mess on your floor."

"Kinda?"

"All right, Sweetness, it's one hundred percent my fault there's a mess. That's why I'm cleaning it up. You may wanna stir your noodles so they don't clump."

"My noodles?"

"Tuesday. Your mac and cheese. Stir the pasta so it doesn't stick together."

She walked to the stove muttering something under her breath. I couldn't quite catch it with the music still on, even though it was at a much lower volume than when I'd come in.

"You really should keep your front door locked. Especially when you're blaring your music. Any psycho off the street could walk in."

"Yeah. I learned my lesson."

I felt, at that point, it was pertinent to hide my smile. She was cute as hell when she was trying to insult me.

"You have great taste in music," I told her.

"You like Elton John?" she asked, looking at me over her shoulder.

I took her in from top to toe. Her face, freshly

washed and devoid of makeup, was even prettier than when she had shiny lips and mascara on, highlighting her already long lashes. I wondered if she even realized it wasn't her looks that made her so beautiful.

"Yeah. "Tiny Dancer" is one of my favorites by him," I answered, noting the song that was playing.

She shook her head, and I watched the long strands of her blonde hair tousle with the movement. Great fucking hair. Perfect to wrap around my fist and tug.

"This is everyone's favorite of his. Even non-Elton fans like "Tiny Dancer." What else do you like by him?"

It was ridiculous how happy I was she was talking to me. If she wanted to argue about Elton John, I'd take it. I'd take anything she wanted to talk about if it meant she wasn't kicking me out.

"Your Song."

"Really?"

"Yeah. Why?"

Her face dropped forward, and I knew she was hiding her smile. A giggle bubbled up and she snorted before she said, "That's a sweet love song."

"And?"

"I don't know. I didn't figure you for a soft ballad kinda guy."

"There's a lot about me you've figured wrong."

Her back snapped straight and her laughter died. "I wouldn't go as far as saying *a lot*."

I opened her trashcan and dumped in the handful of chips I'd picked up and waited for her to say more. When she remained quiet, I decided to test the waters. "How was your trip to New York?"

"How'd you know I went to . . . Mercy." It wasn't a question, she'd merely figured it out on her own. "It was long."

"How do the shows work? You were gone for two weeks; do you work the whole time?"

She walked the pan to the sink and used the lid to strain the water out while answering. "This show was only two nights. Last night and the night before. The days leading up to it are for fittings, choreography, rehearsals, that kind of stuff. But I went up a little early to meet with my manager and agent."

I didn't like the way she winced when she mentioned her manager and agent. "Everything all right?"

"Everything's great on my end. Though my agent wasn't entirely happy when I told her I wanted to slow down on my bookings."

"Why do you want to slow down?"

"I . . . never mind." She caught herself getting ready to tell me something personal and changed the direction of the conversation. "The designer I was working with this time is relatively new. In the last six months she's landed some big gigs, sold some of her designs to high-end stores overseas, so now she thinks she can be as bitchy as she wants to be and everyone around her has to put up with it. She also changed up the show three times, the last being an hour before it started which led to numerous meltdowns. By the time I left I'd vowed never to work with her again. I can put up with a lot, I know the attitudes and egos that are synonymous with this industry. What I have no tolerance for is mean people. And the way she was acting was just plain ol' mean."

I watched as she finished making her mac and cheese. She was a stunning woman, more so while she was in her kitchen in a pair of loose-fitting sweatpants and a tank top. I figured she'd be that way in a brown paper bag. I wondered why she wanted to slow down; with her beauty, I figured she'd be in high demand.

"I'd like to go to one of your shows."

"You've already said that," she reminded me.

"Well? Can I go to one?"

"Um. No."

"Why not?"

"No one watches me work. It's distracting. Besides sitting in a room full of hoity-toity executives would be boring as hell. It's not like what you see on TV."

She grabbed her popcorn out of the microwave and

her bowl of mac and cheese and made her way back to the living room. It wasn't lost on me she hadn't offered me any.

"Well, you have your watch. My dinner's ready. Since you let yourself in, I assume you know how to let yourself out."

Tuesday unceremoniously plopped down on the couch, dismissing me.

"Why do you want to slow down with work?" I asked, sitting next to her, ignoring her request for me to leave.

"What are you doing?" she snapped.

"Talking," I stated the obvious.

"Seriously, why are you doing this? You have your watch. We've already talked about how the other night was a mistake. One that will not be repeated."

She sounded convincing enough, and I almost would've believed she meant her words if she hadn't glanced at my mouth with every other one.

She was lying.

Again.

"No, Sweetness, we didn't talk the other morning. You said some words, and I didn't agree with any of them. Other than, maybe, when you said we had fun. Though, I'll reiterate, I could then and, now two weeks later, still can come up with a fuck of a lot better ways to describe our night. And there was not a damn thing that happened by mistake. I promise you, every swipe of my tongue, every touch of my hand, and stroke of my cock was deliberate. And when you were moaning your passion down my throat, and I was swallowing that pleasure like a dying man, that was not a mistake either.

"You have a way of distorting the truth, but if you try and deny for one second you weren't with me every step of the way, you're a damn liar. As to why I'm sitting here talking to you? That's what two people do when they're friends."

"Are you calling me a liar?" I'd watched her pretty cheeks blush as I reminded her of our night together, now they were getting redder by the second, and I suspected it was not lust tinging them.

"You denying you weren't on board with everything we did?"

Her jaw clenched, and I knew I had her. She'd been right there with me.

"And we're not friends," she added.

"We're not?"

"No."

"Well, that's disappointing."

"What is?" Her brown eyes narrowed, and I was fully enjoying riling her up.

"Here I thought my charm was irresistible."

"More like annoying," she huffed.

"Tell me about work."

She slammed her bowl on the coffee table and stood.

"Are you always this hardheaded? I don't want to talk to you about work, or anything else. You and me? Never gonna happen."

Tuesday crossed her arms over her chest and hurt flashed. Hurt I didn't put there. But I sure as hell was going to figure out who or what had.

"Why not?"

"You want a list?"

"Sure, if you have one."

"Let's see, Mercy is engaged to your cousin." She held up her pointer finger then her middle finger. "Next, You're annoying." She flicked another finger up adding her ring finger to the two other digits. "You don't listen. You barge into my life and think you can ask me personal questions. And when I tell you I don't want to talk about something, you push."

I slowly stood trying to gather my thoughts. It was time Tuesday Knowls understood a few things.

"Yeah, I'm totally barging in, Sweetness."

"You just can't listen, can you?" She threw her arms out in front of her. "You wanted reasons. I gave them to you, and you *still* ignore me."

"Because they were all bullshit and you know it. Mercy and Jason have fuck all to do with us. And you only find me annoying because I won't let you push me away. Which leads to the question, why the fuck you're trying so hard to lock me out? You had no issue being my friend before I took you to bed, but now you're doing everything you can, including acting like a bitch, to make sure I don't get too close. Why? No more bull-shit, Tuesday."

She flinched and stepped back.

"I'm not interested, Jackson. You're too damn young for me. You're like a boy—"

I didn't let her finish her statement. Two strides and we were nose to nose, my hands moved to the side of her neck, and then up until I shoved them into her hair. "Do not bullshit me. And I think I've already proven I am not a fucking boy, but in case you need the reminder, baby, I'm more than happy to oblige." My lips crashed onto hers, it took a moment before she soft-ened but when she did, I went for it. And thank God I did, because the second she opened her mouth to me and our tongues touched it was explosive. Tuesday deepened the kiss and a sexy growl bubbled up from the back of her throat. I went from semi-hard to pound-fucking-nails hard in a heartbeat.

As much as I wanted to take her back to her room and devour every inch of her, I was going to make her wait. I slowed the kiss and pulled away. The hazy way she was looking at me had me questioning my sanity.

Once she blinked the lust out of her pretty bourbon eyes, I knew it was time for me to leave.

"I'll see you around, Tuesday."

"What?"

I didn't answer her, not with words. I leaned forward and gently pecked her lips. "Have a good night."

I straightened and made my way to the front door. She was still standing where I'd left her, only she'd turned to look over her shoulder, watching me go. Yeah, I was making the right decision. When the time came to move the festivities into the bedroom again it will be because she was as desperate for me as I was for her. And not a moment sooner.

I got into my truck and started to drive away. I wondered how long it would take her to notice I'd left my watch on her kitchen counter.

8

I was going to kick Jackson's ass. Scratch that, no, I wasn't, because I was never going to see him again. It had been days since his little stunt in my living room. Though I'm not sure I'd call anything about Jackson little, which was part of the reason, days later, I was still thinking about him.

Again.

Or thinking about him more than I had been.

He was annoying as hell, he didn't listen when I spoke, he'd scared the holy bejesus out of me and had smirked about it, he then had the audacity to kiss me. That was the part I was still thinking about. I'd had a lot of first kisses over the years. I was the Queen of Second Dates but rarely thirds. It was normally sometime during after dinner cocktails on the second date that a man showed me who he truly was, negating the sweet he'd shown on the first date, therefore, not getting a third. Let alone to the horizontal tango part. If I couldn't stand sitting through dessert and drinks with a man, he certainly wasn't putting his penis near my girly parts.

So, there I was Queen of Second Dates still thinking about all of Jackson's not so little, very hard parts, and how he'd left me hanging. Jackson Clark's non-first date kiss had been better than all the others that had come before. He'd kissed me the first night we were together, he'd demanded it actually, but the kiss in my living room was different. It had been slow to start, a tingle that turned into a tremor. He'd built the blaze until I was burning for him. Then he'd pulled back, broke the kiss, and walked away.

I have never, and I mean, never, had a man work me up just to casually stroll to the door with a wave. Not that he'd even waved. I'd spent hours in my bed thinking about him and his hard-on. He'd made sure it'd been pressed against my stomach well and good. Not that I needed to feel it again to remember what he could do with it. And he'd left his fucking watch— again—which I was taking over to Jason and Mercy's the first chance I had. No more excuses for him to pop over for another chat.

There was a twinge of guilt that wouldn't stop nagging me about the way I'd treated Jackson. He'd been so close to the truth my claws had come out. Unfortunately, for him, they were not kitten claws. They'd been sharpened by experience and regret. I'd been taught by the best what happens when you let down your guard and allow yourself to be played.

I sucked in a lungful of oxygen and pushed aside the shame that came with being so naïve. I should've been more concerned with keeping Jackson away from me than I was about the manner in which I was doing it. He was a complication I didn't need. A big fat complication with a capital C. He was sweet, sexy, funny, great in bed, had a great smile, and obviously wanted more, even if it was only another roll in the hay. All reasons to stay away. He was not simply first date material, he was a man I could have feelings for. Those types of men were off limits.

I was putting a stop to this madness once and for all. I had no other choice. I dated. That was it. No boyfriends. No emotional entanglements. No feelings of any sort.

I had so much baggage I was the poster child for fucked up. The worst part was I knew it. I knew why I dated the wrong men. I knew why I never went on a third date. And I knew why I hadn't had sex in the last five years since I'd left Travis. I never wanted to feel anything ever again. I was happy for others who'd found it. I was thrilled that Mercy was crazy in love with Jason. But that was not a risk I was ever willing to take again. So, I went out on dates to pass the time. I dated so Mercy and my grandmother would stop harping at me and telling me they were worried about me. But I didn't ever go out on a date with a man whom I found I was remotely attracted to. I didn't allow anyone close. And sex was absolutely never on the table.

Until Jackson.

In less than an hour sitting at a bar with him he broke my five-year dry spell. He made me feel. He made me wish I wasn't so fucking broken. He pissed me off and I wanted no part of him. Because, if I thought Travis Manning wrecking my heart with all of his bullshit was horrible, I had a feeling Jackson Clark would kill me. I'd never recover.

Jackson was not an option.

He couldn't be.

"Hi, Tuesday." I was greeted as soon as I entered the Autumn Lakes Nursing Home.

I turned toward the voice and there was . . . Rudolf . . . Ralph . . . Richard. I couldn't for the life of me remember the man's name. It wasn't too long ago I'd seen him at the bar and he'd offered to buy me a drink. His beard was still scruffy and unkempt. Good to know he still hadn't started a personal grooming regimen.

"Hey, darlin'," I said in place of the man's name

and threw a hand over my shoulder as I walked past him.

I didn't want to have a stop and chat or possibly give him another opportunity to ask me out for drinks. I wanted to visit my grandmother and talk to her doctor and see when we could bust her out of this joint. My grandmother was a stubborn woman, I still wasn't happy she'd refused to allow me to help her while she was recovering from her latest surgery. Now, the crazy old woman said she loved it at the nursing home.

Who loves a nursing home? Patty Knowls, that's who.

The hair at the back of my neck was tingling. I could hear the footsteps behind me as I made my way down the wide, brightly colored corridor that led to my grandmother's room. I didn't have to turn around to know Mr. I Need to Trim My Facial Hair was behind me. I could feel his eyes on me and hear his heavy footsteps. It was kind of creeping me out. I didn't like the way he looked at me at the bar and wouldn't take no for an answer. And I really didn't like the way he was following me now.

Gran's room came into view and I hurried to get to the door. Thankfully, it was open and I stepped in, closing it behind me before the man could catch up. The first thing that hit me as the door clicked shut was my grandmother's soft smell of Wind Song. The powdery scent never failed to soothe me. It was the aroma of my childhood. She'd worn the perfume all my life. I could feel the stress melting away.

"My sweet granddaughter. What are you doing here?" Patty asked from her wheelchair. "I was just going to go play some bingo with Franco and Phil."

See? She totally loved the nursing home. My grandmother was a stunning woman, even as she aged, she never lost that beauty.

"Phil and Franco?" I smiled.

"My suitors, dear. They are both trying their best to get an invitation to supper."

"Gran!"

"Speaking of suitors, have you seen anymore of the fine young firefighter?"

That was another reason I wanted to kick Jackson's ass. My grandmother hadn't stopped talking about him since the day she'd briefly met him in the parking lot after the fire in the craft room of Autumn Lakes. I'd heard all about how tall he was—tall enough to tuck me under his chin even if I was in heels. She'd told me how good looking she thought he was—he came from good stock. She'd droned on about his smile and how, when it came time, I wanted to settle down with a man with an easy way and quick smile. It would make for a happy life.

Little did she know I'd stupidly screwed his brains

out then shoved him out the door. Not that I'd ever tell my grandmother that. And not for the same reasons that most people wouldn't talk to their grandmothers about sex. Gran would happily mix herself a martini, pull up a chair, and listen intently if I wanted to share my sex life with her. She was an open book. Often times, she over-shared. It was like living with my own personal Dr. Ruth. Only Gran wasn't a sex therapist she was just wise to the ways of the world.

"Jackson, Gran. His name is Jackson. And, yes, I saw him the other day." Her sweet face lit and it sucked I had to take that look away, but I did. She was a dreamer and a romantic. I'd heard the story about how my grandfather had swept her off her feet thousands of times. "He's just a friend. He will always be just a friend, and I'm not interested in anything more."

"That man is smitten," she told me.

"He's hardly a man, Gran. He's a baby."

Thank God, Jackson wasn't there to hear me call him a baby. The last time I'd made a comment about his age, he'd thoroughly reminded me he was all man. However, age-wise, he really was too young for me. He hadn't even begun to live out his twenties. He had a lot of exploring to do before he settled down, and I wasn't going to be his tour guide into all things relationships and women. That sounded like heartbreak to me.

"Is that what your problem is? He's younger than

you?" She waved her hand in front of her face. "Did I ever tell you the story about the summer I spent in Wildwood before I met your grandfather?"

"No. And I don't think I want to hear it either."

My grandmother was raised in a Southern Baptist home. The way she tells it, her parents were very strict, and the minute she turned eighteen she shot out of their house like a bullet. She'd always told me she was too much of a free spirit, to be stifled by hellfire and brimstone. She'd wanted to live her life and experience everything. By the stories she'd told me over the years, she'd lived it up all right. And she had no hang-ups telling me all about it.

"Picture this, Wildwood, New Jersey, 1966. Hot as blazes, people everywhere. I was working there for the summer as a hostess in the Caribbean Hotel. I was strolling the boardwalk with some of the girls from the hotel. We sat down to people watch on the benches off Hunts Pier. Boy, that place was something. We'd barely stopped walking when a group of young men coming out of the surf caught my eye. Even through the mass of people I noticed him right away, taller, broader, and more handsome than his friends. He was far away, and I watched his every step. When he got closer, I turned my head back to the pier so he wouldn't think I was looking, but he walked straight to me. Imagine that, through the gaggle of girls, right up to me and looked down at me where I was sitting on the bench. His first words to me were, come on, doll, let's go get you a cream soda. The audacity of him, coming straight to me and telling me, not asking, he was going to buy me a cream soda."

At this point in my grandmother's story, I noted two things: the first, it didn't surprise me one bit my grandmother was hit on in such a fashion. She'd been absolutely gorgeous when she was younger. The second, and more importantly, I thought the same thing about Jackson when he'd kissed me.

I pulled out of my thoughts and continued to listen. "I had a choice to make, Tuesday. I could've told him to take a hike for having the nerve to be so forward, or I could've stood and taken the hand he was offering."

"I'm assuming you took his hand."

"You bet your britches I did. He bought me that cream soda and one every day after that for six weeks."

It was a great story, but I wasn't sure why she was telling it.

"Well? What happened?"

"What happened was, I had the best summer. We were inseparable. He was funny, smart, and so darn handsome I couldn't believe he'd picked me to spend the summer with. We danced and swam and went to the amusement park. By the end of the summer, we were very much in love."

Nineteen sixty-six? My dad was born a few years later. But this was not the story of how she'd met my grandfather.

"What happened to him?"

"At the end of that summer he went off to Vietnam. He'd just graduated high school and had enlisted in the Army. He spent his last six weeks with me, in Wildwood."

"Eighteen? Gran, you were like . . ." I tried to do the math in my head while remembering how old she was when she'd had my father.

"I was twenty-four. He was six years younger than me."

My mouth dropped open, and my eyes bulged. My grandmother had a summer fling with a teenager. A teenager who'd just graduated high school. Holy shit. She'd told me a lot of crazy stories over the years but never this one.

"I'm telling you this, dear, to remind you age is but a number. And I can assure you, just like your Jackson, there was no *boy* in Thomas. I suppose there are those who are simply born with it, not exactly an old soul, but all man. Tommy was all man, just like Jackson."

My Jackson?

Was she crazy?

I think someone was slipping something into my grandmother's meatloaf in this place. Jackson Clark was not mine. My mind was still reeling from learning my grandmother had been in love with a man named Thomas. I didn't have the mental brain power to sort through all of the reasons Jackson was not, and would never be, my man.

"What happened to him?"

"He died, dear. When we parted, we agreed it was best for both of us to move on. We'd shared a wonderful summer together. But he was leaving and I had a life to keep living. I met your grandfather that Christmas and we were married shortly after that."

"Did Grandpa know about this Thomas man?"

"Of course, he did. There were no secrets between the two of us. We were already married when I got word of Tommy's passing. He held me while I cried and carried on. Your grandfather knew that while Tommy held a special place in my heart, he didn't need to worry. I loved your grandfather beyond reason. He knew that."

We sat quietly for a few moments before her eyes got soft, and I braced. "You need to start living again."

"What? I am."

"No, dear. You work. You're successful. You date. But you are not living."

"Um, Gran, everything you just said means I'm living."

"How many of those men you date have you let in?"

Why was I having this conversation with my grandmother? I was now regretting telling her the misadventures of my dating life. Some of the stories were entertaining and made for a good laugh. Now I wished I'd kept my mouth shut.

"Why would I let someone in when I can't see myself going on a third date with them? The last second date I had blew his nose at the table. It was gross. He didn't just blow it, he had his finger shoved so far in he was mining for gold. I'll repeat, it was gross. I wasn't going to let a nose picker into my life."

"And the nice physical therapist you went out with last year? What was wrong with him?"

"He wore flip-flops with jeans. Out to dinner. At a nice restaurant. Flip-flops. And he needed a pedicure."

"Right. And the accountant had knuckle hair. Are you seeing a pattern, Tuesday? You find fault in every-thing. In everyone. And it's not because you're a judg-mental, mean person, it's because you're hiding away." Gran sighed and brought her soft eyes to mine. "My sweet, sweet girl. I know why you keep going out with these boring men. Nothing about them gets your motor running. They're safe because they're disposable. Not every man is Travis. He was a weasel. He used you. Sweetheart, I know he hurt you, but it is time to move on." She held up her hand. "Don't shake your head. You're transparent. Just because I've never called you on it before doesn't mean I didn't know what you were doing. I hate seeing you so lonely. You should be happy."

"I'm not hiding," I whispered.

"Then why aren't you giving Jackson a shot? It's obvious he wants one."

I was going to note his age again, but thought better of it.

"He's annoying," I blurted out. "And presumptuous."

My grandmother's face brightened, and a broad smile graced her lovely face. Damn.

"You only find him annoying because he won't take no for an answer."

I wanted to ask her how she knew that, but refrained. My gran was a smart woman and had an uncanny ability to read me. She always had.

"I thought we were going to go play bingo. Wouldn't want to keep your suitors waiting."

She shook her head and gave me a small, sad smile.

Fuck.

Damn.

There had been a time I'd wanted what my grandparents had had. The kind of love that lasted decades and didn't dim. I'd always thought I'd find it. I'd lived fast and loose with my heart. I'd worn it on my sleeve proudly, for the world to see, not knowing how fragile it was.

Now that I knew, it was protected. I hated that my grandmother looked so unhappy, but not even for her could I risk it again. It may've made me a horrible granddaughter, but there was only so much humiliation one person could take.

9

"Yo, Jackson. You headed to the bar with us?" Brice asked as I was closing my locker.

"Nope. Got shit to do."

"It's after nine. What shit you gotta do this late at night?"

It wasn't late, but I was dog assed tired. We were working ten-hour shifts for three days in a row with twenty-four hours off, then back to our tens. Thankfully, this would only last another two weeks then we were back to our normal rotation.

"The none of your business kind." I smiled to take some of the sting out of my words.

"You still tryin' to work that girl around? What's her name? Friday?" He was busting my chops. He damn well knew her name.

"Tuesday," I unnecessarily corrected.

"Yeah, Sweet Tuesday. You wear her down yet?"

Brice was one of my closest friends. We'd met at the academy and had been stationed together at the same firehouse. Good friend, great wingman, so, he knew all about Tuesday.

"Nope." I smiled. "Not even a little."

"You seem awfully happy for a man who keeps gettin' shot down."

"Gotta tell you, I'm enjoying the chase," I told him.

The town we lived in wasn't small, nor was it big. Most of the women around the local bars made it their business to know who the firefighters and police officers were. At first, it was gravy. Easy to get laid and not much effort had to be put into it. But the appeal died quickly, and when it did, it became annoying. I'd rather have to work for a woman than have her offer.

"You chasing a new piece, Clark?" Samuel asked as he walked into the room.

My jaw clenched and I tried to check my irritation. "Not real fond of you referring to any woman as a piece. But I'm *really* not happy hearing you call my woman one," I told him.

The man was a dick. He'd been divorced three times, and it was no surprise. Not only had he treated his wives like shit, but all women in general. His last wife had scraped him off exactly two months into the marriage. That was three months ago. Since then he'd gone through every badge bunny in every bar within a thirty-mile radius.

Funny part was, they never went back for seconds, even if he asked. Which confirmed that, not only was he a dick, he was shit in bed. The thing about these women was they'd put up with you being a dick if there was something in it for them. They wanted to hook their star on a firefighter and it didn't take much to please those types of women. A few barbeques with the guys, so they could brag to all their girls about the man giving it to them good and regular, and filling their heads full of bullshit stories about the dangers of fighting fires, and they were happy.

I'd never understand it. And I didn't want it. Tuesday was the exact opposite of easy. She couldn't care less that I was a firefighter.

"Damn. Clark's got himself a woman," Samuel continued, never knowing when to keep his mouth shut.

I ignored his comment and, with a fist bump as I passed Brice, I was out the door. "Catch ya' tomorrow."

I didn't have time to educate Sam on his bullshit. It was going on nine-thirty, and if I wanted to catch Tuesday before she hit the sack I needed to hurry. I got into my truck and spent the drive hoping Tuesday would be in sweats and a tank top singing and swaying her hips again.

———

THE MUSIC WAS ONCE AGAIN PLAYING. I could hear it through Tuesday's front door. This time it was some country jam. I was thinking it was much better than the seventies rock mix she had on last time I was here when I tried the door handle.

Unlocked again.

Goddamn, I was going to tan her ass for not bolting her door. It didn't matter she lived in a decent neighborhood. It was dangerous for a woman who lived alone to leave the door unlocked, especially while she was playing loud music.

I let myself in and there she was. This time she had on a pair of men's boxer shorts rolled at the top sitting low on her hips. Hips that were indeed swaying to the beat of "Girl Like You," and holy shit the song couldn't have been more perfect. I felt the words deep in my chest, and her sexy movements in my dick. I stood and watched, taking in my fill. It was an asshole thing to do, and I should've made my presence known, or maybe even knocked, but I was enjoying the show too much to care.

Suddenly, her body stiffened, and she jerked around. Seeing me standing there she screamed and the papers that were in her hands went flying. Then she flew into me.

"You fucking dick. What's wrong with you?" she yelled as her tiny fists pounded on my chest. "God-damn, you gave me a heart attack."

No, I hadn't. But she needn't worry, I knew CPR and it wouldn't have been a hardship to give her mouth-to-mouth. As a matter of fact, I was thinking that was a good idea. I grabbed her hands in an effort to stop her assault and tugged her closer. She yanked herself free and stepped back.

"Stay away from me. I hate you."

"No, you don't."

"Yes, I do. I hate you so hard right now I want to kick you in the balls. So if you're attached to them and would like to keep them in full working order, I suggest you leave."

"Sweetness, you don't hate me."

"I really do, Jack. Why are you here?" Her breath was coming out in huffs. And I watched the rise and fall of her chest. Her perky boobs had caught my atten-tion and all I could think about was what she sounded like, looked like, and felt like when she'd been panting my name as I'd moved between her thighs.

"Wanted to come by and say hi," I answered.

"Say hi?"

"That's what I said."

She was cute as hell when she was pissed, which would really piss her off if she knew. Her hands were on her hips and a scowl was on her face. But it didn't stop me from taking her in top to toe, this time from the front. She had a great ass, but looking at her face-to-gorgeous-face was a much better view.

"Are your toenails painted different colors?"

"Yes," she snapped.

"Why?"

"Why not? I like my happy toes."

"Happy toes?"

"That's what I call them. The different colors make me happy when I look at them," she explained.

Well, there I had it. Happy rainbow-colored toes made her happy.

"Have you eaten dinner?"

"Why are you asking me about dinner? It's almost ten."

"Because I just got off a ten-hour shift, we had four jobs during that time, which means I didn't eat. Came straight here after work and I'm starving. So, have you eaten?"

"Four jobs?"

"Fires."

"Is that normal? Four fires in ten hours." Her eyes widened and she almost sounded concerned.

I was happy to see she was no longer pitching a fit telling me she hated me but I wasn't lying, I was hungry.

"How about I answer that after I order a pizza? Pepperoni and sausage, okay?"

"You're not staying. Go home and order your pizza."

Damn, I loved how feisty she was.

"Babe, I'm staying. I missed you. I wanna talk to you and see how you've been the last few days but I wanna do it eating. Pepperoni and sausage?"

She stared at me long enough I was getting ready to pull out my phone and order, if she didn't like my choice, she could pull off the toppings, when she finally answered.

"No sausage."

"Pepperoni it is."

I pushed the call button when she added, "Add bell peppers and garlic."

I placed our order and disconnected. I'd never had garlic on a pizza before but at the late hour, I was willing to eat just about anything.

"First, how has your week been?" I asked.

"Fine."

I wasn't stupid, I had a mother and grew up surrounded by female cousins. I knew when a woman said fine, she meant anything but. I was going to have to drag it out of her. Luckily, I didn't work tomorrow so I had all night.

I glanced at the floor and noticed the papers she'd

dropped. I knelt and started to pick up the loose sheets around my feet. A quick scan told me it was a contract of some sort.

"Everything okay with work?"

"My agent doesn't want to allow me out of my contract."

"Can she do that?"

I didn't know anything about the modeling world, contracts, or agents. But I'd certainly learn if it meant wiping the scowl off her pretty face and the lines marring her forehead.

"No, she can't. I can end the contract at any time, for any reason. She'll still get her cut of anything she's booked up until the time the contract is canceled. But she can't force me to stay with the agency or take on more work."

"Then what's the issue?"

"I make her a lot of money," she stated. "She doesn't want to lose it. While we were in New York she was sweet and pleasant and begged me not to cut back. Now that she's not getting her way, she's threatening to sue me and booking me double what she was. I was supposed to be in a fashion show in Florida this afternoon."

"Why would she do that?"

"Ruin my reputation. I declined the Florida show,

she still booked me, now I'm a no show and it makes me look like an asshole."

What a bitch. I finished picking up the papers and handed them to her.

"Damn, Sweetness. That sucks. Anything I can do to help?"

Her eyes flashed before she blinked and the look was gone. "No. I need to read through my contracts and hire an attorney, I guess. Which is gonna be hella expensive. But I can't have Meredith running around telling designers and photographers I'm going to be places when I didn't agree to it. Not only to protect myself, but them as well. It sucks when a model doesn't show; it throws everything off. It screws with the vibe of the show, too. Everyone is stressed and trying to rearrange things. Not to mention, it's also a waste of a photographer's time. It's not right."

I was surprised, though I shouldn't have been. It sounded like she was more upset about the undue hassle the other models would go through than her reputation.

"What else is bothering you?"

"Nothing."

"Babe. You look like you have the weight of the world riding on your shoulders. I understand this shit with your agent has you bent, but that's business, and an irritation. The look you have right now screams personal."

She looked like she was getting ready to answer when she closed down tight. I had three uncles and a dad who were all badasses. All of them had perfected masking their emotions. Tuesday Knowls had them all beat. In an instant she'd wiped all emotion off her face, it was completely devoid of any reaction. I hated that she knew how to do that. But more than that, I hated she felt like she had to do it with me.

That shit was going to stop. I didn't care how long it took, but she was going to learn to let me in.

I'd thought I'd come up with an action plan. I was going to slowly start integrating myself into her life. I had a feeling it was going to be at a crawl's pace. I'd have to slip past her defenses until it was too late, and I'd made myself an integral part of her life. But, now, after seeing that shit? No way I was going to continue to let Tuesday live in a world where she thought she had to hide. There would be no going slow and sneaking in. I was going to trample and push until she told me why. Then I was going to set about making sure she never went back.

10

"Why are you here again?"

I'd had a momentary lapse of judgment and almost answered his question. I'd also forgotten I was irked at him. Well, I was irked before he'd shown up and let himself into my house. Now I was downright angry. And I'd let him order his stupid pizza.

How dumb am I?

"I wanted to say hi." He repeated his lame answer.

"Ever heard of a telephone?"

"Don't have your number, babe."

"Did you stop to think why that was?"

"Nope."

"Right. Ever heard of knocking?"

"Didn't bother. Seeing as your music was so loud you would've never heard. And for the record this playlist is the bomb."

My playlist *was* the bomb. But it pissed me off he was standing in my living room listening to it. It further made me mad he'd once again scared the crap out of me.

"And you didn't lock your fucking door."

A sudden and unwelcome thrill raced through me. He sounded like he actually cared.

"Whatever." It was an immature response, but I was still trying to figure out why my heart was now pounding from something other than fright.

"Not *whatever*, Tuesday. It's dangerous. Lock the goddamn door."

I wasn't sure why he thought it was his concern and I really wasn't sure why I liked that he was worried. I was a grown woman, after all, and had lived on my own a long time. A lot longer than him.

"I think when your pizza gets here you should take it and go home."

"Oh, no, I ordered bell peppers and garlic for you. We're gonna sit down and eat it together."

"Why?" My hands went up in frustration. "Why are you doing this? I'm sure there are about fifty other women you could call up and they'd be pleased as shit you wanted to have pizza and a sleepover with them."

The thought hurt my heart.

"Sleepover?" He laughed.

I wasn't trying to be funny. The last thing I needed

was him in a good mood. He had a great laugh, deep and rumbly. It wasn't lost on me how much my girly parts liked it. And his lips, mouth, and tongue. They really loved what he could do with those three things. I'd spent days imagining him doing them to me again.

Nope.

No way.

Not going to go there. He had to leave.

"What are you thinking about?" he asked.

Jackson stepped closer while I was daydreaming about his expertise in the bedroom. This wasn't good either. I didn't want him in my personal space. It seemed my common sense took a vacation when he touched me.

"About how I want you to leave."

"Liar. Your cheeks are pink and your eyes are glazed over. The last thing you were thinking about was me leaving. If I had to guess, I'd say you were thinking about what it feels like when—"

Ding dong.

Thank God. Saved by the bell.

Jackson smirked before strolling to the front door. I used the time to pull my shit together. I'd have to be more careful. He was far more observant than I'd given him credit for.

He came back in, dropped the box on the coffee

table, went to the kitchen, cabinets opened and closed, then he reappeared with plates and napkins.

"Make yourself at home, why don't you?"

"Planned to."

All of this happened while I stood woodenly in my living room wondering how the hell this was happening. The only good part about Jackson showing up was that I'd stopped thinking about my grandmother.

"Come eat, Sweetness," he invited.

"Why are you doing this? And please answer me this time. I don't like having to repeat myself."

This had to end. Everything about him drove me crazy.

"I've already told you why. It's not my fault you don't like my answer."

"Seriously." I couldn't stop the growl as it ripped from my throat. "Why the fuck do you keep showing up here?"

He stood up from my couch and stalked toward me. Yes, he stalked, like he was a sleek panther and I was his prey. He stopped inches from me. So close I could smell what was left of his cologne. I'd stupidly noted how much I liked the smell, specifically when it was on my pillowcase. I shouldn't have. I should've been paying attention. One of his arms wrapped around my middle and hauled me flush to him, and his other hand made its way into the back of my hair. He unnecessarily tugged, as I was already staring at him.

It was then he spoke. "Who hurt you?"

"What?" His question felt like a physical blow.

"Who the fuck hurt you so badly, you've closed yourself off?"

"No one," I lied.

"Do not bullshit me. No woman or man goes to such great lengths to push people away if they haven't been burned."

Now he was pissing me off, he'd hit the truth, and I wanted him nowhere near it.

"Did you ever stop and think that maybe it's just you I don't want around? Or are you so arrogant you believe that all women should fall at your feet?"

"Who burned you, Sweetness?"

"No one. We've been over this."

"The first time I came back was to get my watch. This time I came back because I missed you. Wanted to talk. And I definitely planned on getting another taste of you. But now I wanna know why you're so hell-bent on protecting yourself."

"Is that what you want? A little more fun? Another taste?"

"Among other things, yes."

"You can't have anything else."

The hand he had in my hair was moving down to

the nape of my neck. He paused there and gave me a squeeze. "Tuesday, Sweetness, I'm not going to hurt you. You don't have to protect yourself from me. I'd sooner cut off my arm than see you sad. Let me in."

I wanted to believe him. Hell, I almost did believe he wouldn't hurt me intentionally, but that didn't mean he wouldn't do it all the same.

"That's not going to happen. And if you'd been paying attention at all, I already told you why."

"No, you gave me shit excuses, one being I was too young. You even went as far as saying you liked your men experienced. Think I proved we're more than compatible in that department and I can be everything you need. And just so you know, I *have* been paying attention. So much so, I know all your talk was utter shit. I also know what we shared meant something to you. I saw it. If I had to guess, I'd say it's been years since you've invited a man to your bed. How that is possible with you looking the way you do, is beyond me, but it doesn't make it any less true." He stopped and leaned in even closer. "And how I know has nothing to do with how tight your pussy was, how wild you got at the smallest touch, or how fast you came for me. It had everything to do with the way you were looking at me. And just so you know, straight up, Sweetness, it meant something to me, too. A fuck of a lot."

I wanted a hole to open up so I could fall through it and disappear. I was embarrassed he could read me as easily as he could, I was mad at myself for letting my guard down, and I was a whole lot turned on. He was right about all of it, and I hated that. I'd used his age as an excuse, but it was a concern. I was seven years older than him. We were in two different places in our lives.

"That's still the case, Jackson," I told him, ignoring the rest.

"Babe, it isn't. It stopped being the case when I kissed you and you attacked my mouth."

More embarrassment.

"I didn't attack your mouth."

"Yeah, you did. And I have to tell you it was hot as fuck, and I would've been damn disappointed if you hadn't."

"So what? One really great kiss and awesome sex and suddenly you've aged ten years?"

"Awesome sex?"

Damn. Shit. Fuck. Why'd I say that? I was losing the argument and needed a subject change pronto.

"Can you please step away from me?"

"After you kiss me."

"I don't think so, Jack. No more kissing."

"Maybe I'd believe that if you weren't melting into me and if your beautiful brown eyes hadn't gone soft."

I tried to shove away from him, but he held on tight. "Jackson!"

This wasn't going well. He saw too much and he had no problem calling me on my bullshit. I didn't like it.

"You're holding on to some stupid reason not to let go and give us a shot."

I could hear my grandmother's words in the back of my mind telling me I was hiding away. Would it be so bad to go on a date with Jackson even though he was younger than me? Yes. It would be bad. Very bad. Because the only fault I could find in Jackson was his age. He was annoying as hell, but, as usual, my grandmother was right about that, too. I only thought that because he wouldn't let me push him away.

I knew I was making a mistake even before I said the words. "I won't let you in. I don't do relationships and feelings. I don't want to talk to you about my day. You wanna work out an arrangement where you come over, we have sex, then you leave? We can talk. But other than that, I got nothing to give you. The reasons why are none of your business and I won't be sharing." He continued to stare down at me. "You were right, it had been awhile. You're good in bed, you want more, I want more, but there will be a few rules."

"Not real fond of rules, Sweetness."

"That reminds me, rule number one: no more calling me sweetness."

His lips curved up into a smile. "Yeah, not following that rule. What else you got?"

"No more showing up unannounced. No going out. No asking me personal stuff. I'm not joking, straight up sex, then you go home. I can't offer you anymore than that."

"None of those work for me."

"Funny. They don't have to work for you. They're mine. You just have to follow them. And if you don't want to make the deal, there's the door."

Why did thinking about him walking out the door hurt? I'd gone from completely pushing him out of my life to offering him sex. Yeah, I was stupid. In that moment looking up at Jackson waiting to hear if he was going to agree to my rules, I kind of felt like one of those too-stupid-to-live actresses in a horror movie. You know, the dumb bimbo who runs toward the danger instead of, say, locking herself in the closet so the bad guy can't find her? Totally me. Too-stupid-to-live starring in my own personal horror show. Fuck. I knew this was a mistake.

Huge.

Big.

Epic.

He lowered his face closer to mine and whispered near my mouth, "Might as well start as I intend to go."

Before I could question what he meant, his lips were on mine. And just like all the other times, I opened for him. Immediately. No hesitation. I didn't understand why, it just felt right. He kept the kiss slow and soft even when I tried to deepen it, he remained in control. He gave me no other option but to follow. It was all kinds of hot. Just as good as our last, but not as wet and wild. Our tongues danced and stroked.

His hold tightened, and I was no longer paying attention to how great the kiss was, being in his arms was better. He was strong, and tall, and held me with a gentleness I'd never experienced. I was protected and cared for. This was why I'd wanted to stay away from him. I didn't want to delude myself into thinking there could be more between us. Before I knew it, I'd never want him to let me go.

Jackson broke the kiss, and before I could get my wits about me, he spoke. His voice was full of gravel and that was hot, too. "I'm gonna lay this out for you, Sweetness. Straight up honesty. Your rules do not apply to us. I'm gonna kiss you whenever I can. Touch you often. I'm going to take you out. I'm gonna spend time with you here at your house. You're gonna spend time at mine. So maybe I can give you not showing up unannounced, because from here on out, I'm not working, you're not working, you can expect me."

His proclamation had me worried. Jackson touching and kissing me muddled my head. I couldn't think clearly. And I needed to or I'd never survive him.

"This isn't a game."

"Damn right, it's not. You're not a woman to be played. But, fair warning, while we're doing this, I'm pulling out all the stops. I'm going to prove you can trust me with your time. I'm not fucking around with your heart, I want in. You can fight and push me away, but I'll still break through."

"Why?"

I sounded like a broken record. I'd asked him so many times, but I still didn't understand why someone as hot Jackson, who could have any young girl he clapped eyes on, would want me. I was a mess and told him flat out I didn't want a relationship.

Hell, I'd basically tried to make an arrangement with him where he dispensed orgasms and nothing else. Yet, he still wanted more. What was wrong with him? What guy wouldn't be down with a no strings sex non-relationship?

"Because I like you."

The ice around my heart had been quickly melting, but with those four words it went back into a deep freeze.

"None of that other shit is up for negotiation. Sex. That's it. Take or it or leave it. But, Jack, you have to know this is me giving you straight up honesty, I'm never gonna fall in love with you. I don't want a man. I don't want touchy feely shit. You broke my dry spell in a way that makes me want more of what you can offer. But that's it. I'll take you up on your offer for seconds, but you'll need to check the rest at the door."

Lies, lies, and more lies.

Jackson's eyes flashed, the brown that was a shade darker than mine turned molten.

"While you're fucking me, no one else touches you. Not a kiss, not holding your hand, and definitely no one else in your bed. Nothing," he bit out, anger rolling off him in waves.

I thought about his request, it wasn't a hardship since none of that was happening anyway.

"Fine."

"You're taking my cock, Sweetness, there will be no dating other men."

"Not part of the agreement, Jack."

"It is now. We make this agreement, I don't take another woman to my bed, that means I'm over here burrowing myself into you. I'm not working my schedule around some chump who has no shot at getting in there anyway."

It was safe to say, Jackson was a little pissed with

me. Which, as fucked up as it was, was easier for me to hide when he was acting like this.

"Fine," I repeated.

"Great."

"You sure this is how you wanna play this, Tuesday? My dick and nothing else?"

"All I'm willing to give you."

Acid churned in my stomach remembering why I had nothing else to offer. Memories that cut so deep they never healed. I'd spent years making sure they were still open and bleeding so I'd never forget the pain of betrayal.

His hands moved to my ass, he lifted me, and my legs wrapped around his waist.

Oh, shit. This was happening now.

"What about the pizza?"

"Fuck the pizza."

Yep, it was happening.

The fucked-up side of me was totally turned on by how pissed Jackson was. The logical side knew I'd just awoken a beast I'd never be able to contain.

11

Tonight hadn't gone as planned.

My strategy had been simple, I was going over to spend time with her and lay the groundwork. Move in slowly, build, and go from there. Nowhere in that tactic had I thought she'd suggest this shit. A booty call. That's what she was pushing for. She wasn't even offering friends with benefits. She wanted the benefits all right, just not the friendship.

Now she was wrapped around me and I was stomping to the bedroom. Even as pissed as I was, I couldn't miss how good she felt pressed against me. If this was all she was offering, I was going to take it. But there wasn't a snowball's chance in hell I was abiding by her fucking rules. Not any of them. I wasn't going to check shit at the door. And if she thought I was going to stop pressing her for answers, she was mistaken.

She wanted to get stubborn, I'd get creative. After the bullshit she'd just shoveled, I knew I'd been right. Someone had fucked her over, and, when they had, it hurt her bad enough she'd retreated, protecting not only her heart but her body as well.

When we got to her room, I set her down by her bed, roughly yanked her tank over her head, and tossed it aside.

Her eyes were wide with shock and a little apprehension.

"You sure about this, Sweetness?"

"Yeah."

"Convince me."

There were a lot of ways Tuesday looked at me that I loved. Some I liked better than others. But doubt and worry were not two of them. If she wanted this agreement, I'd play along until I could break through. What I wouldn't do was be the asshole she wanted me to be, laying her shit on me so later she could pin me down and paint me as the bad guy.

"Convince you?" she asked.

"Yep. You want this, show me."

Her shaky hands went to my shirt and started to pull it up.

"Look at me," I demanded.

Her eyes snapped to mine and there was still trepidation. She had under two minutes to prove she was on board with this until I shut it down. She continued to fumble with my shirt, and I knew I couldn't do it.

"Tuesday." My hands went to her waist, hitting bare flesh just above the rolled-over boxer shorts she was still wearing. Her palms landed on my pecs, abandoning her efforts, short tipped nails dug in. "Baby," I whispered.

Her gaze softened, and her hands roamed. "I want this."

I watched and waited, keeping my eyes on hers, which was no small feat considering she was standing in front of me, heaving in oxygen, perky breasts on display. She wasn't wearing a bra, and as desperately as I wanted to look, touch, and taste I didn't.

Tuesday was back to pulling my shirt off this time with more certainty. Still not enough for me to touch her, but enough I'd let her continue.

Her lips touched my skin just below my throat, and I moved my hands back to her hips, mainly so I wouldn't touch her other places. Goddamn, her mouth felt good. The tentative kisses were turning into nips, moving up my neck.

Her hands shoved under the back of my jeans, fingertips digging into the muscles in my ass, and she pressed her tits against my chest. "I want this, Jack," she whispered, then licked the shell of my ear. "So are we gonna stand here all night discussing it, or are you gonna fuck me?"

One hand came out of my jeans, traveled up my spine, the back of my neck, and, finally, into the back of my hair.

"Kiss me," I demanded. Her eyes flashed, and I knew she didn't want to. She was planning on keeping this exchange as impersonal as the first. She hadn't wanted to kiss me while I'd been fucking her then. But this was personal, as personal as it got, and I was going to make sure she understood. "Baby, when we are in this room, you are mine. If I wanna spend hours kissing my woman, I'm gonna. If I want to play with your body until you're boneless, I'm gonna. Because, in here, like this, every last bit of you belongs to me. I can wait you out all night long, and, Tuesday, I am not fucking you until you kiss me."

"That's not—"

"In here, that's exactly the way it is. You laid out your rules, I'm laying out mine. In here, I call the shots, every last one of them, all you need to do is trust that everything I do, I'll make it good for you. So, kiss me, baby. I'm fucking starved. All I've been doing these last three weeks is thinking about how good you taste. Can't tell you how many times I've stroked myself thinking about the way you look, the way you sound when you're coming around my dick."

She didn't hesitate, her lips hit mine hard, and she went for it. All the other times we'd kissed she'd let me take control, but not this one. She wasn't giving me an inch. Her tongue wasn't gently gliding against mine, she was taking, owning, claiming.

Fucking perfect.

Without breaking the kiss, I shoved her shorts and panties down over her ass and let them fall around her ankles. This time it was my hands that were shaking when I picked her up, put my knee to the bed, and hefted us both up and into the middle. We came down, both my palms flat on the bed by her head, not giving her all of my weight. Her hands were getting desperate, they moved from my back to the button of my jeans. I grabbed both of her wrists and stopped her.

"Hands above your head."

Tuesday looked so pretty under me, lids at half mast, makeup free, guard down, nothing but lust shining back.

"But I want—"

"Baby, I wanna take my time and enjoy your perky tits, then I'm gonna enjoy exploring all the ways I can make you come. I cannot do that with your hands on me."

Her lips twitched and one side curved up, a few beats later, she was smiling wide. "Can't say that sounds all that bad." She moved her hands to the bed then up over her head. The movement slow and sexy. The side effect to that was her back arched and her tits looked fantastic on full display.

With my cock throbbing, begging to be released, I set about seeing the ways I could make her scream.

In the end, I found out she could orgasm with nothing but nipple stimulation and me talking dirty. She could also let go with just my mouth sucking on her clit, with *her* talking dirty. And I found she could be filthy. But the best way to turn Tuesday wild was finger fucking her while I played rough with her tiny, sensitive nub. She went wild, her hips bucked, her head thrashed, she screamed out, and I licked up every last drop of excitement that leaked from her pussy. I did it for a long time, not wasting a drop. She tasted good, fabulous. When she lost her control, it was so fucking beautiful I didn't know what to do with it all. But I was going to learn.

By the time she'd exploded the fourth time, which took a good amount of effort on my part, getting dirtier with my words, she was so exhausted she hadn't protested when I gathered her into my arms, and she passed out.

My unused dick was still hard, still throbbing, and in serious need of attention. Attention I would give it later when I was alone. There were many ways I could play this, but I only had one shot. I'd give her as many orgasms as she wanted with my mouth and fingers. But she wasn't getting more until she gave more.

Tuesday thought she'd manipulated the situation, getting what she wanted. She had no idea all she'd done was give me the opening I needed.

And I wasn't stupid, not only had I walked through the door, but I'd locked it behind me. She wanted me out, she'd have the fight of her life trying. I'd dead-bolted that fucker closed.

I drifted to sleep with a smile on my face and an armful of my woman.

12

I woke up and the first thing that hit me was heat at my back. I was on my side, Jackson behind me. The next was the strong arm that was wrapped around me, holding me close. This was not part of the sex-only agreement. Not that I had firsthand knowledge, but I was fairly certain this was not how this was supposed to go.

I'd never done it, but I did have friends, both female and male that regularly participated in no strings sex and, not that they'd waxed poetic about every detail and nuance, I didn't think cuddling or even spending the night was a part of the program.

And, if it was, it wasn't going to be a part of mine.

That didn't mean I wasn't going to take a minute and enjoy how good it felt having Jackson in my bed. Stupid. I was so stupid allowing myself to sink into his embrace. But I wanted to know. Just for a few minutes while he was asleep and it was safe, I wanted to feel normal.

If Travis hadn't come into my life, if I hadn't trusted him, if I hadn't been so blinded by all his bull-shit, I could've had this. A man, a real relationship, love and faithfulness. I *would've* had it.

There'd been a time in my life I'd needed to be loved so desperately I'd lived with my head in the clouds when I'd thought I'd found it. When I'd heard rumblings around the fashion shows that Travis was cheating, I confronted him, then believed him when he'd said it was nothing but jealous gossip. The rumors flew, then they turned into something worse, people no longer gossiping, instead looking at me like I was a clueless chump. I'd allowed that. But even all of that didn't compare to his kill shot, his ultimate betrayal.

I was no longer the naïve idiot who'd needed to be loved. He'd taught me that the love I'd envisioned for myself wasn't real. I knew my grandparents had shared it, I'd watched them. So I knew. But a love like that had come about during a different era when people were still kind and honest. What they had was an old-fash-ioned love. It was pure and honest. That kind of love didn't exist. Not anymore. My parents didn't even have it. I was stupid to think I could have had something from days gone by.

Travis had provided a valuable education, and I'd graduated with my Ph.D. I was never going there again. But I would take this, Jackson's warmth surrounding me while it was safe, and he was none the wiser.

"Morning," Jackson whispered into my hair.

His sexy, gruff sleep thick voice doing nothing to help me pull back into my cocoon.

"Sleep okay?" he went on.

"Yeah."

"Good."

His arm around me tightened, and his hard-on pressed into my ass. Realization hit. He hadn't spent the night to hold me, he hadn't finished. Last night I'd fallen asleep before I'd paid him back for his generosity. And he'd been generous—with his mouth and his fingers.

Despite what I wanted Jackson to believe, I was sure he had more experience than I did. But that didn't mean I hadn't had a few men over the years and none of them had taken their time or given me anything close to what Jackson had. Nor had I ever lost control and spoken to any of them like I had to him last night.

My face went up in flames remembering all the things I'd said. All the things I'd begged him to do to me, and everything I'd said I wanted to do to him. No wonder he was still here. I hadn't made good on my promises. God, even when I knew what this was, I'd still stupidly thought he'd spent the night for different reasons.

The denim scraped my bare legs as I turned in his arms to face him. Jackson Clark was a good-looking guy; he was no less hot first thing in the morning with his hair messy and face mellow. He was calendar worthy. I could see him in his uniform pants, boots on, shirtless, posing in front of a fire engine. Mr. July. I could totally see women buying that calendar and never flipping to the next month when they got to him.

What the hell did he want with me? I was thirty-one, emotionally bankrupt, untrusting, with an uncertain career and nothing to offer.

"What has you thinking so hard, Sweetness?"

Hell no! We were not talking about what I was thinking. We weren't supposed to be talking at all.

"Sorry I fell asleep on you last night."

My hands went to his chest, and I'd like to say I was unaffected; more than just my palms were tingling as I touched him. My brain short-circuited and all my common sense took a hike. If I was smart, I'd end this now.

I wasn't made to be able to carry out this type of arrangement. I was destined to live the rest of my life celibate, because there was no way to deny I felt more than physical attraction when I touched Jackson.

"What are you doing, baby?" he asked, placing a hand over mine as I went for the button of his pants.

Well, if that wasn't mortifying, I don't know what was.

"I'm . . ." I trailed off because I was embarrassed that I was so bad at this he had to ask.

"Tuesday?" His tone was gentle. "Look at me."

Why did he always want me to look at him? And kiss him. What the hell was up with that? Couldn't he just fuck me and leave? That's all this was.

"Tuesday." My eyes snapped to his and he was studying me. Dammit.

"I believe payback is in order for last night. You want it now or are you gonna come back later to collect? But I've got shit to do today, so you need to make your decision quick."

All the sleep fled from his face, all the gentleness, *poof,* gone.

Back was the pissed off man who'd taken me to bed. The one that didn't look at me with kindness. This was who I needed him to be.

"Later," he growled. But not in the sexy, feral kind of way he did when his mouth was between my legs.

He pressed a hard kiss against my lips and rolled out of bed.

I watched in horror as he tagged his tee off the

floor, gathered his socks and boots, and headed for the door.

Not even a goodbye.

Not a look back.

Not a wave.

He slammed the door behind him, and was gone.

I fell back on the bed, stared at my ceiling, and wondered what the fuck was wrong with me.

Then the answer came.

Travis Manning and all of his lessons.

13

Payback?

What the fuck?

I fought the urge to throw Tuesday's coffee pot across the room. I was so pissed I had to get away from her. Even knowing she would throw some fucked-up attitude my way I hadn't been ready for *that*.

I hadn't been ready for the sting to twist into a burn that hurt so damn badly I couldn't swallow it. I couldn't stand the look on her pretty face when she spewed out the words. If she thought I'd missed the hurt that had flashed when she'd tried to paste on the fake bluster, she was wrong.

I saw what it took for her to utter those words. When I'd had her body blazing, she could moan all the dirty things she wanted to do to me and make it sound so fucking sweet. But lying there looking at me with hurt flashing, talking about payback coming from her pretty mouth, was the nastiest, jacked-up shit I'd ever heard in my life.

I'd never felt so dirty.

And that was saying something. I wasn't a monk. I'd had my fair share of one-night stands, drunken encounters I can't say I'm proud of, but none that I regret. Yet, never had I walked out of a woman's bedroom feeling like I needed a shower to wash away words spoken.

Fucking payback?

Was she for real?

I was watching the coffee brew with my back to the entrance of the kitchen. I couldn't see her, but I felt it the minute Tuesday hit the room. The air crackled, and I struggled to get a hold of my temper.

"Jackson—"

"Don't."

"Maybe we should—"

"I said, don't. Leave it, Tuesday."

"I thought you'd left."

Yeah, I bet she had. Or more to the point, I bet she wished I had.

"You thought wrong."

I turned to face her and found no joy when she flinched. I was pissed and made no effort to hide it. This was me. I was honest to a fault. I didn't hide shit, if someone asked me a question, they were getting honesty. If I didn't like something I came straight out and said it. I wasn't changing who I was, therefore, she caught the brunt of my anger. It was written all over my face.

I glanced over her shoulder, a big bouquet of flowers sitting on her dining room table catching my attention. Her gaze followed mine slightly, turning to see what I was looking at.

"Thank you for the flowers. They're beautiful," she told me.

"Come again?"

"They're beautiful. Roses are pretty enough, but I love wildflowers. The color of those brighten the room."

She was still looking at the bouquet, and I saw her in profile, I didn't need to see her face to know she'd softened.

"Babe, I didn't send you flowers."

"What?" Every muscle in her body went tight. "But the card—"

"What did it say?"

Tuesday walked over to the flowers, found the clear plastic stick, and pulled the small card free with a shaky hand, and read it out loud.

"It was nice seeing you. You looked as beautiful as ever." Her voice wobbled as she read.

Something was wrong. She seemed almost scared. I took the three strides needed and pulled her into my arms, some of my anger ebbing away.

"Sweetness?"

"I'm not listed, Jackson. I've gone to great lengths to keep my phone and address private."

"When were those delivered?"

"Yesterday."

"This happen a lot?"

"What?"

"You getting flowers from admirers."

The thought of men sending her flowers did not sit well with me.

"Not any . . . um. No." Her answer was shaky and unsure.

"Why go to great lengths to keep your information private?"

Tuesday stiffened before she started trembling and then started to pull away.

"Babe, what the fuck?"

"I just don't want people knowing where I live."

That was a lie and something we'd come back to.

"Could those be from your agent? The card said, it was nice seeing you."

"Jackson, my agent is threatening to sue me. At this point, I think she'd send me a pipe bomb, not flowers."

We'd be coming back to that, too. Right after I

figured out why she went to "great lengths" to keep her address private. I get a single woman not wanting her information on blast but her shaking in my arms, freaking out about goddamned flowers went beyond general precautions.

"Anyone from the show?" I continued.

"Maybe. But it would be unusual. And I'd think they'd sign their name. That's actually why I thought they were from you."

"Why's that?"

"Don't take this the wrong way, and no offense, but I kinda thought not signing the card was pretty arrogant. Like, I should automatically know who they were from."

My lips twitched despite how pissed I still was and now concerned. "None taken."

"You really didn't send them?"

I hated that she sounded scared, hated even more that something didn't feel right.

"No, Sweetness, I didn't send them."

"I think I want to throw them away now."

I let go of her and watched as she turned, picked up the glass vase, walked to the sink, dumped the water, and tossed the flowers in the trash, glass container and all.

"I've Googled you," I said conversationally.

"You did?" Her face paled and a new look crossed her face. It wasn't fear, she looked like I'd slapped her.

What the fuck?

"Yeah. I found a video and watched you strut your fine ass down the catwalk, saw your picture in advertisements. I'm actually more than surprised I hadn't recognized you. I had no idea how much of a celebrity you were."

"You're taking it a little too far. I am hardly a celebrity." She still looked flushed and her hand was shaking so badly it'd taken her more than one try to pull the carafe of coffee off the burner. "I'm a nobody."

I came up behind her and pulled her back against my front, pinning her between me and the counter.

"Babe," I spoke near her ear. "You've been on dozens of fashion magazine covers. You're in print ads for perfume that costs as much as most people's weekly paycheck. Your sexy feet showing off shoes I know cost more than my monthly salary. I'm not exaggerating. You're hardly a nobody."

She shook her head and was putting forth so much concentration into stirring her coffee you'd think she was performing brain surgery. She was shit scared, and I didn't have the first clue what she was afraid of.

"Listen, Jackson, I've got a lot of errands to run and I still need to shower. I should get on that."

She was sporting her getaway. Retreating to her corner.

"Why's your agent threatening to sue you?"

"I already told you why."

"Explain it to me again."

With a huff, she abandoned her coffee and turned to face me.

"This is not us, Jackson. Remember? We have sex, you leave. No personal conversation."

"Bullshit."

"What do you mean bullshit? That was what you agreed to."

"Sweetness, if you think I'm gonna stand here watching you shake like a leaf, looking upset, and not ask questions you've lost your mind."

"You're right. I have lost my mind. I was crazy to think this could work. It can't."

"It's working just fine," I told her.

Or it would be once I got her to open up to me.

Tuesday's posture changed, and she rearranged her features with a look of defiance. It was cute she thought her being stubborn was going to push me away.

"I think we're done. You can let yourself out."

She tried her best to push me away, the movement only bringing her closer to me. I loved she was so tall, her height meant I didn't have far to go when I leaned down and brushed my mouth against hers, then to her forehead where I let my lips linger for a moment, breathing in her gardenia scent.

"I'll see you soon, Tuesday."

"No, you won't, Jackson. We're done. This isn't going to work," she whispered.

"Bet?"

With one last peck on her forehead, I set her aside and moved toward the door. I heard her mumbling something but didn't stop.

I was in my truck, backing out of Tuesday's driveway thinking about the best way to get her to open up to me when a horn blared. An old, beat-up Nissan Sentra was pulling away from the curb, and my head was so full of thoughts of Tuesday, I hadn't even seen the car.

Fuck.

I needed to get my shit together.

TWENTY MINUTES LATER, I was pulling into my parents' driveway. They still lived in the house I grew up in. It was outside of the city limits and one of the last few places that hadn't been taken over by developments. When my dad bought the house, he was still in the Army. After a deployment, he'd needed the space and quiet. After he got custody of Nick and married my mom, the space was needed for a different reason, he had a family.

It was a good thing I'd left Tuesday's when I had. I'd forgotten I'd agreed to help my dad repair and paint an old wooden fence that really needed to be pulled out and replaced altogether, but my mom refused. She wanted it repaired. Reagan Clark was sentimental. Dad had put the fence in after I was born to help contain me. Not that I hadn't been able to crawl under or over the split rails, but it gave them enough time to get to me before I disappeared into the woods behind the house. Mom refused to let Dad take it down, she said she liked to sit on the back deck and remember us boys playing. Not that Nick had done much playing back there, he was much older than I was.

I parked my truck and saw my dad already in the backyard. I was late, no doubt I was going to get an earful.

I jogged to the side of the house, and my dad turned, did a once-over, and shook his head.

"You lose your watch, son?"

"Nope."

He shook his head again, noticing my blue cargos and station 57 tee and asked, "You been home since your shift?"

"Nope."

"Boy, I know you've made it your life's mission to

tag every available piece of ass south of the Carolinas, but don't you think it's time to slow down?"

There were two things to note: first, when my dad said piece of ass, he wasn't being a disrespectful prick like Sam, therefore, I didn't correct him. The second was, I didn't hide shit from my dad. I also didn't lie. I'd gone to him when I knew I was close to losing my virginity and we'd talked. He was honest, he explained things that teenage boys don't talk about with each other, and he told me straight up what my responsibilities were toward the girl. Being that we had an open relationship, he hadn't held much back, and in the years since then we'd talked some more.

He also understood that my options were vast, and while I'd learned to be more discerning with the women I took to my bed, I hadn't always been.

"Working on it."

"Working on it? Doesn't look like you're trying all that hard, wearing yesterday's clothes looking like you just rolled out of bed."

"Yes, but the woman whose bed I just rolled out of is the woman I'm trying to nail down."

"By the looks of it, I'd say you managed the nailed part."

Smartass.

"Where'd you meet her?"

"Nick's house."

"Come again?"

It was rare I got to surprise my dad. And his look of confusion was priceless.

"Remember Mercy's friend Tuesday Knowls?"

Not only did it take a lot to surprise Nolan Clark, it took a fuck of a lot to shock him. And staring into my father's wide brown eyes, I knew I'd shocked the shit out of him.

"That is not a good idea, son."

"I think it's a great idea."

"Jackson, that woman is gonna chew you up and spit you out."

Now I was getting a little irritated. "And why is that?"

"It wasn't lost on me, under all that pretty and great smile, that woman is an island. She ain't letting anyone near her, Jackson."

"You don't know the half of it," I muttered.

"Right. So, all you'd be doing is spinning your wheels. And, son, a woman like her, one that looks like she has a lot of experience shutting men down, can be lethal. I suppose it'd be painful when that door slams shut. You may want to rethink having a go at Tuesday Knowls."

"Too late."

"No, Jackson, it's not. You also have to think about

when this goes bad, where does that leave her? As far as I can tell Mercy is her only friend. Mercy is now a part of this family, which means she's gonna want to bring her friend around. Tuesday might not feel like coming around if that means you're there. There's more at play here than you wanting to nail a beautiful, leggy model."

"Now you're pissing me off, Dad. I'm not trying to nail her, if I were, I'd be there taking her up on her offer of servicing me as payback for what I gave her last night. But as you can see, my tired ass is standing here in front of you. And since when do you care about the possibility of screwing up family ties? Mom and Uncle Jasper go way back, don't they? Mom came to Georgia to meet his family. That didn't stop you from going after her."

"And that almost backfired. Since you remember the story so well, you'll remember I also had to let her go."

"No, Dad, you didn't let her go because of Uncle Jasper. You let her go because you weren't ready to claim her and admit you loved her. And, I get why. What Nick's mom did to you was low. So low, I understand why a man would never want to take a chance again. But I'm standing here instead of tangled up in bed with Tuesday because I know I want more than a tangle. I don't want payback. I don't even want to be in this fucked up sex-only arrangement she's come up with."

"What exactly did you agree to?"

"Sex. That's it. No strings, no commitment, no talking, no relationship. A fucking booty call. It's the last thing I want, but I agreed, because I know this is the only way I can get in. You got one thing right; it's gonna be painful. She's gonna fight me tooth and nail. You should know, I've learned a lot from you about the man I wanted to be. Part of that was paying attention and learning from my mistakes. It took one goddamn smile for me to know I was all in. One. That's it."

"Damn, son." My dad's gaze held mine and I braced. "Maybe you need to slow this down."

Fuck that. I learned my lesson about going slow with Tuesday. Slow meant retreat. I was moving forward. And I was going fast. It was the only way, keep her off balance, and satisfied. If that didn't work, I'd come up with something new. One way or another, she was gonna cave.

"You know what she was doing the first night I walked in her house? Dancing. Hips swaying, and singing out of key, not giving the first fuck she sounded like a dying rhinoceros. I had to stop and savor it. At first, I thought she just liked good music and liked to dance. Now I know the only place she's comfortable is when she's locked herself behind closed doors and she can be herself. And the way she does it, she sucks every bit of goodness she can out of it. Because when she walks out the door, she knows no one sees her. Not the real her. Partly because she hides it, but mostly because people are shallow and only see her pretty face and look no further. She's also scared of something or someone but won't open up the smallest fucking bit to tell me. You know anyone like that, Dad? Someone so sweet and pretty you'd do anything to protect that soft spot you know they have under all their fake smiles?" I stopped to let that sink in.

"You're setting yourself up for a world of hurt. You think she's locking herself away hiding from a world that doesn't see her but you are wrong. That's not why she hides. Someone fucked her over. Bet my house on it. And they fucked her good." Pain flashed in my dad's eyes, and I knew he was remembering the woman who'd fucked *him* over. "I haven't looked in the mirror and seen that look for over two decades now, but I still remember it."

"You're right, someone did. And you may remember the look, Dad, but you no longer feel it. Mom healed it. I want to do that for Tuesday, I want to be the one to soothe the hurt, but she won't let me in. She was freaking the fuck out because someone had sent her flowers. Flowers, non-threatening flowers. That's fucked. She was scared because they had her address. Her words were, I go to great lengths to keep my address private. Why would she do that? Then when I told her I'd Googled her, you would've thought I'd hit her. Something's not right."

"Shit." I waited while my dad worked through everything I'd just said. He scrubbed his hand over his face and asked, "You're sure about this? Really fucking sure, Jackson?"

"Positive."

"What do you need from me? We can run her. See if there's anything on record that would explain why she doesn't want her address out there. But I will say, it's a smart thing to do. She's in the public eye, she lives alone, and that makes her an easy mark."

Warmth spread over me, and it had nothing to do with the hot Georgia sun beating down. There it was, my dad would take my back.

"I agree with you, it is smart. But it doesn't explain why she was shaking. I want her to tell me. I'm gonna give her a week. If she doesn't, I'll take you up on your offer."

My dad nodded then asked, "You about done yappin'? We got work to do."

He was so full of shit. My dad had all the time in the world to stand around and talk to me. But he was right, the fence wasn't gonna fix itself, and I did need to sleep.

"I'm ready if you are, old man."

"Old man? Shit, boy, I can still—"

"Please don't finish that, Dad."

My dad's head tipped back, and he barked out a laugh.

"I was gonna say outwork you. Good to know where your head's at."

"Sure you were."

His hand pounded my shoulder and he started toward the fence. "I'm rooting for you, Jackson. If there's anyone who can get her to come around it's you."

It was a good thing I had him in my corner. I had a feeling I was going to need him more than I knew.

14

My phone ringing cut through the song playing through my car's speakers. The display announced Mercy was calling and I felt like shit. She'd called me three times in as many days and I hadn't answered.

I hit connect on my steering wheel and answered. "I'm so sorry I'm such a shit friend."

"Mm-hmm. Shit friend for ignoring my calls? Or have you been a little busy?" She laughed.

"Um..."

This felt like a trap, and when Mercy busted out into a fit of laughter then said to someone that was not me that they owed her five bucks, I knew I'd been busted.

"So, how's Jackson?" I could hear the humor in her singsong voice.

Damn!

"Um . . ."

Fuck me running. How the hell did she know about Jackson? I was going to kill that little weasel if he'd shared.

"What's the matter? Cat got your tongue or is your mouth simply too tired to form words?" She was still chuckling.

I didn't find any of that funny.

"Neither," I snapped. "And there's nothing going on with Jackson."

"Right. That's why he was at my house for dinner and wanted your address because he'd left his watch there. Now, if I'd just fallen off the turnip truck, I may believe there's nothing going on. But, being your best friend and knowing no man is ever invited to your home got me thinking. What I'm thinking is, my BFF got herself some and didn't call to tell me she'd lifted her ban on sex."

"I can't believe you just said that in front of Jason."

"Oh, please, like I would, he already left my office. So, spill."

"There's nothing to spill, Mercy. I screwed up. Wish I could say I was drunk and not thinking straight but that's not the case. Momentary lapse in judgment is all I've got. It happened but it's not happening again."

"Why not?"

I pulled up to a stop sign, flipped my blinker on, and thought about her question. There were a thousand reasons why not. But only a few I was willing to share.

"For one, he's too young for me. Another reason is he's Jason's cousin. And—"

"Okay, you can skip the practiced answers and tell me the truth. And don't try and use me and Jason as an excuse. Neither of us care."

You know the problem with having a best friend for as long as I've known Mercy? I couldn't bullshit her. And when I tried, she called me on it. Always had.

"Tuesday . . ."

"Fine. We had sex. It was good. Really good. He came back over to get his watch, kissed me, and walked out. Then he comes back again to get his watch because he thought it was cute leaving it at my house a second time, only on purpose so he'd have a reason to come back.

"So, he does come, back, that is. That time he was pushing with the, let me get to know you speech. I shut that down and offered him a friends with benefits relationship, minus the friendship. He took me up on it. Promptly got started, did a bunch of really great things to me. I fell asleep before I could return the favor. He spent the night.

"This morning I offered him his payback, and he

got pissed. He started asking personal questions that weren't part of our arrangement, then he left. Now, I understand there's no way he's going to be able to have sex with no strings, so I cut them. Done. That's why there's nothing to tell you about."

"Seems to me like there was a lot to tell me about."

"Well, now I have."

"You offered Jackson Clark no strings sex?" she asked disbelievingly.

"Sure did."

"Then you offered him payback this morning when you woke up?"

"Yep."

"That's fucked up." She wasn't laughing anymore. "Actually, all of this is really fucked."

"Why's that? Men do it all the time. Why's it fucked-up when I offer it?"

"Honey, I love you. And there's nothing wrong with a one-night stand or a booty call. What is fucked is that you offered Jackson payback. I bet he was pissed. Nothing like a slap in the face waking up next to a woman who you like and hearing her say that. The second reason it's fucked-up is the reason you offered it in the first place. Jackson is not Travis. And you've sat back and nursed those wounds long enough. It's way past the time you started opening yourself up again."

Not a single person in my life had mentioned

Travis's name to me in years. Many years. And now, in the last few days, the two people who mean the most to me have both said his name to me. I hated thinking about him, the only thing I hated more was talking about him. His name said aloud was enough to make me gag.

"I'm over Travis. Way fucking over that asshole. And trust me, I know that Jackson is nothing like him. Travis was smooth, all class, nothing but silver-tongued compliments and promises. Jackson isn't that. But it doesn't matter, because I'm not interested. I ended it this morning. It's over."

"You ended it?"

"Yep."

"And how did you do that?"

"I told him it wasn't working out, and he could let himself out."

"Right. And let me ask you this, since this whole thing was your brilliant idea. At any time did Jackson tell you he wanted more than just sex?"

"Sure. That's why I shut it down and said sex only." Mercy didn't say anything; she just laughed. "What?"

"Nothing."

"Did you call me just to ask about my sex life?"

I was pulling into the grocery store and needed to get off the phone.

"Nope, two other things. Next weekend my house for dinner and wedding plans—"

"Yay. I'll be there. So you set a date?" I asked, genuinely excited for my friend.

"We did. Location, too. It's going to be out at the pond behind the Clarks' house. We'll have the reception in their backyard. The property is huge and beautiful."

The Clarks'. Great, Jackson's parents' house. Special, really freaking special.

"And I also wanted to ask, is Gran still at Autumn Lakes?"

"Yeah, for another week, why?"

"This is to be kept private," she was whispering. "I just caught a case; the nursing home is under investigation. Prescription fraud."

"Oh, shit. Is Gran in danger?"

I pulled into a spot and thought about my sweet grandmother.

"No. But I still wanted to give you a heads up. You may want to look through Patty's itemized bill and compare it to what's gone through her insurance. But, physically, she's not in danger."

"Okay. Thanks for the heads up. I'm at the market so I have to go. Can we do lunch soon, there's other stuff I need to catch you up on?"

"Yes. I miss you."

"Miss you, too, soon-to-be Mrs. Walker."

"God, I love the way that sounds. I'll let you run."

Mercy disconnected, and I checked the parking lot before I unlocked my doors to exit. Since this morning, when I'd found out Jackson hadn't been the one to send me the flowers, my imagination had been in hyperdrive. It was happening again. Last time it had started with flowers from unknown men, then it had escalated. And I could swear someone was watching me.

Why is all of this starting again?

15

I was sitting outside Food Lion in my truck watching Tuesday get out of her rental. An electric-blue Mini Cooper. I was thinking about how I could fit the damn thing in the bed of my pickup when I noticed her looking around. For someone who was on high alert, she wasn't very observant.

I'd pulled into the grocery store parking lot two cars in front of her and was parked within her field of vision, yet she hadn't seen me. But she was looking. Her head was on a swivel, and she looked just as scared as she had when I'd left her in her kitchen this morning.

I was supposed to go into work that afternoon but a buddy had wanted to switch shifts so he didn't miss his son's birthday party next weekend. The captain approved it, and I was all too happy to get the day off to rest after working in my parents' backyard all day. My dad had informed me Jason and Mercy were getting married next to the pond he'd put in for my mom, so there was going to be lots of work to be done over the next few weeks.

Tuesday got out of her car still looking around. I was happy to see she'd stowed the phone but had kept her keys in her hand. I'd planned on giving her a reprieve and going back to my place after I hit the store. After seeing this shit, Tuesday was having a visitor.

I opted to wait in my truck instead of running into Tuesday in the store and arguing. Undoubtedly, she'd reiterate the arrangement she'd come up with wasn't working and tell me to stay away from her. I could've told her that her plan sucked and was never going to work, but I was willing to keep my mouth shut if it meant I got closer.

Ten minutes later, she walked out with a bag, and repeated the same process as she did going in. After she got inside her car, I waited until she was out of the parking lot and followed her to her house, the whole drive over wondering why she was so nervous. By the time I was pulling in front of her house I'd almost convinced myself I was overreacting, she was just being smart and vigilant. But then I remembered the flowers and how worried she'd been.

I gave her time to get inside and got out of my truck. I got to the door and noted no music was playing. I tried the handle and it was locked.

I knocked. I waited. Then I pounded.

A minute later, the door was thrown open and a very pissed off Tuesday was standing there.

"You should've checked the peephole or looked out your curtains before you answered," I told her and pushed past, not giving her a chance to slam the door in my face.

"Why are you here? I'm too tired for this."

"And what is *this*, Tuesday?"

"Your games, Jack. I had a bad day, I have shit I have to work out, and nowhere in that do I have time for you and your games."

"This is no game, Sweetness. And the last thing I'm doing is playing. Why was your day bad?"

"Jackson, go home."

"Not until you tell me why those flowers freaked you out so badly that you practically jogged into Food Lion."

"Are you following me?"

"Babe, if you had been paying attention, you would've noticed *you* were following *me*. Now, tell me why you had a bad day."

She was three feet away from me, in what I was finding was her signature pose when I was around.

Hands on her hips and a scowl on her face. I had all fucking night to repeat the same questions. Sooner or later, I was gonna wear her down.

"Please go home."

"What are you afraid of?"

"I'm not afraid of anything."

"You are shit scared and jogging into a grocery store. This morning when I told you I didn't send you flowers you looked like you were ready to pass out. So, with all that, you wanna try again?"

"Get out."

Yeah, now she was mad. We were getting somewhere.

"Someone used to send you flowers? Secret admirers? A boyfriend? Who?"

Her face paled, and I knew I was on the right track.

"Get out!" she screamed.

"Tell me, Sweetness, why did the flowers freak you out? Why'd you have a bad day? Why are you so scared? You're running from something. Just—"

"You wanna know why I had a bad day? My car's totaled, got that news today. Went to visit my grandmother today. She informed me she's moving into a fifty-five and older community. My agent filed a lawsuit against me. Which means I had to hire an attorney. I started my day fighting with you. And, now, after dealing with a bunch of crap, I'm dealing with you, again. Oh, and my grandmother's nursing home is under investigation."

My body locked tight thinking about helpless elderly people being abused.

"For?"

"Prescription fraud."

"Most important out of all of that is your grandmother. Is she safe?"

Her face softened the barest of a fraction when I asked about Patty.

"Mercy loves my grandmother like her own. If she thought Gran was in physical danger she would've already gone and taken Patty kicking and screaming from the nursing home. But Mercy wants me to check the bills from Autumn Lakes and compare them to insurance statements to see if they match."

The nursing home being under investigation wasn't good, but there were things far worse than doctors writing fake prescriptions. I thought back over the rest and even though she'd shared, she still hadn't told me why she was scared.

"Baby, I need you to tell me why you're so scared."

"No way. That's not for you, Jackson. It's none of your business."

"Why not?"

"Because that is not who we are. I already—"

"But it can be. All I need you to do is trust me." I was done with the distance between us. "I am not whoever hurt you."

Tuesday recoiled then started to back up.

"You have no idea what you're talking about."

"I do. And I know I'm not him. I'm not the one who hurt you and put that fear in your eyes."

Her back hit the wall, I brought my hand up to brush her hair off her face and she flinched. Anger started to well in my gut. Someone had done a number on her, and the thought made me want to punch something. I counted to three and tried to leash my fury.

"Sweetness, did he hit you?" I whispered.

"What? No."

"You can tell me anything."

"Travis did a lot of fucked-up shit but hitting me was never one of them."

Travis.

"What'd he do that has you so scared?"

"*He* didn't do anything to scare me."

"But someone did."

"God, Jackson. Can't you leave it alone? I don't want to talk about it. I don't want to talk period. I just want you to leave."

She wanted me to leave so she could curl that security blanket around herself and keep me out. That wasn't going to happen. She'd told me more in the last thirty seconds than she had the whole time I'd known her. Travis may've hurt her, but he wasn't the one to scare her. Interesting.

"Have you had dinner?"

My abrupt change of topics had taken her by surprise. Her eyes widened then narrowed. It was a fucked-up thing to do, but it was my only option. I needed her off her game, and the only way to do that was to keep her off-kilter. If she got behind those walls she loved so much, she'd shut down.

"Dinner?"

"Yeah, Sweetness, are you hungry?"

"I'll make something after you leave."

Cute.

"You had a bad day, you're not cooking. Either I'll make dinner, or we can order Chinese."

"You can cook?" she asked disbelievingly.

"Your choice."

"I choose to eat alone."

"Chinese it is."

"Do you ever listen, Jackson?"

Super fuckin' cute when she was mad.

"I listen to every word you say. I just choose to ignore the shit I don't like."

Commence the stare down, which I liked a helluva lot. Her face was unguarded, her eyes unafraid. Oh, yeah, I liked it.

I kissed her forehead and backed away. I patted my pocket not feeling my phone, looked around, saw her keys on the counter, nabbed them, and headed for the door.

"Where are you going with my keys?"

"Gotta get my phone out of my truck."

"And you need my keys because?"

"Because I'm not stupid. I know you'll lock the door behind me."

Tuesday's mouth curved up into a smile before she looked at her shoes, her hair falling around her face. I may've been a pushy asshole, but I was not an idiot.

I opened her front door and pushed the storm door open. A white sheet of paper floated to the concrete steps, I bent to pick it up and continued to my truck. Tuesday's motion sensor tripped, and the driveway was flooded with light. I glanced down at the flyer and my blood ran cold.

I send you flowers, and this is the thanks I get? I should've known you're just like the rest. Ungrateful bitch!

What the fuck?

Ungrateful bitch?

Hell to the fucking no!

I yanked open the passenger side door and nabbed my phone out of the cup holder. Scrolled through my recent calls, found the number I needed, and hit go.

Two rings later, Ethan picked up. "What's up, Jackson?"

"Hate to call you out this late, but I need you."

"Where are you?"

I heard my cousin moving around and telling Honor he needed a minute.

"Tuesday's. Found a note shoved in the storm door. Fucked up and picked it up off the ground when it fell."

"What's it say?"

"I'll show it to you when you get here. But I want this on record."

"Tuesday got problems?" Then Ethan was talking to Honor again telling her he had to run out.

"She got a flower delivery, it freaked her out, but she won't say why. Now this. Yeah, I'd say she has problems."

"Shit. Text me her address, I'm on my way."

"Thanks, cuz."

I disconnected and texted Ethan Tuesday's address.

Movement from the porch caught my attention. Tuesday was standing there holding open the glass door with a different kind of scowl. One that was more concern rather than her earlier irritation with me.

"Everything okay?"

Shit.

Hell, no, everything was not okay. And now it just became even more *not okay*.

16

I stood leaning against the wall thinking. I'd done this for what seemed like a long time. And while I was standing there, I was trying to get my temper under control. I'd screwed up. Jackson had pushed me to the point of extreme anger, and I'd blurted Travis's name out.

However, while I was thinking about all the ways I wanted to kill Jackson, I realized I wasn't freaking out about saying Travis's name. There had been a time when hearing his name would cause me to feel physically sick, saying it would send me into an anxiety attack. Five years was a long time to be harboring a grudge. But it wasn't long enough to forgive the man that had violated my privacy, my trust, and had turned my life to shit. He'd profited from my misery. Monetary gain from my humiliation. He'd degraded me in the worst way.

So, the way I saw it, five years wasn't long enough. A lifetime wouldn't be. But at least I now knew I could say his name without wanting to curl into a ball, like I'd done many times before and wished my life away.

Jackson and Mercy were both right, Jackson was nothing like Travis. I may've been screwed up in the head when it came to trusting people, but I wasn't so stupid I couldn't see the difference between the two.

I knew Jackson would never betray me like Travis had. It took a special kind of douchebag to go to the lengths Travis had to deceive, cheat, and steal my self-worth.

But I also knew that Jackson could still hurt me. And I needed to be careful. Him pushing for details about my life was annoying but his reasons weren't. Neither was his honesty. Even if I didn't like what he was saying, he told the truth. And when he showed concern for my grandmother, that was almost enough to make me want to talk to him.

The seriously crappy part was I knew he'd understand. I knew he'd listen. But that would mean opening myself up, and that was too scary.

Jackson had been gone long enough that my thoughts had gone from what I'd revealed to food. I'd had a few bites of a sandwich with my grandmother this afternoon when I visited the nursing home, but after she'd told me she wanted to move out of her house and into a townhouse in a fifty-five plus community, my appetite had taken a nose-dive.

I walked to my front door and pulled it open. Jackson was pacing, talking on his phone. I caught his profile from my security light on the corner of the house and he looked mad. Not like the mad he got at me when I argued with him or shut him out. Not even the same kind of angry as when I'd offered him payback for all the awesome orgasms he'd given me. It was ferocious and coming off him in waves.

What the hell?

He disconnected and looked down at a piece of paper. He was studying it like it had all life's answers.

I called out to him, and when he looked over, I took a step back into the house. I'd been right. He was mad. By the time he'd made it to the door I'd already backed up three feet into my house and wasn't sure I wanted him to come inside, this time for a different reason than him always being nosy.

"What's wrong?"

"Sweetness, I need to show you something, and when I do, I need answers, not you shutting down on me."

I contemplated arguing for a nanosecond before

the look on his face told me it wasn't the time. This was so unlike the annoying, playful Jackson I knew.

"Okay."

He walked into my dining room and placed the paper on the table. Before I could look at it, he pulled me into his arms and slipped his hands up to my face. "Please, Tuesday. Do not shut me out."

I nodded because I was scared. "Brace, Sweetness."

Without moving my body, my eyes slid to the side and I read the note. Clean, bold, block letters. It was only two sentences, but it took up most of the paper. I'd never been so grateful for Jackson's touch. If he hadn't been holding me, I would've crumbled.

"Oh, God. It's happening again."

"What is, Tuesday?"

"The flowers. The notes. It's happening again."

"Who, baby? Who's doing it?"

I shook my head. I didn't know. I never knew. Flowers. Cards. Marriage proposals. Threats. This could not be starting again. I hated Travis Manning.

"Sweetness."

His voice was getting further and further away.

Fucking, *fucking*, Travis. He ruined me. Took everything. I was stupid thinking it was over. It would never be.

The internet. The information highway of misery.

I was moving but I was not walking. My mind was

racing a million miles an hour trying to figure out why now. Why, after all this time, was it starting again?

Jackson sat down with me in his lap, his arms like steel bands wrapped around me, holding me together. I wished he'd let go and let me fly into a million pieces. I couldn't do this again.

"Sweetness, you gotta talk to me. Who's doing this?"

"Travis," I spit out. "He did this. This is his fault. All of it."

The doorbell buzzed, and I nearly jumped a mile. "Easy, baby. That's Ethan."

"Ethan?"

Why in the world would Ethan be at my house?

"I called him so we can report this."

"No!" Panic flooded. "Please don't. There's nothing he can do."

"Tuesday! Stop." His arms tightened even more. "Maybe not, but we're still going to report it. At the very least it's trespassing."

"No, it's not," I told him. "I've been down this road. Just leave it."

"Fuck no! Sweetness, Ethan's here, he'll take care of it."

"I don't want this." Oh my God! They'll find out. Mercy's new family will find out. "I'm serious, Jackson."

He stood and steadied me on my feet. "I need you to trust me."

"I won't ever trust you if you do this."

Wrong thing to say.

Way wrong.

His face was back to granite and his eyes roamed my face, searching, and when he found what he was looking for he growled. "Baby, I do not care how pissed you get. I do not care if you go back to telling me you hate me. The look on your face tells me you're not just scared, you're shit scared. I will do anything I have to, to wipe that look off your face, including going against your wishes."

He left me standing near my couch and stalked to the door and let Ethan in.

I remained silent as Jackson told Ethan about the flowers and where he'd found the note. I didn't contribute a word. I was no longer giving head space to Jackson, he was out of my life, for real this time. I was going to have to move again. I couldn't live through another day of this. It was going to get worse.

Ethan asked me a few questions, my answers were short and to the point. I knew I sounded like a grade A bitch, and the two men had shared more than one look confirming my attitude was not missed.

It couldn't be helped. I wasn't going to taint Mercy's relationship with her new family with my problems. She was finally happy, and I was not going to ruin it.

Jackson walked Ethan to the door and then joined me in the kitchen.

"Sweetness. What the fuck? Why wouldn't you talk to Ethan?"

"Leave."

"No way. I told you not to shut down on me."

"This is not me shutting down. This is me cutting you out of my life. I asked you not to do that and you didn't care. You have no idea what you've done. Now get out of my house."

"Tell me why. Explain to me why you're so scared. Tell me, Tuesday."

Jackson standing in my kitchen with his arms crossed over his chest and a smug look on his face shattered what was left of my sanity. I felt it slipping and before I could stop it, fury and righteous indignation simmered until it boiled over.

"Fuck you!" Tuesday screamed.

I'd pushed too far. This was not right. I needed to know why she was scared but the cost was too high. Her body was shaking with rage, her eyes unfocused, and she looked like I'd gutted her.

No, the cost was way too fucking steep.

"Sweetness."

"Don't you dare. You wanna know my dirty little secret, huh? I might as well tell you. It's not like you're not gonna find out anyway. Actually, everyone already knows. The whole goddamn world knows."

"Baby—" I tried to stop her.

"Don't. While I was so caught up defending and turning a blind eye to Travis running around on me, fucking every model he worked with, I totally missed the real betrayal. See he was smart, full frontal attack so I wouldn't notice he was diggin' in from behind."

"Tuesday—"

"So when the knife plunged, it was too late. They were out there and there was nothing I could do. Nothing my attorney could do. Nothing the PR firm I hired to fix my tarnished reputation could do. And there was nothing *anyone* could do about my shattered soul and humiliation. I was naked for the world to see. Me sleeping. Me changing. Me in the bathroom brushing my goddamned teeth. Me standing in my closet, innocently looking for something to wear. *Naked!*"

Her arms were thrashing, and her chest was heaving. I couldn't take anymore. Not the story, but seeing her like this.

"Baby—"

"No way. You wanted it. So there it is. The man I trusted. The man who promised he loved me. The man I shared my home with was not only fucking my friends," she jabbed a finger at herself, "but he was also taking nude photographs of me without my knowledge. While I was sleeping in my bed, somewhere I was supposed to be safe, the motherfucker took pictures. Then if that wasn't bad enough, he sold them. He made money off my humiliation."

"Jesus Christ."

"Oh, no, it gets worse." I didn't see how there was anything worse than someone you trusted and loved betraying you like that. He'd deceived her and, in his deception, he'd brought her low. "Once the pictures were out, it was open season. Cards in the mail. Love notes. Emails. Men sending me vile, disgusting pictures of themselves. Voicemails from strangers telling me they loved jacking off to me. Every day. Every fucking day something new, something more. It never stopped. So now you know, there's nothing Ethan can do to stop this, because the first five hundred and fifty-two other times I reported it nothing happened. So I stopped. I moved, hired someone to wipe my personal information clean, and started over. But now, it's happening again. Fine. I can handle it. What I cannot handle is you completely ignoring my wishes and telling Ethan."

"Tuesday, baby. Come here."

"Now Ethan'll know. Now the minute he looks up my name he'll see all the reports. He'll know why. And that is embarrassing. I don't want Mercy to be judged because I fucked up—"

I. Was. Done.

I didn't wait for her to come to me, I moved to her with purpose. I swept her up into my arms. One arm under her knees, one behind her shoulders and cradled her. Any other time I would've enjoyed the feel of her weight.

Not this time.

Before she could struggle, I carried her to her bedroom. One knee on the bed I heaved us both on, went to my back, her to her side, half on top of me, and held her tightly.

She tried to roll away and break free from my hold. "Settle, Sweetness."

"Let go of me." She tried to shove away.

"Tuesday! Stop it."

I pressed her closer and waited. She was breathing heavy and was vibrating with so much hostility I knew if she really wanted to fight me it'd be difficult to contain her.

"First, you didn't fuck up. Not in any way. None of what he did to you is your fault. None of it. You do not have a single thing to be embarrassed about."

She stopped moving. Completely. I wasn't even sure she was breathing.

"Sweetness, I know you don't know my family very well, so I'll let you in on something. Not a goddamn person will judge Mercy or you for something someone else did. Especially about something like this. It would seriously piss me off hearing you say that, but I know you don't know them."

I waited a second, hoping my words were penetrating. I also needed a minute to calm myself down. I knew, from day one sitting across from her, someone had done her dirty. There was no reason for a smart, funny, beautiful woman to be standoffish if someone hadn't hurt her.

She laughed, made jokes, smiled, but gave nothing else. She used her sassy attitude and wit to dazzle you, hoping you'd be so ensnared by her beauty and lively disposition you wouldn't look any further. I bet that worked well for her. I bet men saw a tall, leggy woman, sexy as all get out and stopped there.

Women wouldn't know what to do with her, friendly, kind, a little bitchy, but again, beautiful. Tuesday could lay it on thick and hide in plain sight. No one would question her, because on the outside she looked great, but her insides were rotting away.

After spending the night with her, I could've guessed someone had cheated on her. She wore her suspicion and distrust like a warm blanket. It would make even more sense why she was holding on to the age excuse. Lots of things were making sense now. However, I'd never have guessed the depth of Travis's mendacity.

What a low-down motherfucker.

He'd stolen her privacy and safety. So, he'd taken everything.

Motherfucking dick.

"Baby, tell me about the cards and stuff that you were sent."

She sucked in an audible breath and shook her head.

"Tuesday, Sweetness, tell me."

"I can't do this again," she whispered. "It was awful."

"I bet it was."

I could feel her heart pounding against my ribs. There was nothing I could do but hold her and wait her out. And it took a long time, lying there in her bed, in the semi-dark. I looked around and in the quiet, I noted this room was much like her living room. Nice, expensive furniture but it was void of any personality. I hated this for her. She should not be living locked away behind white walls and loneliness. Hated it.

"At first I didn't understand why all of a sudden I was getting notes and flowers sent to me," she started. "Travis told me it must've been because I'd done my first billboard and my face was plastered all over. Stupidly, I bought it." There was nothing stupid about it. Travis was a master and it was a perfectly plausible reason. Proving, yet again, he was a dick. "At first the notes weren't all that bad, just creepy. Men asking me to marry them. Telling me I was beautiful. It seemed like a new bouquet showed up every day. But then it got worse."

She finished on a whisper. I didn't rush her, just let her process what she needed. All I could do was gently stroke her back and wait. It was a long time before she spoke again and when she did, she broke my heart.

"The declarations of love and proposals never ended, and then the death threats started. People started telling me I was a whore and going to hell. Some of them said that I should be beaten for defiling my body. Others said it was because of women like me that men were tempted and cheated. I've been called every name in the book."

I felt the first of her tears start to soak through my tee. Pain leaked from Tuesday, and I desperately wished I could take it from her.

"Pictures." Her voice hitched. "Of men touching themselves. Asking me if I liked what they were doing. I was being mentally assaulted every day. I was forced to see things I never wanted to see. Forced to read the vilest things about myself. And I didn't understand why people hated me so much."

"How'd you find out what he'd done?"

"My manager hired a PI after the police said they couldn't do anything. The death threats were the only thing taken seriously, but those were a dead end. The PI tracked down the photos. He moved quickly to get them taken down. I was kept in the dark about what the PI and my manager were doing until one of the websites who'd received a cease and desist letter produced a model release."

"A model release?"

"Travis was a photographer. He'd done headshots of me and portfolio building work using images he took of me. I signed a blanket model release. Now do you understand why this is my fault?"

"Tuesday, none of what happened is your fault."

"Yes, it is. I trusted him. So stupid. Beyond fucking stupid. I gave him permission to sell images. That's it. Just images. Not a release with specific file numbers. Not specific shots. Just a fucking, *fucking*, generic blanket release saying he could sell *anything*. And, boy, did he sell them."

Big, wracking, violent sobs shook her body.

She was done.

And I couldn't bear to hear anymore. *Mother-fucking prick*. His abuse of her trust was outrageous.

Tuesday cried and I held on. There was nothing else for me to do. No promises could be made that I would make it better for her. I couldn't. The only vow I could make was that I would stand by her side and get her through this. I'd carry her and help her heal. But she wasn't ready to hear it, nor would she believe me.

No, there was nothing to do but hold my woman

and pray I had the strength to battle her demons. They'd dug in deep and laid claim. It was going to take time and effort to dig them out, both of which I was willing to put in.

The hardest part was going to be getting Tuesday to trust me when she had no reason to ever trust again.

18

It had been three days since I'd woken up in Jackson's arms after I'd cried myself to sleep. And that was after I'd spilled my guts. Now he knew what an idiot I was.

So what?

I'd wanted this, right?

Wanted him to leave me alone. Wanted out of the dumb sex-only arrangement. I'd made my bed and now I was lying in it. The only problem was, if I'd wanted it so badly why did it hurt so much?

Jackson was nice about it. He'd tried his best not to make it awkward when I'd woken up with swollen eyes and a stuffy nose. He'd made coffee and stayed for a few minutes after he'd finished his cup. He was soft and gentle. Steered the conversation to safe topics like Mercy and Jason getting married in his parents' back-yard. He'd told me he'd helped his dad fix a fence and he and his brother, Nick, would be spreading mulch for their mother and helping them get everything ready.

I'd succeeded in making everything so uncomfortable between us the only thing left to talk about was landscaping. I bought that, too. Distance. After he'd waited the appropriate amount of time, he bailed. I didn't blame him. Especially now that I'd laid all my baggage at his feet.

Travis had made me incapable of trusting or loving anyone ever again. Jackson had hightailed it out of my life and that was a good thing. One less complication. I had enough to worry about. And just because I was irrationally missing Jackson didn't mean I hadn't kept myself busy.

I'd met with my attorney, who was charging me out the ass to fight a lawsuit that was unwinnable on my agent's part. She knew it, I knew it, and both lawyers knew it. Though they were happy to rack up billable hours, the question remained: why was Meredith pushing so hard to keep me under contract? My manager, Lambert, was at a loss as well.

The craziest part was, in the beginning, I didn't want to leave Meredith, I just wanted to slow down. It wasn't until she booked the Florida job, I'd expressly told her I wasn't doing, that I'd fired her. Lambert understood why I wanted to cut back. He knew how much I hated modeling. I'd confided in him a lot over the last ten years he'd been with me.

Both Lambert and Meredith had been with me when I'd endured the nightmare that was Travis Manning. Lambert had worked tirelessly to get all the pictures off the internet. He'd helped me find a computer genius who may or may not have done some not so legal things to make sure the images were as gone as they could be in today's internet world. It had cost me a fortune, and it didn't mean that people still didn't have the photos stored on their computers. All it meant was it wasn't in my face 24/7. It was something. *And something was better than nothing.*

So, while Meredith was behaving like a complete bitch and money was flying out of my bank account, I was wondering how many photoshoots I was going to have to subject myself to in order to pay for everything and not cut into my savings.

I'd also gone over my grandmother's insurance statements. I'd picked up an itemized bill from Autumn Lakes and combed over both and compared the numbers. Something was off. The insurance had been billed for prescriptions that were not on the nursing home's statement. I'd called Mercy and told her what I'd found, and she asked me to come in and meet with her.

Now, I was in my cute little Mini Cooper rental

hoping I got to keep it another week so I could post-pone car shopping. Which was only one step lower than getting a bikini wax on my favorite things to do list. The fact I'd rather lie spread eagle while an esthetician spread near boiling wax on my lady parts and ass crack, right before she ripped it off in the most painful way was saying something. And what it was saying was, I'd rather have my pubic hair torn out by the root than shop for a car.

I found a parking spot in front of the DEA office, grabbed my folder, and made my way into the building. I dashed by Jason's office and hit the elevator. It was incredibly rude of me, but I didn't want to see Jackson's cousin. I didn't want my inability to be a normal, func-tioning person to be rubbed in my face. Not that Jason would be ugly about it, but maybe Jackson had told him about my two-hour crying jag before I'd passed out, and I didn't want to take the chance. Mercy would ask me about him again, but she'd understand why I'd pushed him away.

Her door was open, and I walked in, stopping dead in my tracks when I saw Jason standing near Mercy's desk.

"Hey, Tues, thanks for coming by," Mercy greeted.

"Yeah, no problem. Here, I'll just leave these with you. I highlighted the discrepancies."

Mercy, being my best friend for a long time, therefore, knowing me well, gave me a once-over, and leveled me with a stare.

"What's wrong?" Her hand went up, halting my answer. "And don't say nothing."

"I'm in a hurry. I want to make it in to see Gran before she goes for physical therapy," I lied, not feeling bad about the untruth.

"Wrong answer."

"What do you mean wrong answer? Gran has PT in twenty minutes."

"I believe she does. What I do not believe is my best friend is trying to run out of my office like her panties are on fire to get to her grandmother before PT. What gives?"

"Jeez. Nothing. I'm just busy."

Mercy commenced a stare down. And when she stared, she could hone in on what the issue was with laser precision. She'd always been able to read me. Mainly because I never hid from her. Now was one of those times I wished I could.

"Did you talk to Jackson?"

My body jerked before I could stop myself. And Mercy, being my bestie, didn't miss it.

"Um . . ."

I didn't want to talk about this at all but especially not in front of Jason.

"Jackson said he called Ethan out the other day.

Some flowers and note had been delivered," Jason said conversationally, not knowing he'd just landed a blow. "Any update from him?"

"What?" Mercy asked in a whoosh, leaning forward she gripped the side of her desk. "It's starting again?"

Fuck!

"Um . . ."

"Why didn't you call me?"

That was a good question with an easy answer. Because she had Jason now. She was happy, and after all she'd lost in her life, I was not dragging her back into this shitstorm while she was planning to marry the man of her dreams.

"What's starting, again?" Jason's normal, happy tone was replaced with a not so happy one.

Jason waited for someone to answer, and I held my breath. I'd rather go back to the Jackson topic and tell him all about my screwed up, non-relationship sex agreement with his cousin than tell him this.

"Tuesday?" Jason practically growled.

Mercy placed her hand on his bicep and shook her head. By the time she'd walked around her desk to me, I wanted to vomit. Why was this happening now?

"Sit down, honey." She led me to one of the two chairs and guided me to sit.

"What did the note say?"

"I don't remember exactly. Ethan has it. After the flowers were sent, I guess I hadn't replied to the anonymous bouquet in a timely fashion. The note just called me an ungrateful bitch. It wasn't bad. Nothing like before. I was just taken off guard. I thought it was over. I didn't call Ethan, Jackson did."

"Jackson was there?" she whispered.

"Yep. He found the note and made the call before he even came back inside the house." I sucked in a breath and held my friend's eyes. "I'm so sorry this shit is leaking into your life again, and now—"

"Stop speaking before you piss me off. You will never apologize for what that scumbag did to you. It didn't *leak* into my life the first time and it isn't now. You're my best friend." She squeezed my hand. "Does, um, Jackson . . ."

I nodded but still answered. "I told him everything. It wasn't my finest hour. After everything, I just lost it, and once I started, it all poured out."

"Everything?" she asked with wide eyes. I knew why she was so shocked. Other than the people who were involved in the situation, I didn't talk about what Travis had done. Not to anyone for any reason.

"Good. That's good."

"Did you hear me? He knows about *all* of it. Now not only does he think I'm a slut and a bitch for being mean to him, he can now add internet porn star and crazy person to the list."

The growl that emanated from across the room reminded me we had an audience. Something I'd forgotten.

Dammit.

"Never, Tuesday, and I mean, never, talk shit like that about yourself again where I can hear. I haven't the first clue what happened or what the two of you are talking about. What I do know is you are none of those things."

I hung my head in shame. He had no idea; I *was* all those things.

"We gotta tell Jason, honey." I shook my head and didn't look up. "You did nothing wrong. We're not alone anymore. He needs to know so he can help protect you." I remained quiet. I'd told the story once and I wasn't telling it again. Not now, not ever. "I'm gonna tell him."

I nodded and continued to look at the tan Berber carpet under my feet.

It had taken Mercy almost an hour to fill Jason in on the worst year of my life. And that was because she'd skipped over the previous four when I'd been dating Travis. You could sum up those years in a few words: lying, cheating, manipulating, son of a bitch. There, done. It was the following year, when the incessant cards, emails, and deliveries had shown up, that took longer.

Travis Manning and his gift that kept on giving. And here we were five years later, and it was giving some more. Like the bad fart that lingered and burned your nostril hairs.

"Motherfucker!" Jason roared, and I jumped. My eyes snapped to his, and I was surprised he had his phone out.

"Nick," he barked into his cell. "There's a situation I need you to punt to the right people."

Nick? As in Nick Clark, Jackson's brother, who also happened to be an FBI agent.

Oh, no!

"Mercy . . ." I whispered.

"It's okay," she replied, and I earned another hand squeeze.

"What's he doing?" I asked.

"Making it right for you."

"What?"

"Tuesday Knowls—" Jason stopped abruptly. "He did?" Another pause. "Yeah, she just told me. Appreciate it. Keep me in the loop."

Jason disconnected and turned to me. It took a second, but he cleared the anger from his face and all that was left was compassion. I'd be lying if I said it wasn't the same look Jackson had given me before he'd gone. Something I was grateful for. He never did look at me with pity, only understanding.

And I'd still let him walk out the door.

"What'd Nick say?" Mercy asked.

"Jackson already briefed him." The side of Jason's mouth curved up. "Actually, he more like demanded Nick look into the situation. Old and new."

"What?"

"Called him three days ago, explained everything but instructed him not to talk to anyone about it. Jackson said it was your business and not anyone else's. The only reason he told Nick was because he's in a position to do something about it."

"But nothing *can* be done," I told him. "We tried. There's certainly nothing Jackson can do."

"Then you don't know my cousin very well."

"Why would he call Nick? He left, and not on good terms. I haven't talked to him in three days."

"And if you have to ask *that*, then you really don't know my cousin."

I threw my hands in the air and declared, "No, I don't know him. That's why I'm asking. Why would he waste his time calling his brother? I've been a complete bitch to him. I pushed him away. Every time I see him, we argue."

Jason looked at me in a way I didn't understand. His eyes were soft but looked conflicted.

"Did you know that Jackson told everyone he was going to be a firefighter when he was in kindergarten?"

That was a bizarre turn of topic.

"Um. No. I didn't know that."

I couldn't help but smile at the image my mind had conjured up. I could totally see a cute little boy Jackson playing with firetrucks.

"Everyone thought he'd grow out of it. Most kids are fascinated by big trucks and firemen. But it was more than that for Jackson. When he sees something he wants, and he knows what he wants the second he sees it, he doesn't stop until he achieves his goal. He's the most ambitious man I know. Him setting his sights on you doesn't surprise me. It also means he knew you were exactly what he wanted in a nanosecond, then set his course to make you his. It also doesn't surprise me that when he found out you had troubles, he waded in. That's Jackson."

"He doesn't know me, Jason. It's been like, a hot minute. And did you miss the part where I told you all we do is argue?"

"That's not all you do." Mercy smirked.

I, on the other hand, didn't see anything amusing. I still felt like shit that I'd offered him payback. Though, at the time, I didn't see anything wrong with my offer. However, after Mercy had pointed out it was totally bitchy and low-down it was all I could think about.

"He knows you. The real Tuesday, not first date Tuesday."

"What exactly does that mean?" My eyes narrowed on him and he smiled.

"Right, see, the two of you talk about men hiding who they are on dates. Women do it, too. And you know it, so don't deny it. Jackson didn't get any of that, he just got the good stuff. The real you."

"None of that matters anyway. He left me."

"So fix it." That came from Mercy, all nonchalant, like it was no biggie.

"It's not that easy," I told her.

"Sure it is. Just call him."

"I can't. I don't have his number. I deleted it. And besides, it's for the best. He left and now we have a clean break."

Man, it hurt just saying that. What was wrong with me? First, I pushed him away when he wanted me, and now that he's gone, having done as I'd asked, I wanted him around.

"What do you mean you deleted his number?" she quietly asked.

"Never needed it. He just showed up." When I wasn't lying to myself, I could admit Jackson walking into my house filling my space with his presence had been the best part of my day. I'd known it the first time he'd dropped in, and the self-imposed isolation had fallen away. I'd purposely secluded myself, controlling the only part of my life I could—who I allowed close. So dumb. God, Gran was so right. I wasn't living.

Mercy's gaze went from me to Jason, before it swung back to me. She looked thoughtful and a little sad. She picked up one of my hands and squeezed.

"Honey," she started on a whisper, and I braced. "Do you want to be right or do you want to be happy?"

Fuck.

I'd said that to her. I'd given her the same line when she refused to take any of Jason's five million calls begging for her to forgive him.

"That situation was different, and you know it. You and Jason were different. He loved you. You loved him. You'd hit a bump and all you needed was a push. It's not the same."

"Tuesday, it is. If you let go of all the hurt Travis left, you could move on. You deserve to be happy. But you have to learn to trust someone other than me and Gran."

"I do." I sat up straight. "I trust Jason."

"Honey—"

"I can't do this right now." I stood and Mercy's hand fell away. "I have to go visit Gran. I'm already late."

Mercy stepped away and the second she was clear of the chair, Jason tagged her around the waist and pulled her close. Both looked at me with disappointment.

"Thanks for all your help. Both of you. Please call me after you look through the statements."

Nothing. Not a word out of either of them. Just two identical, sad smiles as I walked out of Mercy's office.

Damn, damn, damn.

Seeing the two of them together never failed to make me deliriously happy they'd found each other and slightly jealous I'd never have it for myself.

I'd never have the kind of love they shared, and it was no one's fault but my own. I couldn't even blame Travis. It was all me. I'd done this to myself.

19

Between work and helping my dad around my parents' house in preparation for Jason and Mercy's wedding, I was dog dick tired. We'd just rehung all of the shutters my mom had wanted painted when I finished telling my dad what Douchebag of The Century Travis had done to Tuesday. His reaction was no less violent than mine.

I'd seen my dad pretty pissed over the years, but upon hearing about Tuesday's troubles his reaction had to have been in the top five. Nick had been furious, too, and promised to look into the police reports.

"What the fuck?" Dad's face was red, and it wasn't from the heat of a day spent busting our asses for Mom.

"I talked to Ethan, and he told me almost the same thing Tuesday did. It's not against the law to send someone flowers. And there isn't much he can do about the note either. Even if he knew who wrote it. Best he could do would be trespassing, and if he could track down the person and explain to them Tuesday doesn't want to have contact, he'd have to wait until they did something else for it to even be harassment."

My dad continued to stare at me, blatant disgust was turning into determination. "I'll have Brady head over to Tuesday's today and install cameras. If nothing else, we'll have eyes on her house."

Brady was one of the men my dad and uncles had working for them. When my dad, Uncle Levi, Uncle Lenox, and Uncle Jasper had retired from the Army they'd started a consulting and security company. They trained the local PD and SWAT teams on tactical shooting and maneuvers. They'd also branched out into private security plans and alarm systems. Over the years they'd built a reputation for being the best, therefore, people paid top dollar for their services.

"I'd appreciate that, but she's gonna have a shit hemorrhage. I think it's best if I'm there when Brady shows."

"We're done here. I'll call Brady and the two of you can go over there."

"I'm giving her time," I explained.

"Giving who time?" Quinn Walker asked, strolling our way.

Shit. I'd been so wrapped up talking with my dad, I

hadn't heard her come out the front door. Quinn wasn't only Jason's sister, she was also my best friend. Always had been, since we were toddlers running around causing havoc. I hadn't told her about Tuesday. None of it. Quinn was a spitfire and hugely protective over those she loved. While Tuesday and I were battling it out, I didn't want Quinn involved.

"Tuesday," my dad answered.

Fuck.

"Tuesday?" Quinn cut her eyes to me. "Mercy's friend? What are you talking about?"

Before I thought better of it, my dirty, paint covered hands scrubbed over my face.

"Nothing—"

"Are you dumb?" she blurted, and my dad chuckled.

"Come again?"

"Dumb, Jack. You know, stupid. Or do you just think I am? If you think any of us missed you looking at Tuesday like she was a juicy ribeye, you're flat out a moron."

"Well, tell me how you really feel," I muttered.

"Okay, I will. I think you're making a play for Tuesday, and she's not catchin' those plays. So, you probably did something boneheaded, mostly because you're a man, but partly because you've never actually been into any of the women you've tagged, so now you're all tied up and you don't know how to untangle yourself."

My dad's chuckle turned into a belly laugh, and Quinn smiled proudly. Smartass.

There were two things I got from all of that: I was not as stealthy as I'd thought and Quinn paid attention. Unless, it was more of the first, and I sucked at hiding my thoughts.

"Truth? She has me tied in knots, but I don't want to get myself untangled. Which means I need to give her time."

"Did you do something stupid? Hurt her feelings?" Quinn continued.

"No. Nothing like that. I've been pushing, and she's been resisting. Three days ago, she revealed why she's been working so hard to get me out of her life. Her reasons for not trusting are valid. After she laid it all out for me, and when I tell you she laid it out, I mean, it leaked from her eyes and didn't stop for hours, I realized I needed to slow down and stop pushing if I want to get in there."

Quinn's green eyes narrowed, and her hand went to her hip. For a little thing, she was fierce.

"Have you lost your ever-loving mind? Let me get this straight. Tuesday opens up to you, tells you something painful, gives you her tears, and you repay that with time?" Her hand was no longer on her hip; it was pointing at my chest and she was approaching quickly. "Wrong. Way wrong, Jackson. When a woman gives you that, you never give her time."

"Quinn, you don't know Tuesday. She orders me out of her house practically every time I step in."

"Um, yeah, I get that. You still don't give her time. I'm sure it took a lot out of her to tell you what she did. And I don't want to know what's holding her back making it so she can't trust you; it isn't my business. But what I do know is she let down her walls and you're giving her time to build them up again."

"I didn't just leave. I stayed all night and held her. I made sure she was okay the next morning before I left."

My dad was staring at me and shaking his head and Quinn looked like she was going to blow.

"I love you, Jack, but you fucked up. Let me tell you this: if it was me and I poured my heart out to a man and the next morning he left, regardless that I was trying to deny I had feelings for him, I'd think he no longer wanted me. That the burden I carried was too heavy for him, and he'd figured out I was not what he wanted."

"What? That's not how I—"

"She's right, son. You fucked up. Tuesday gave you a golden opportunity, she opened up, she was vulnerable, and you should've taken the opening and wedged yourself in."

"Fuck!"

"That about sums it up. Time is not your friend. Not when you have to fight to gain every inch of ground."

My phone vibrated in my pocket, and I reluctantly pulled it out, praying it was not the station.

Ethan's name flashed on the screen and I took the call.

"Where are you?" he asked before I could say hello.

"The 'rents house," I told him.

"Get to Tuesday's now. She just called. There was a note waiting for her when she got home. I'm headed there now."

"Fuck. Did she tell you what it said?"

Not bothering to say goodbye to Quinn or my dad I jogged to my truck.

"Man, she could barely get out that she needed me to come over. She was crying but managed to get out that the note mentioned you, too."

"Me?"

I was opening my door when my dad's hand shot out, and he stopped me with a shake of his head.

"I'm leaving now. I'll meet you there."

"Out."

I disconnected and turned to my dad and filled him in. He told me he'd meet me there after he handled

Quinn and my mom. Five seconds later, I was in my truck peeling out of the driveway. I broke every posted speed limit between my parents' and Tuesday's house and pulled up right behind Ethan. He'd just gotten out of his car and was scanning the area.

Tuesday's car door opened, and she stepped out looking over the roof. Her red, puffy eyes got big when they landed on me. Damn, I'd screwed up, I should've never left. I slammed my truck door and stalked to her. This was not the first time I'd seen her cry. But it was the first time I'd witnessed it being done in fear. And this would be the last.

I did my best to check my anger at seeing her scared before I stepped into her space and pulled her to me. She let out a squeak of shock but a heartbeat later, her arms were wrapped around me and her face was buried in my neck.

"Everything's okay, Sweetness."

"N-no, it's not," she cried.

Ethan joined us at the car, his gaze hard as he took in a sobbing Tuesday. He gave her the time she needed before he asked, "Where's the note?"

"On the front porch. I didn't touch it."

With a nod, he was gone.

"Open your garage. We'll go in through there."

"I don't have an opener. I never use the garage."

Another thing that needed my attention. I'd meant

to ask her why she didn't park in the garage. It wasn't safe for her to park in the driveway, especially when she came home late from a work trip.

I watched Ethan pick up the paper with a gloved hand and straighten. His face was unreadable when he gestured for us to go into the house.

"Come on. Let's get you inside."

She didn't say a word, just allowed me to lead her to the front door. Ethan stepped aside and Tuesday unlocked and pushed the door open.

Once we were inside, she visibly relaxed. Motherfucker!

"What does it mean?" she asked Ethan.

"Not sure."

He walked farther into the room, fished a large plastic bag out of his pocket, placed the note inside, and set it on the dining room table for me to read.

Back off, bitch, and tell your fucking boyfriend to mind his own business. I'm not fucking around, bitch. This is your only warning. If you don't stop, you'll both be sorry.

"What the fuck?" I seethed.

"'Bout sums it up. Hopefully we can pull prints off this one. If we can, you both can file an order of protection."

I clamped my mouth shut. An order of protection

was bullshit and Ethan knew it. Not to mention, there'd been no prints but mine on the first note.

"Sweetness?" I waited until she looked at me. Anxiety clear as day was written all over her face.

I thought about what Quinn and my dad had said. I'd messed up big time and given her space when I should've been crowding her. I should've continued as I was and not given her a chance to rebuild.

Fuck.

I moved the two feet needed and gathered her in my arms.

Kissing the top of her head I whispered, "Everything's okay."

"It's not."

"I'll rephrase, everything is *gonna* be okay. Trust me."

Her body went solid in my arms and Dad and Quinn were right. I'd fucked up thinking time was the answer. She'd rebuilt her fortress.

Nothing like starting back at square one.

20

My heart was pounding in my chest; it had been for the last thirty minutes. It had started when I'd opened my storm door and the note had flitted to the ground, face up. With each word I'd read the beating had intensified. I'd run back to my car, got in, locked the doors, and called Ethan. Then I waited. Ethan had shown up with Jackson in tow.

Jackson. He came.

Now I was in his arms and he was asking me to trust him. That was why my heart was threatening to explode from my chest. Not because of the note, though it was creepy and frightening. Especially the part about if we didn't stop, we'd be sorry. I didn't want to be sorry, but I didn't know what I was supposed to stop. And I *really* didn't want Jackson to be sorry.

Someone banged on the front door and I nearly

jumped out of my skin, almost nailing Jackson in the nose. "Jesus, Sweetness. That's just my dad."

This time when I whipped my head to look at Jackson, he was prepared and dodged another near miss. "What?"

"I was at my dad's when Ethan called," he said by way of explanation. Though it didn't explain anything.

Ethan was already at the door letting Nolan Clark in. He moved out of his uncle's way and the imposing man stepped into my house.

"Brady's outside scoping out locations for cameras," he weirdly stated.

I couldn't take my eyes off the man as he prowled farther into the room. For a man who was coming up on his sixtieth birthday, he looked good. So good, in fact, I momentarily forgot why he was in my house. He and Jackson were the same height, I'd guess six two, maybe six three. Where Jackson was lean and buff, his dad had bulk to him. The gray peppering his brown hair, predominately his sideburns and up, framing his face, did nothing to take away from his good looks. Jackson came from good stock, there was no doubt about it.

"Tuesday," Nolan's gruff voice greeted me.

"Hello, Mr. Clark."

"Nolan, or just Clark will do," he corrected just as he had the day of the barbeque when I'd first met him.

"Did you bag the note?" That was directed at Ethan.

"Yeah."

"Let me see it," Nolan demanded.

Ethan handed him the letter and Jackson held me close. I watched as Nolan's face took on a hard edge. "Right. The cameras will be installed today. We'll get the street, too. I didn't see an alarm when I came in. That will take longer, but Brady will get on that, too."

"I can't afford an alarm and cameras," I told them.

"There's no charge," Nolan argued.

"Of course, there would be. Alarms are expensive."

"Family doesn't pay," he continued.

"But I'm not family."

"You're Jackson's. And you're Mercy's best friend. That makes you family, and family does not pay. Cameras in the front of the house will make it much easier to nail this guy. Faster, too." Nolan turned to Ethan. "I'd like it if you could keep us up-to-date on what you find. Nick is digging in and he'll be sending you what he finds this afternoon. The more eyes on this the better."

No, *no*, no. I still didn't want Nick looking into anything. He'd dredge up the past, if he hadn't already. He'd see all the horrible pictures Travis had taken of me. He'd know everything, then he'd pass the information on to Ethan and Nolan. The whole family would have a front row seat to my humiliation and shame. *Jesus Christ, when would this end?*

"I'm gonna get this to the station. I'll call you when I have something," Ethan told Nolan. "Hang in there, Tuesday. We're gonna get this mother . . . to the bottom of this soon."

"Thanks, E." Jackson lifted his chin in his cousin's direction but still hadn't let me go.

Something I was grateful for but shouldn't have been.

"I don't want Nick looking into my past," I whispered to Jackson.

"Why not?" He didn't whisper; he spoke loud enough for his father to hear and now he was staring at us.

"You know why not."

"No, Sweetness, I don't."

He couldn't be that obtuse. I tried to push away. I needed distance to remind myself I wasn't living in some fantasy world where I was well adjusted and Jackson was a possibility.

"Let me go," I demanded.

"No. Tell me why you don't want Nick looking into who sent the letter."

He was looking down and I was looking up. There wasn't that much space between our faces. And I could remember, even though I was trying hard not to, what his lips felt like on mine. Not to mention, all the other places they'd been. The way they made magic wherever they skimmed along my flesh. Dammit, why couldn't I forget?

"Because it's embarrassing," I seethed.

"Embarrassing? Tuesday, you do not have one goddamn thing to be embarrassed about. I've told you this. You didn't do not one single thing wrong. Travis is to blame."

"But I did. I trusted him."

"And? He took advantage of that trust. He's the one who should be embarrassed. He fucked over a good woman who didn't do anything but love and trust him."

"But—"

"He's right, Tuesday," Nolan started. "I'm not going to pretend to know how you feel. He violated you. I have no doubt that mark is deep. But, darlin', that asshole is to blame. He did this *to* you. I know it doesn't make it easier, I suspect, if I were in your shoes, I'd feel the same way. However, in this family, our family, there is no judgment. If you let us, we will rally around you and protect you. Whatever Nick finds, he'll be discreet. What he passes to Ethan, he'll be discreet, too. You'll never know what they see because they'll never discuss it with you. So, while it doesn't make it any easier, I hope it makes it a little better knowing we've got your back."

When his dad was done, Jackson was smiling. I could see him out of the corner of my eye but didn't stop looking straight ahead.

"They're bad," I muttered.

Nolan's features softened and nothing but compassion shone in his eyes. "I figured they were, darlin'. Anytime someone abuses trust to inflict harm it is. But he did it in a way where you were unaware and vulnerable. That shit ain't just jacked, it's criminal. Nick's working on that, too. He has a copy of the model release, and he's trying to work around it. If something can be done to prosecute Travis, Nick will find it."

"But—"

"No sense arguing, Sweetness." Jackson gave me a squeeze. "When my brother sniffs injustice he doesn't stop. He might not be able to find something, but he's gonna try. In the meantime, we have to concentrate on making you safe and catching whoever is leaving you notes now."

I was overwhelmed by their kindness. Other than my grandparents and Mercy no one has ever offered to take care of me, not in the slightest. I'd been on my own since the week after I turned eighteen and my parents had declared they'd done their duty and had gotten me to adulthood.

They'd promptly packed up the house, told me they were leaving, and were on a plane to Hawaii before the house sold. They were nice enough to allow me to live in the home I'd grown up in, until they found a buyer. The only room that they'd left furnished was my bedroom. I didn't take them up on their *generous* offer, instead, I'd moved in with Gran and Pop. I stayed with them for almost a year then I was ready to be on my own.

"With cameras and an alarm," I muttered. "I have money in my savings I can—"

"No use arguing about that either, Tuesday. Dad already told you, family doesn't pay."

"But I'm not—"

"Explained that, too," Jackson cut me off again.

"Sorry to interrupt," a man said, walking into my living room.

"No problem, Brady. Need me?" Nolan asked.

"Yeah, if you wouldn't mind. I'm ready to install and want to run over the site plan," Brady answered.

He was a nice-looking guy, sandy blond hair, a little shorter than Jackson, he, too, looked like he put a lot of time and effort into keeping himself in shape. But that wasn't what had caught my attention. There was something in his eyes that was sad.

Nolan didn't say anything else he just followed

Brady out the door, leaving Jackson and me alone for the first time.

"You doing okay?" Jackson asked.

"No."

"Break it down. And we'll figure out a way to make it okay."

Before I could answer him, my cellphone rang. I pulled it from my back pocket and saw the number I'd been avoiding answering. She wasn't giving up and she wouldn't. Seeing as today had already been shitty, I decided I might as well answer it.

"Hi, Mom, right now's not good. Can I call you back?"

"No, you *may* not," she snapped. "I've called you four times in the last two days." It wasn't a statement, it was an accusation.

She had indeed called me four times, and I'd hit ignore each time. While I didn't ever find speaking to my mom a good time, the last two days really hadn't been good.

"What can I help you with, Mother?" I sighed and did it in a way she knew I was doing it. Nothing annoyed Gladys more than my "childish behavior," as she called it.

"You can start with explaining why you're giving Meredith such a hard time. She's worked hard for you over the years and this is how you repay her?"

"What?"

How did my mother know about my troubles with Meredith? She hadn't been involved with my career since I'd cut her out in every way I could. Mainly because she'd been stealing from me. Though she hadn't seen it as such. To her, she'd been taking what she was owed for making me somebody, when, clearly, I hadn't had the intelligence or ambition to do it myself.

"A lawsuit? Do you have no shame?" she sneered. "Do you have any idea what you're doing to the family name?"

The family name? That was all she cared about?

"She's suing *me*, Mother. And how do you even know about the lawsuit?"

"Yes, she is suing you because you are being an irrational bitch. Meredith had—"

"Irrational bitch?" I bit out. "Irrational because I wanted to cut back on my schedule to pursue other avenues. A bitch because I'm not caving to Meredith's demands? Why is this your business? Oh, that's right, Mother, it's not. And I'm not sure why Meredith called you in the first place, but knowing she has means I'm absolutely doing the right thing by severing ties. You do not enter my life but two times a year. Christmas and Gran's birthday. Both of those occasions are the only times you and Dad feel it is imperative you behave like parents to put on a big show for Gran. Though, after all this time you have to know she's not senile and has caught on to your game."

God, why couldn't I have a normal mother? She'd always had a stick up her ass when I was a kid, but as I got older her attitude surpassed annoying and went straight to mean. She'd become the worst kind of stage mom.

"That is the second reason for my phoning you. What is this I hear that Patricia has decided to move into an old folks' home?"

She hadn't even attempted to hide the disdain. "Geez, Mother, it's a fifty-five and older community. She wants to be around people her own age instead of alone in that big house."

"I don't care where she wants to live. What I care about is why you think you're entitled to the house."

"The house? What house?" I had no idea what had my mom so worked up. She was telling the truth. She didn't care much about anything except herself.

"The Manor. I'm warning you, Tuesday, you do not want to fight me on this. I will take you down."

"Take me down?" I breathed. "What?"

The next thing I knew, the phone was snatched from my hand. I'd forgotten Jackson still had his arm around me. Testament to how angry my mother had gotten me.

"You're done. When Tuesday's ready she'll make contact. Until then, you do not bother her."

Holy shit.

Jackson was taking on my mother.

"No. You listen. And listen carefully. I don't care who you are. When my woman starts trembling in my arms and it's not from what I am doing to her, instead what her bitch of a mother is threatening, you get me. Tuesday is off limits."

His woman?

Oh, boy.

Oh, shit.

I liked that. I liked how it made me feel having Jackson take my side.

Do you want to be right or do you want to be happy? I didn't want to be right. I didn't want to believe that Jackson would tear me to shreds. I wanted to be happy. But I didn't know how to be that. I'd been miserable and alone for so long, I wasn't sure if I could let down my guard—not even for Jackson. Though if there were ever someone I'd be willing to try with, it would be him.

Maybe . . .

I think . . .

Shit!

21

Tuesday's mom was a total bitch.

I could hear the entire conversation they'd had through the phone. I wasn't sure how someone as wonderful as Tuesday could come from someone as nasty as the woman who was currently screaming in my ear.

"I cannot believe my daughter would choose to be with someone as vulgar as you. Though I should, she always did like to scrape the bottom of the barrel."

"I don't care what you believe. But I will tell you, it says a lot about the type of woman you are speaking about your daughter that way."

"Put Tuesday on the telephone."

"We've been over this and that's not going to happen."

I wasn't sure what was working behind Tuesday's

eyes but clearly, with this new drama, she'd forgotten she was supposed to be pushing me away, because the more I spoke to her mother the softer her features became.

"Tell my daughter, I'll be over soon."

"You show up here, we've got problems."

I disconnected before she could answer. There was no point in arguing with a bitch. She'd dug in and so had I.

"She's coming here?" Tuesday squealed.

"That's what she said."

"She can't come here."

"Sweetness." I pulled her tight against my chest. "Let's finish up with my dad, then we'll talk about that conversation. How far away do they live?"

"Uh, Hawaii."

The fact I didn't know her parents didn't live close or that her mother was a complete bitch was a reminder of how little I knew about her. Something that was going to be rectified starting immediately.

"Then we have time."

"Who's coming here?" my dad asked, coming back into the house.

Tuesday stiffened in my arms. "Her mother threatened to come over, but she's not going to."

I heard the tiny gasp, it was better Tuesday learned now, I didn't keep shit from my dad. I'd learned early on that if anything important was going on in my life, he'd have my back. And it was best he had it from the start.

Just as I suspected he would, his gaze hardened and he asked, "Threatened?"

"I had a five second conversation with the woman. She took the opportunity to insult me, insult her daughter, then informed me she'd be over soon. After I told her she wasn't going to speak with Tuesday again, until Tuesday was ready."

"She insulted Tuesday?"

My dad was a good father and a good honorary uncle. A man like him wouldn't be able to fathom insulting his own child. Never once growing up had my dad ever been anything but supportive. I was disciplined when needed, but I'd never been talked down to.

"That's just her. She always—"

"That's just her?" my dad interrupted.

Tuesday didn't answer she just nodded in the affirmative and rested her head back on my chest. I was thrilled she hadn't yet pushed me away, though I knew it was coming.

"Right. Brady's heading to the office to get the rest of what he needs. He'll wire up the front today, but he's gonna run out of light soon, so he'll be back to do the rear tomorrow. He's also gonna check what equipment we have and what needs to be ordered. It may be a few days until that's set up. When's your next shift?"

"I have the next two days off," I told my dad.

"I'll make sure it's done before you're back to work."

I knew what that meant. I was guessing Tuesday did, too, when her head lifted and her eyes came to mine.

"Jackson. I'll be fine."

"I know you will."

"So—"

"Because I'll be here with you."

"Jack—"

Her cheeks were getting pink, and the cute look she got when she was pissed was blooming. Yeah, my girl burned hot. And I'd bet she'd have no issue unleashing on me in front of my dad. Which I had no problem with either, but Brady was standing at the door. He seemed cool enough, not that I knew him well, but Dad and the uncles having hired him in the first place told me he was solid. That didn't mean I wanted him to witness Tuesday in a snit.

As I'd noted, she was cute as fuck when she was mad, when she activated the head tilt and hand on hip maneuver, it drew your attention to all the right places. As much as I enjoyed the show, Brady wasn't getting a front row seat.

"Sweetness, let's let my dad head out."

"Maybe you wanna go with him and help?" she sassed. My upper body started to shake as I held in a silent chuckle. "I'm not being funny. I think they may need help. And you need a shower, you smell like the inside of the men's locker room."

"You know what a man's locker room smells like?"

"Yeah, like sweaty balls and your shirt."

My dad and Brady both started laughing, and, before I could brace, her lips tipped up and her face split into a smile.

Holy fuck, I'd missed seeing that.

Beautiful.

I caught Brady out of the corner of my eye watching Tuesday with a look that could only be described as wistful. Time to shut this shit down.

"Thanks for all your help, Dad." My curt statement only made him laugh harder.

With a chin lift he started to the door. "Call me if you need anything."

"I will," I called out to his back.

He stopped and turned. "I got it before. But I really get it now. Be smart." And with that they were gone.

I was frozen in place with Tuesday's arms still wrapped around my middle, but she was staring up at me. She opened her mouth to speak, but I beat her to it. "Please, just give me one hour."

"One hour?"

"Before you batten down the hatches and start kicking me out. One hour."

She didn't respond verbally but she nodded. But more than that, her eyes gave me the answer I needed. They were soft and receptive. With a gentle kiss I broke away.

"Be right back."

I left her in the living room and jogged out to my truck, grabbed my gym bag, and headed back inside. After I made sure the door was secured and locked, I gave Tuesday another lip touch, and made my way to her bedroom, tossed my bag on her bed, and headed for the shower. I quickly rinsed the heat of the day off my skin. Taking a moment to breathe in her gardenia shampoo, I thought about how I was going to play this.

Apparently, giving her time was the wrong way to go, and after what Quinn had pointed out, I realized she and Dad were right. I shouldn't have left the way I had. I also realized that while I'd been pushing her to let me into her present, I hadn't been asking the right questions about her past. What I did know, I liked. All of it. Enough that no matter what, I wasn't letting her keep me out.

I dried off, threw on my clean gym clothes, and went in search of Tuesday. She was sitting in the corner of her couch, heels up, knees to her chest, and her chin was resting on them. She looked tiny folded into herself. Which was a goddamn crying shame. There was nothing small about Tuesday, not her height, not her personality, and certainly not her attitude.

I sat down next to her and tugged her leg so it fell off the couch. Taking advantage of her being off balance I continued to pull her until her body collided with mine. She was at an awkward angle, not nearly close enough.

"Scoot over," I told her.

"But—"

"Please, Sweetness."

She did as I asked and once her head was on my chest and my arm was around her, I started.

"Tell me about your parents."

"What about them?"

"Anything. Your mom. Has she always been like that?"

"For as long as I can remember," she mumbled.

"And your dad?"

"My dad tries, sometimes, though he's a 'yes man.' What Gladys wants, Gladys gets. George doesn't stand a chance. When my mom first brought up modeling, my dad put his foot down and said no. She ignored him and I had my first studio session with a photographer a week later for headshots."

So, her trust issues didn't start with Travis. They ran much deeper, back to the first man in her life who should've been her champion but wasn't. From the phone conversation I'd had with Gladys I could totally see the woman having no regard for anyone but herself.

"How long have they lived in Hawaii?"

"They left Georgia right after I graduated high school."

"Come again."

I couldn't imagine living so far away from my parents. Then again, my family was tight. My ass was planted at my mom's dinner table at least once a week. And if I missed a meal it was only because I was working.

Reagan Clark loved her boys and could get pissy if my brother or I didn't give her ample opportunity to show it. Over the last decade, this had also included Meadow, Nick's wife. And now that they had babies, my mom was thrilled she had more people to love.

"They left a few months after I graduated. I moved in with Gran and Pop. They were more than happy to have me. I'd spent a lot of time at their house when I was growing up. I don't think it's too hard for you to believe Gladys wasn't real hip on being a parent. Sometimes I think the only reason she had me in the first place was to make my grandparents happy."

Jesus, the woman was more of a bitch than I'd

thought, and I already thought she was a raving asshole the way she spoke to Tuesday with such venom.

"Which reminds me, I need to talk to my grandmother about her house."

"What's The Manor?"

I'd heard her mom mention it right before she vowed to take Tuesday down.

"The Manor is my grandmother's house. More than a house, really. When my Gran told Pop about the house of her dreams, he got it for her, tenfold. She wanted a beautiful wraparound porch; she got a three-story home with one on each level. She wanted a place where she could have a family holiday meal and dinner parties, he made sure she had a ballroom. She wanted a place she could sit and quietly read a book or work on sewing, he made sure she had an entire wing that was just hers. It's an honest to God southern mansion. My grandfather was brilliant with money and he purchased it for a good price, she owns it outright and the nine acres surrounding it. And, unlike my mother, Gran appreciated everything my grandfather gave her. He loved to spoil her, and there was nothing else on this earth she loved more than to spoil him right back."

Over the next thirty minutes, Tuesday went on to tell me about the big windows in the front room and the huge weeping willows and magnolias that surrounded the house. With extreme reverence, she told me how her grandmother had taught her to bake in that kitchen and how to sew. Tuesday smiled when she explained how her grandmother would play music and they'd dance in the ballroom with Tuesday dressed up in Patty's furs and silk. She also told stories about her grandfather watching grandmother and granddaughter twirling around the house and how happy he'd been. He'd take her outside and walk her around the property telling her stories about all the adventures he and Patty had gone on.

"I loved being there more than any other place. It's not just a house to me, it holds all of my best memories." She stopped and took a breath before she admitted. "It breaks my heart thinking of strangers living there. I know that's selfish, but I always imagined walking my children through the orchard one day. Dancing with them in the ballroom. Cooking with them and Gran in the kitchen. I understand why Gran wants to move. The house is too much for her. I get it, but it still hurts."

"Sweetness, that's not selfish. That's beautiful. My parents still live in the house I was raised in, I couldn't imagine them ever leaving it. All my childhood memories are wrapped up in that house. All the little things that mean everything."

Hearing her talk about her grandparents, the way she spoke with such fondness, made me fall a little more in love with her. It said a lot about her, the adoration she had for them. It was more than how a grandchild loved her grandparents, it was pure, and she'd made it obvious how much family meant to her.

"I need to ask Gran what my mom meant. Gladys Knowls on the warpath isn't pretty. She brings so much ugliness with her, it takes months for it to wear off."

"I'm sorry, Sweetness."

"I'm used to it. She is the way she is, and my dad is how he is. Thankfully, they now live far enough away I don't see them very often. There isn't much that can tear my mother away from her perfect life living in paradise."

So much made sense now. A few days ago, I'd thought my only battle was the ghost of Travis, and what he'd left behind. Now I knew better. Trust was only a small part of what I'd have to win from her. The damage her parents had done was far more lasting.

"Thank you for sharing all that with me." I kissed the top of her head. "How about I make us some dinner?"

She was silent for a beat, before she answered, "I'd like that."

Hell, yes. Progress.

22

Yesterday was eye opening.

From my talk with Mercy, to the note that was left, Nolan Clark showing up, Jackson sitting and listening to me talk about my childhood, and, last, the fact that I shared in the first place.

Jackson cooked and while he did, he told me some stories about growing up. Jason had already told me that Jackson had declared he was going to be a fire-fighter by the age of five, what he didn't tell me was Jackson was obsessed with all things fire: from acceler-ants and investigations to suppression and prevention.

Throughout our conversation, I couldn't figure out what he loved more, firefighting or his family. He spoke about both with fervor. I knew he loved his cousins, Quinn had been his best friend since forever, which I could totally see; Jason's younger sister was a blast. He and his brother Nick were extremely close despite the age difference. He was so happy to be an uncle times two, since Meadow and Nick had adopted twins.

However, he spoke about flashover and thermal decomposition with just as much passion. Autoignition temperature, hot smoke, flammable gases, and back-drafts shouldn't have been exciting topics, but hearing him talk about them, while gesturing with his hands and using different kitchen utensils as props, I was enthralled.

He loved his job, that much was obvious. But I think it was more than that. Though he'd never admit it, it was that every day he got to help someone. I was slowly learning who Jackson Clark was and about his deep need to protect.

Jackson had no problem wading into my situation. Not with the flowers and letters and not with my mom. He just dove straight in, and, even though he'd been threatened, he hadn't backed away. As a matter of fact, he'd double downed. He proved that to me last night after dinner when we were watching TV. He hadn't asked anymore about Travis or my mom, but he did ask about how I got into modeling. Shockingly, I'd opened up about that, too.

Sitting on my couch with a movie playing in the background I told him how much I'd liked the work in the beginning, but the more my mom had pushed, the less I'd wanted to do it. However, by the time she'd become a complete nightmare I was tangled up in contracts and couldn't stop. I could feel the air in the room changing when I explained why I'd had to fire my mom. It was nearing close to combustible from one of those flashovers or rollovers he'd explained earlier when I told him the amount of money my mother had made off me during the years she'd *managed* my career.

There had been a time I'd felt like I owed her something. Whether it was out of duty or guilt, I allowed her to draw a paycheck. I hadn't known she was strong-arming my account and taking more money on the side. When that came to light it was the last straw.

Now we were both in my kitchen drinking coffee the morning after conversation and confessions of the soul. I should add, Jackson had stayed the night. He'd explained that it was because while Brady had finished installing cameras, how many I didn't know, the alarm equipment still needed to be ordered. He did offer to sleep on the couch, that would've been the smart thing. But I hadn't felt like playing it safe, so I'd invited him to sleep in my bed. This morning when I'd woken up, cuddled to his side, I understood what a monumental fuck-up it had been.

He was warm and hard in all the right places. I felt safe. Not physically—emotionally. I was free to be me, and Jackson would still be there in the morning. One of the other things he'd explained was why he'd disappeared after I'd told him about Travis. I didn't want to be relieved he hadn't run a mile after hearing there were nude photos of me out there in the world, but I was.

Each time I felt like retreating, both last night and this morning, I'd remember the last part of what Mercy had said to me: do you want to be happy?

I wanted to be happy. I just wasn't sure I had it in me. But I wanted to try. I'd been lying to myself for so long about all the reasons why I never went on a third date. I'd convinced myself it was the truth. In reality, I didn't care if a man wore flip-flops, though I totally did if we were going to a nice dinner, but it wasn't a deal breaker. Neither was a man having knuckle hair, though the nose picker was legitimate, and I'd argue that to the grave. I'd been unfairly judgmental over the years to protect myself and I didn't like what that said about me, though I wasn't sure how to change it.

"Are you ready to go see Patty?" Jackson asked, shoving the last piece of toast in his mouth.

"Yeah."

Jackson was leaning one hip on the counter, ankles crossed, his feet bare. The pose was intimate, just as all the conversations we'd had over the last eighteen hours or so we'd spent together.

"Thanks for all your help and for staying here," I told him.

His bright smile flashed, and I was taken aback by how content he looked.

"No need to thank me, Sweetness. I got to hold you in my arms all night. Believe me, I should be thanking you."

That was sweet. I wished I was able to express to him how much I liked hearing him say that.

"And thank you for taking me to—"

He pushed off the counter, instantly was in my space, and a beat later his hands were on the sides of my neck, his thumbs grazing the apple of my cheeks.

"You don't need to thank me for anything," he said, his brown eyes sparkling.

The longer I stared into them, the more lost I became and the more I thought about how they'd looked the night he'd demanded I kiss him before he took me. Then I remembered the last two times he was in my bed and nothing had happened. One of those times I was sobbing in his arms, so that time didn't count. But last night, we lay in bed and talked, and he hadn't tried anything. Nothing. He hadn't even tried to round first base. All he'd done was hold me close and kiss the top of my head.

Had he changed his mind? Was he no longer interested in me that way? I couldn't blame him. I had put some effort into making him want to stay away from me, however weak my objections, I'd told him I didn't want a friends with benefits relationship.

"Don't," he growled.

"Don't what?" His rumbly voice pulled me from my mental freak-out.

"Whatever you're thinking, stop. Please, Sweetness, do not shut me out again."

"What?"

I didn't know what he was talking about.

"I see you closing down. Don't do it. Please stay here with me."

"I wasn't . . . I mean, I didn't . . ." Shit, was that what I was doing? Shutting him out. "I didn't realize that's what I was doing."

He dropped his forehead to mine and whispered, "Please just give me another twenty-four hours. Don't close down on me."

"Okay, Jackson."

"Okay."

His reply came out in a relieved rush of air.

"Sorry," I mumbled.

"What were you thinking about?" he asked, lifting his head but not going far.

I pinched my lips together and tried to come up with something other than the embarrassing truth.

"Well, hell, the way your cheeks are burning up, this oughta be good."

"No, no, it's not good. I wasn't thinking about anything," I lied.

"Sweetness . . ." He chortled.

He wasn't going to let this go and maybe it was best to simply ask than wonder.

"Why didn't you make a move last night?"

"Come again?" Jackson jerked back.

"You didn't even kiss me. I mean, we've slept together before, and you've done other stuff. Is it because you're not interested?"

"Fuck, no." The vehemence in his tone made me feel a little better, but now he looked pissed. "I'm not an asshole, Tuesday."

"I know you're not. That's not what I meant. God, I'm screwing this up. I was just wondering if you'd changed your mind."

"I have," he affirmed.

My heart sank. I'd pushed too far.

"Oh."

I tried to pull myself together and not let my disappointment show. Of course, he would be done with me. Who wanted to continue to deal with a wishy-washy twit?

"Sweetness, I am not interested in a booty call. I didn't want it in the first place, but you had my hands tied, and I felt like the only way for me to get close was to agree. That isn't what I want for us and that's not where I'm gonna let us go. Last night when you were in my arms, opening up to me, I had to fight taking things further. The only thing I want more than getting back inside of you is having you trust me. So when I say I've changed my mind, what I mean is I want it all."

Holy shit.

"I want to be crystal clear. When I say all, I mean, all of you. The friendship, the commitment, the sex, the conversation, the intimacy, along with you knowing I'd never break your confidence. I know it will take time. I know it's going to be hard. I know you're gonna push back, get scared, and want to run. I'm good with all of that. I will fight for it and, Sweetness, I get that, too. Travis may've fucked you over, but every insecurity you have started way before him. So, fair warning, I'm not going to let you quit because someone broke your heart. I'm not going to let you hide because your mom is a raving bitch and has never shown you any kindness. But, mostly, I'm going to show you how a real man is supposed to treat a woman. Because I'd bet, other than you seeing how your grandfather was with your grandmother, you've never experienced it. Never had a man honor you the way he should have." I was heaving in air trying not to let it show I was going to hyperventilate at any moment. "Ready or not, Tuesday,

I'm playing for keeps. Buckle up, baby, it's about to get bumpy."

I couldn't get words out through the crush of emotions flooding me. He was right. Everything he'd said was spot on. He saw through all my bullshit. Saw past what Travis had done, to the heart of every bad decision I'd made. I'd spent so much of my life wanting to be seen and loved that I'd chosen poorly. I'd fucked up, and that was mine to own. I was responsible for myself and my actions and just because my dad hadn't stood up for me and my mom hadn't shown me love didn't make my poor judgment any less mine.

I'd learned the hard way. But I'd learned. And through those lessons I knew Jackson was different. So different I was afraid of him for new reasons.

But I'd never know unless I tried. Never know if I could truly be happy unless I let go and let him in.

I wanted to be happy, and since I couldn't talk because I was choking back tears, I nodded my acceptance.

"Good," he whispered.

Now there was a new question hanging in the air, would I be able to make him happy?

23

"Jackson! How lovely to see you again." Patty beamed as I walked into her room with Tuesday by my side.

This was not my first time in Autumn Lakes Nursing Home, but it was the first time I'd paid attention to the décor. The first time I was in the building, I was more concerned with a small fire in the arts and crafts room. My attention had not been on the well-appointed lobby nor had I noticed the numerous clusters of comfortable chairs positioned around the large space. One side of the entryway had a hallway that led to the activity rooms, including a gym. The other side had a corridor that led to the occupants' private rooms.

When we'd stepped into Patty's room, I hadn't been expecting soft gray walls and furnishings that looked like they belonged in a residential bedroom. Even the paintings on the walls looked like they didn't belong in a nursing home. I could see why Tuesday's grandmother enjoyed the facility. Other than the nurses and other staff roaming around nothing indicated nursing care. It was clean and well kept.

"Nice to see you, too, Mrs. Knowls."

"Patty," she corrected.

The older woman took us in, and her soft face broke into a wide smile. Tuesday, on the other hand, was not smiling. She was nervous and looked like she'd been forced to eat a lemon, or a dozen.

On the way over we'd talked more about Tuesday's parents. The more she told me, the more I understood her worry about Gladys showing up. It seemed Tuesday's mother had a flair for drama, and had no issue spreading it far and wide. At least in private. She'd also explained that her mom was big on appearances and thought the Knowls name should be held in high regard.

"Tuesday, dear, you're going to give yourself wrinkles with that scowl."

"How's your day been, Gran?" Tuesday asked, ignoring her grandmother's comment.

Patty didn't miss a beat. "By your sour puss look, I'd say better than yours."

I lost the battle and a chuckle slipped out, and Tuesday's eyes cut to me. "What's so funny?"

"You are, Sweetness."

"There's nothing funny," she hissed.

"Right."

Patty's laugh cut through Tuesday's snit, and when the old woman snorted, Tuesday finally smiled. It seemed she got her pretty laugh, complete with the cute snort, from her grandmother. I looked to Patty, sitting in a wheelchair, and really took her in for the first time. She was all sunny disposition and smiles.

Nothing but love and warmth shone in her eyes. Patty Knowls was a woman who'd had a good life. And from the stories Tuesday had told, she'd known love, lots of it. She'd had a husband who'd adored her. He'd given her so much during their marriage that even after his death Patty was still feeling it. I liked that for her. I liked how she'd had so much it spilled over and she'd given it to Tuesday.

"Listen, Gran, I hate to bring this up, but my mother called me last night and well . . ."

Patty's smile faded, her eyes slowly drifted closed, and when they reopened, she looked thoughtful.

"She threw a fit," she surmised.

"You could say that. She mentioned the house."

The thoughtful look was wiped clean off Patty's face, and in its place was anger. "The house?"

"Yes. She said she heard you were moving and said—"

"That damn son of mine. He could never keep his

cotton-pickin' mouth quiet. I'm sorry I didn't tell you. I wanted it to be a surprise. I told George that. I didn't want it spoken about until the paperwork was finished."

Oh, yeah, Patty was mad. A great laugh wasn't the only thing Tuesday had inherited from her grandmother. Seems both Knowls women had a fiery temper.

"What about the house?" Tuesday inquired.

Patty sighed and invited Tuesday to sit on the bed. When she did, Patty wheeled herself closer and picked up her granddaughter's hand.

"I've found a townhouse in Leisure Village I like. I made an offer, and it was accepted."

"That's wonderful," Tuesday said and smiled.

Patty offered her one in return even though it was evident Tuesday's wasn't real. She was putting on a show to cover the pain she felt about losing what she considered her childhood home. There was no missing it, therefore, Patty hadn't.

"It is. The movers will be at The Manor this week to pack up my personal belongings."

"Do you need me to pack the rest? Will you be having an estate sale?"

With each word Tuesday spoke, my heart was breaking for her. I hoped to God, Patty would not allow her to pack up the house for her.

"No, my sweet girl. The rest is staying, for you. Anything you don't want, it's yours to do away with."

"Mine?"

"The Manor is yours, along with everything inside."

"Gran." Tuesday's voice was strangled. "I can't."

"You can, dear. It's yours. Whether you receive it after my death or now. And, personally, I'd rather be alive to see you enjoy it."

"It's too much," she whispered.

"Nonsense. Your grandfather worked hard. Harder than any man I've ever known. He did so because he wanted to give to those he loved. This is what he'd want. I know, because we discussed it. He knew how much you enjoyed visiting us. It was his greatest joy watching you dress up and dance in the ballroom. He could watch your smiling face for hours, and he did. He watched you in the kitchen baking your first apple pie and ate every last bite on his plate even though you forgot the sugar, and I swear it was the tartest pie I'd ever tasted. But he did that because you made it. You smiled and giggled the whole time you were slicing the apples the two of you had picked from the orchard. That tree is still there. It's meant to be yours. For you to make a home and carry on the tradition of love and happiness."

There it was, everything I'd thought was correct.

Tuesday's grandfather had given his love and done it in abundance.

"Gran," she repeated.

"That home served me well. It will you, too. I want you to have it, Tuesday. I want to see you in it. I want to watch you dance again. I want to be invited over for Sunday dinner and eat your apple pie. I want this and it is not for you to turn down an old woman's dying wish."

Patricia Knowls had brought out the big guns. Emotional blackmail. Good for her.

"You're not dying!" Tuesday blurted. Her spine straight and eyes leveled on her grandmother. "What about Dad?"

"What about him?"

They both had seemed to forget I was in the room and I momentarily considered stepping out so they could have their privacy. Before I could come up with an exit strategy Tuesday looked at me then back to Patty.

"Won't he be upset? He's your son, the heir, shouldn't the house go to him? I mean, it will still be in the family, that's all I want. I can't bear to think about strangers in your house," she admitted.

I knew it took a lot out of her to confess that to her grandmother. She felt selfish for thinking it and didn't want to stop Patty from moving.

"Your father never loved the house as much as you do. Not even when he grew up in it. And don't you worry about your father, this was how it was meant to be, how it was set up. It's time for me to move on, dear. That house is too big for me. I haven't been on the third floor in years."

Tuesday still didn't look convinced. So Patty continued, "Besides, your mother has made it clear she wants to live out her days in the sun and surf. She's perfectly happy in Hawaii, and I think she should stay there. It's my house, and I get to choose to whom I'm going to leave it. I've never asked anything of you, my sweet girl. Give me this. Nothing will make me happier than to see you in that house."

Tuesday glanced at me again, and I was surprised how conflicted she looked. "What's worrying you, Sweetness?" I asked.

"You heard her," she whispered.

"She will not get close to you, baby." I tried to assure her. "Besides it's not up to her who gets to live in the house. And I think your grandmother has made it clear who she prefers."

"Who is *her*? And what did she say?" Patty's tone had changed from sweet old woman, albeit not a happy one since her son had spilled the beans, to a seriously pissed off woman.

"Um," Tuesday started then stopped.

"Gladys," I told Patty. "In her call last night, she informed Tuesday she was not pleased about The Manor. And expressed her displeasure by telling Tuesday she'd bring her down. I then had a brief conversation with the woman where I explained to her she was not to contact Tuesday until Tuesday reached out. Where she then informed us, she would be seeing Tuesday soon."

"You spoke to Gladys?" Patty asked.

"I did."

Her face lit with humor before she roared with laughter ending on a snort. "I'm sure that was hostile."

"You could describe it as such, yes."

"Tuesday, you let me deal with your mother and my son."

"Excuse me," a male orderly called from the doorway before Tuesday could answer Patty. It took me a moment to place the man.

"Yes, Randolph?" Patty answered.

Randolph, that was his name. The man from the bar who'd been hitting on Tuesday and wouldn't take no for an answer. We hadn't talked about him or if she'd known him.

"I wanted to remind you there's a bridge game scheduled for this afternoon."

He was talking to Patty, but his eyes were on Tuesday.

"Tuesday," he greeted.

Yeah, I didn't like his stare on my woman one fucking bit. I walked the few steps needed and put my arm around her waist and pulled her close. I didn't give the first fuck I was acting like a caveman. Randolph's eyes dropped to my hand. His eyes narrowed, not missing the claiming gesture.

"Hey." She added a smile, but it was worth noting, she hadn't tried to pull away.

"Thank you, dear, but I have an appointment this afternoon. I won't be making the game."

"Sure." Randolph gave me one last, hard look—or at least he tried—but it looked more like he was constipated than tough before he turned to leave.

"I know the way!" a woman screeched from the hallway.

Tuesday went solid and Patty's eyes widened.

"Ma'am. All visitors need to be announced," a second voice demanded.

"I do not need you to announce my visit to my mother-in-law."

"Shit," Tuesday whispered.

A woman stormed into the room, the clacking of her heels stopped, and her gaze zeroed in on Tuesday.

"I've been looking for you," she accused.

It didn't take a genius to figure out who the woman was.

"Get out," I demanded, stepping between Gladys and Tuesday.

To say Gladys was not what I'd expected was an understatement. Tuesday was tall and willowy. Thin without being overly, great legs and ass, perfect smile, and beautiful, shiny hair. Gladys was short, squatty, and unattractive. She dressed like she was the one walking the runways but didn't have a single ounce of Tuesday's beauty.

"I'm sorry, Mrs. Knowls," a nurse said from behind Gladys.

"You should be. I want this . . . this . . . man out of my mother-in-law's room. I cannot believe for the amount of money you charge you would allow such filth to enter," Gladys sneered.

"I was speaking to Patricia." The nurse corrected. "Would you like me to call security?"

"No, thank you, Emma. I believe Jackson can escort her out when I'm done with her."

The nurse left and Gladys's face pinched into a look of disgust. "Really, Tuesday? This?"

"Tuesday, dear?" Patty called.

"Won't you please step outside and let me speak to your mother for a moment?"

"I'd prefer to stay, Gran."

"I know you would, but the conversation is going to be unpleasant. As your grandmother, I've always promised myself I would never speak unkindly about your mother in front of you. To keep that promise, I'll need you to step out."

"I came here to speak to my daughter, Patricia." If I wasn't mistaken, Gladys had turned a shade or two paler.

"I'm sure you did. That's always been your way. You like to corner my granddaughter because you know she is kindhearted despite having you for a mother, therefore, she wouldn't dare tell you to jump off a bridge. But you stormed into my room causing a ruckus. You wanted trouble, and you've found it."

"I don't have to stand here and listen to an old woman—"

"Watch it, Mother." Tuesday stiffened in my arms.

"Or what, Tuesday? Don't you think you have enough problems right now?"

"Come on, Sweetness. The faster your grandmother speaks to her, the sooner I can toss her out on her ass."

"I cannot believe—"

"Yes, you can. What you won't believe is I don't give a shit what you think of me. You are a nobody. Absolutely meaningless in my life. Tuesday and I are gonna give Patty the privacy she's requested, then you're gone."

Patty's gaze hit mine, and she nodded. "I'll be right

outside, Patty. But if I hear one nasty thing come out of her mouth, I'm coming in and dragging her out."

"I appreciate it, Jackson."

I gathered Tuesday in my arms and started to walk to the door but she stopped as we neared her mother.

"We're done. I hope you know that. We haven't ever had a loving relationship, but we've both managed to tolerate each other. After this stunt and your last threat? We. Are. Done."

"It was not a threat. I'm warning you, little girl, I will burn your life down. You think what that dumbass Travis did stung? That pissant didn't even have what it took to follow out a simple plan. I will destroy you," her mother said, snickering.

Tuesday was vibrating, and Patty sucked in an audible breath from the other side of the room and stood. I didn't know if Patty was supposed to be standing after her hip surgery, but it seemed she was more than capable of doing so and was more than willing to put herself out there for her granddaughter.

Tuesday was right, we were done. Gladys was leaving.

24

I felt like I was floating on a cloud of fury and devastation. Jackson was guiding me back to my grandmother's bed, but I couldn't feel my feet.

Simple plan?

What did my mother know about Travis's plan?

I wasn't sure what was more disturbing, my own mother threatening to destroy me or her knowing about what Travis had planned and saying he hadn't been able to follow it through. How much worse could it have been?

"Out," Jackson demanded.

"You cannot—"

"I can and I am. Get. Out."

"Patricia said she—"

"Don't care about that either. Either you step out, or I'll put you out."

"You wouldn't dare put your hands on me. I have more attorneys—"

My grandmother moved to the side of the bed and picked up my hand. The gesture was comforting, it always had been, but it did nothing to alleviate the hurt my mother had caused.

"You don't have anything, Gladys." My grandmother started, not letting go of my hand. "I never thought I'd have to say this in front of Tuesday, but you've left me no choice. I never did see what my son saw in you, other than what you gave him on the first date. Easy, that's what you were. A gold-digging ninny then, and you have been every day for the last thirty-some-odd-years. You've lived off what my husband afforded his son. You've taken everything and the only thing you've given this family that's worth a damn is my granddaughter. But you've treated her like garbage since the day she exited your womb. Jackson's correct, you're done. You've stepped over a line, this time, I will not ignore. Either you inform my son he should call me, or you may tell him yourself he is no longer welcome in my home so long as you accompany him. As for any future money you or he thought you would inherit from my estate, it's gone. I certainly hope you can make what's left of George's trust last, because you will never see another red cent from me or mine ever again. The house is Tuesday's. You and George have always known it was to be willed to her. Yet you stormed in here as if you have a claim to it. You have the nerve to threaten my granddaughter. When I say you're done, Gladys, I mean that in every way possible."

"You can't tell me what I can and cannot do with my daughter," my mom spit out, bending at the waist toward my grandmother. "I've put up with thirty years of you thinking you were the queen of this family. You always bossing George around. The will's already drawn up, and the trust has been filed. We'll just have you declared unfit before you can change it."

A cruel smile played at Gran's lips. "I thought you and my son would try something like that."

"What does that mean?"

Had my mother always been this shrill? The answer was a resounding yes. She was nasty to me ninety percent of the time, the other ten percent she'd been decent was only because Gran or my pop had been around.

She had always been a bitch. Gladys treated everyone as if they were beneath her, especially the people I'd worked with in the modeling industry, and she'd acted, in particular, as though Meredith was lower than dirt. Yet, another reason I couldn't understand why she was taking her side now. She'd always despised the woman, and blamed Meredith for her money train ending.

But I had never, not a single time, heard her speak to my grandmother this way. I'd overheard her bitch to my dad about why he allowed me to spend so much time with his parents, even though she didn't want me around. She'd thrown a fit when, after speaking to my grandfather, my father had changed his mind about sending me off to boarding school. However, to Patty's face she was sugar sweet, fake through and through. It was disgusting to watch. I'd always thought it was out of respect.

It wasn't.

It was greed.

She thought she would come into Gran's fortune.

What a bitch!

"The papers have been drawn up; you and George get nothing. I'd rather leave everything to an animal shelter. At least I'd know the bitches who inherited it would appreciate it."

"You can't do that!"

"Jesus, woman, stop screaming," Jackson told her. "Patty's said her piece. This conversation is over."

He moved to stand in front of her, and she stepped back.

"This isn't over," she threatened.

"God, mother, haven't you said enough? You're embarrassing yourself and me."

"You ungrateful bitch." She turned toward me, and I flinched at the hate that shone on her face. "After everything I've done for you. All you had to do was stand in front of a camera and you couldn't even do that right. Your career would've been over years ago if it weren't for me."

After all these years, you'd think I'd remember that my mom didn't love me. She never had. But each time she spewed her venom, I'd have forgotten, and her sharp tongue would slice deeply. Even years of scar tissue couldn't stop the pain her words caused.

"What does that mean?"

"It means, you were stagnant. You were yesterday's news. And you weren't doing anything about it. Meredith saw it, I saw it, even Travis saw it. But not you. You were too busy living with your head in the clouds, letting your career tank. Someone had to step in and make you relevant."

My insides started to burn. "You didn't!"

"Nothing makes you relevant like a scandal. Everything was almost perfect, all Travis had to do was get one sex tape out on the internet and your career would've exploded, but he got camera shy. And the videos of the men we sent to you would've been a goldmine, the media would've eaten those up, but that idiot

Lambert had to get involved and ruined everything with his PIs and computer experts and had them deleted before we could leak them." She squared her shoulders and smiled. "You should be thanking me."

The scorch quickly turned to ice. *A sex tape? I was going to be sick.* My own mother had worked with Travis to cook up a scandal, and she thought I should thank her? Naked pictures were still floating around of me, and I should thank her for that? Her own flesh and blood had been violated and stalked. Harassed.

I was going to kill her. I was off the bed and on the move. "Did Meredith know?"

"Who do you think came up with the idea?"

"You bitch!" I lunged at my mom.

Jackson grabbed me and swung me into his arms. A bone-deep cold settled over me, as my shitty life flashed in snippets behind my eyelids. My mom screaming at me on my sixth birthday because I dropped cake on my dress and embarrassed her. It was done away from the guests, of course. When I was ten and I couldn't memorize all the state capitols, I was stupid. At sixteen I was fat. Seventeen when a boy asked me out on a date, she called me a whore when I got back from the movies. At eighteen I wasn't working enough. More photo sessions. More runway shows. More money. More, *more*, more.

"Why does she hate me?" I whispered.

"She doesn't, Sweetness, she hates herself. She's so jealous of you she is overwhelmed by it." Jackson rested the side of his face against mine. So close our air mingled. "Patty, can you come here and sit with her while I escort Gladys out?"

"Yes, dear."

My grandmother's sweet voice filled my ears as Jackson sat me on the bed. Gran took slow tentative steps and sat next to me, her frail arms wrapped around me and all I felt was her love.

"Gran."

"My beautiful girl." I'd been holding back tears but at hearing my grandmother's whispered words, the dam broke.

"She knew," I cried. "She helped them."

"She did, dear. I'm so sorry."

There was nothing else left to say. My own mother had worked with Travis. Meredith? I couldn't believe it. She'd always acted appalled at my mother's behavior. We'd discussed her antics over drinks many times. She'd helped me when I was trying to untangle the mess my mother had left when I'd pushed her out of my finances and management. Meredith had taken on the task of helping me rebuild my life after all the money my mom had stolen from me. Why would she betray me? Why would she help my mom and Travis? Why would Travis, for that matter? Gladys had treated him like he was scum. None of it made any sense.

"I hate her," I told my grandmother. "I hate them both. Dad never did anything to stop her. He knew. He knew how she treated me, yet he did nothing. He just stood there and listened to her call me fat and stupid. He didn't ever stand up for me. Not once."

"Did you know it was your father's idea to move to Hawaii?" she asked.

"No. Neither of them ever talked to me. All Mom said was they'd done their job and now it was time for them to move on with their lives."

My grandmother was silent for a moment then she softly told me, "Your dad is not a strong man. Part of that may be our fault. Mine and your grandfather's. We should've made him work harder. Should've made him earn the things he had. For that I am sorry. Your grandfather grew up in a family that struggled. Often times, there was barely enough food. He scraped and saved and worked himself to the bone to build something that was great. When we had your father, he didn't ever want his son to feel that kind of burden, so we spoiled him.

"But there was a change in him when he met your mother. He was in love. The sun rose and set with her. It didn't matter how many times we warned him. She had her hooks in him and there was no stopping him.

The only thing my son has ever done for you that I'm grateful for was moving that woman far away from you. He didn't have the backbone to stop her, but he could entice her with the promise of a lifestyle she couldn't say no to. So he packed up their life here and got her away from you. It doesn't abolish his sins, but that's why he did it."

It was not my grandparents' fault their son was a spineless asshole who didn't love his daughter enough to stand up to his wife. But at least I now understood the abrupt move right after I graduated high school. Of course, my mother had to put her own twist on it and dig her knife in.

Gran sat next to me, rocking me gently while Jackson was escorting my mother out of the building. I hoped he wasn't doing it kindly. She would hate being told to leave, but she would seriously hate being told by someone she felt was below her social status. God, she was such a bitch.

"Gran?"

"Yes, dear?"

"Thank you for always loving me."

"Oh, my sweet granddaughter, you never have to thank me for that. You are one of the greatest blessings in my life. Your grandfather's, too. I hope you remember how much he adored you."

"I do. I could never forget."

And I couldn't. My grandfather had never been selfish with his love. He'd been open and had communicated how much he loved both my grandmother and me. He'd always had a smile on his face, a hug to give, and a kind word to say. I missed him so much.

I needed to get back to Patty's room, but I was giving myself a few minutes to calm down.

Gladys was not only the world's worst mother, she was also a crazy bitch.

As soon as we'd cleared the threshold and hit the hallway a security guard met me and helped guide her to the lobby. The woman shrieked all the way there. Threatening lawsuit after lawsuit. It was ridiculous.

The guard couldn't care less what Gladys was saying. Though, I'd never wanted to gag someone as badly as I wanted to her. The only good news was, once we were outside of Autumn Lakes and taking her to her car, she started to incriminate herself more. The smug bitch had reiterated her role in the scandal to revitalize Tuesday's career. She was pleased with herself that the scheme had worked brilliantly, even if

Lambert, whoever that was, had tried to shut it down before it had hit the newswire. The stupid bitch hadn't cared that her daughter had been humiliated. She'd been an active participant in Tuesday's mental abuse.

"Sir?" the receptionist called as I walked past her desk.

"Yes."

"I'm sorry to bother you, especially after that scene. But Ms. Knowls requested Mrs. Knowls' current statements. Normally I wouldn't give them to anyone but our patient." She lowered her voice to a conspiratorial whisper. "You know, with the laws the way they are. Anyway, we all heard what went on with her mother, and, well, I *really* don't want to bother her, but she said it was urgent. So, I want to give them to you. They're sealed. Just, um . . . please don't open them, or tell anyone I gave them to you."

I took the envelope the woman was handing me and smiled. "Thank you." I leaned in and added, "It's our little secret."

"I hope Tuesday's okay," she offered.

"Thank you for that, too. And she will be."

With a lift of my chin I walked down the corridor taking those last moments to control my anger. Patty and Tuesday both needed me to be levelheaded. I was about to enter the room when movement to my right caught my attention. Randolph was in a heated conversation with a woman. She clearly wasn't a patient. When they noticed me staring, they broke apart and the woman walked away at a fast clip. As much as I'd like to know if Randolph was harassing the poor woman like he'd done to Tuesday I had more important things to do.

When I stepped into the room, I found the two women huddled together on the bed. Patty's frail arms wrapped tightly around her granddaughter while Tuesday cried softly. It would've been picture perfect if I didn't know what had caused those tears. A moment so sweet and protective, I didn't want to interrupt.

Patty's eyes came to mine, and she gave me a small, sad smile. She looked absolutely heartbroken, and I knew she was because Tuesday was. Not because she'd taken anything Gladys had directed toward her to heart. Patty didn't care for the woman and had made that clear, too, something she'd gone to great pains to hide from Tuesday. Though, it was doubtful Tuesday hadn't seen through her efforts.

I was sure the older woman had found the entire confrontation distasteful for a variety of reasons. The biggest being she had class and dignity, and there was nothing classy about the drama Gladys had caused.

"Would you like to come sit with our girl?" Patty asked, and Tuesday lifted her head.

"No, ma'am," I said with a smile. "She looks good right where she is, with you."

"Well then take a load off, you're making me nervous standing in the doorway."

I was happy to hear some humor in Patty's tone. I walked to the nearest chair and took a seat, smiling as I did.

"Is she gone?" Tuesday asked.

"Yeah, Sweetness, she's gone."

"What's that?" Tuesday's eyes went to the envelope in my hand.

"The receptionist gave it to me. She said you'd requested some additional statements," I told her.

"Statements? What kind of—"

"If you wouldn't mind, Patty, perhaps we can tell you about it a little later."

I didn't want to be rude, but I also didn't want to discuss the investigation while the door was open or while at the nursing home at all. Right now, there was no danger to Patty, however, if someone overheard that Tuesday was providing her best friend, who happened to be a DEA agent, proof of prescription fraud both women could be in trouble.

"Who do you have an appointment with?" Tuesday asked her grandmother.

"What, dear?"

"Earlier you said you wouldn't be playing bridge because you had an appointment."

"Oh, yes, Mr. Palmer, my attorney."

"Are you really going to . . ." Tuesday trailed off, leaving her question hanging in the air.

"Yes, Tuesday. It's already been done. I had the paperwork drawn up months ago. As distasteful as it is, it needed to be done. Unfortunately, your parents have bought themselves some financial issues. And it's not because of poor business decisions or a declining market. It's simply due to overspending. I've bailed them out before, more than once. If my son is not responsible enough, at his age, to manage his money properly, I'm not giving him mine to waste. Your grandfather worked too hard for it to be squandered."

Tuesday simply nodded and looked back at her clasped hands in her lap.

"One more thing, then we're moving on to something happy," Patty continued. "The Manor is yours. No arguments. I would like it to remain in the family after I'm gone, but it is yours and you may do whatever you'd like with it. The new arrangements will make it so you'll be able to financially take care of the property indefinitely. Now, about what your mother said about Travis and Meredith. I'm not sure what can be done about it at this point, but I do hope you will be doing what you can to make sure that all three pay for what they did."

I waited for Tuesday's response. And the whole time I was waiting, all I could think about was how badly I wanted to be the one sitting next to her with my arms wrapped around her. And how difficult it had been not to take Patty up on her earlier offer. But I knew both women needed each other close. Being in the room to watch over them should've been enough, but it wasn't. Tuesday looked beaten down. Shattered. It was becoming harder and harder sitting so close but not being able to hold her.

Finally, she looked up with some of her earlier anger on her face, and while I never wanted her mad it was a fuck ton better than seeing her forlorn.

"Jackson's brother, Nick, is with the FBI. He's been looking into some stuff for us. When we get home, we'll call him and tell him."

Us.

Home.

We'll.

Warmth hit my chest and spread like wildfire. Maybe she wasn't thinking clearly due to the latest trauma. Maybe it was a slip. Whatever it was, I was taking it and savoring it. I also wasn't going to let the opportunity slip by. I was grabbing it—and holding on.

If this was her letting me in, it was a bloody miracle and hallelujah.

"Good. That's really good." Patty smiled. "So, what do the two of you have planned for the rest of the day?"

"I was hoping to catch a few games of bingo while we were here," I told Patty. "Tuesday tells me you have quite the winning streak."

"Did she?" Patty laughed just as I'd hoped. "Bingo is a game of chance. I'm not sure you can call it a winning streak. Maybe I've caught some good luck."

"But from what I hear, I may have to fight for a seat next to you."

"I don't think the old men in this joint would be too much trouble for a young, handsome firefighter such as yourself."

I was holding back a chuckle by the barest of fractions, but when Patty added a wink to her statement, I lost it.

"Gran!" Tuesday tried but failed to sound chastising. She could barely cover her own giggle.

"Unfortunately, you're out of luck, there are no games scheduled for today. We could, however, sit and play a few hands of five-card draw. But there is something you should know about my Tuesday," Patty started. "Just so you're aware, she likes to win. Always has. And she's a card shark. Sometimes I think it's the only reason she likes to come here and play poker against the old men. She takes their money and they don't care because they get to sit across from a beautiful, young woman and watch her dance a jig when she wins a hand."

"You take old men's money?" I asked Tuesday, still chuckling.

"We play for quarters." She rolled her eyes at me. "And I do not dance a jig, Gran."

"Well, then, I don't know what it's called, but you dance."

"Victory. It's a victory dance." Tuesday rallied.

I was enjoying watching the women smile at each other, even if it was forced. I didn't want to think about how many times Tuesday had been subjected to her mother's bullshit, and evidence was suggesting quite a bit. It seemed experience meant she could pull herself together quickly. Albeit most of Tuesday's recovery, if you could call her fake smile such, had been for Patty's benefit. She loved her grandmother and didn't want her to worry.

The rest I would take care of when we got home.

"I think it's time we left," I announced.

I didn't want to play cards, but when Gran had suggested it, I couldn't say no. I knew it was her way of keeping me close until she deemed I was no longer going to have a nervous breakdown. Though, I did think she'd needed both Jackson and I to help settle her as well.

"Don't pout, dear," Gran said and collected the cards.

"Well, I'm out of quarters." I pointed out.

"I'm not," Jackson gloated.

So, there we were playing five-card draw in Gran's room and I was losing—badly. Jackson, however, was not. He was cleaning up and Gran was coming in a close second.

"You know what they say about being a sour winner, right?" I crossed my arms over my chest.

"Nope. Sure don't."

He was smiling, and Gran was looking at him like he was the best thing since sliced bread. She was beaming, therefore, I didn't really mind I was losing—that much. I still wasn't sure what exactly I was doing.

Jackson had asked for twenty-four hours. At the time, with all the craziness that had gone on, it was easy to agree. Well, maybe it wasn't easy, but it hadn't been as hard as I'd thought it would be. But, this morning, when he'd asked for another twenty-four there was no big, traumatizing event, just us in my kitchen. I'd agreed again, and now it was hard. I wanted to shut down and pull back.

Watching Gran and Jackson laugh and joke together, even if it was in an effort to erase what my mother had said to me, felt good. I liked seeing it. I liked that he made her smile. I liked that she liked him. I just plain liked it, and that scared the hell out of me.

I was gonna screw this up and when I did, it was gonna hurt. Big time. Maybe even more than seeing a naked picture of myself on the internet. And that knowledge was so terrifying it made me want to tell Jackson his time was up. But, once again, I had Mercy in my ear, *do you wanna be happy?*

I felt his eyes on me, and, sure enough, they were

narrowing, like he could read my mind. But then he tensed, turned his head to the side like he was trying to listen really hard, then he was suddenly standing.

"What's wrong?"

"Stay here."

He strode to the door at a fast clip but didn't even make it out of the door before he turned back.

"Tuesday, help Gran into her wheelchair," he barked.

"What? What's happening?"

"Now, Sweetness, hurry."

He rushed into the en suite bathroom, and I helped my grandmother who, apparently, could follow directions without asking why, was already out of the chair she'd been sitting in and was walking to her wheelchair. Something she didn't need anymore, unless she was tired.

Jackson came back out with two wet towels and handed one to me.

"There's smoke coming out of one of the rooms. Both of you keep the towels over your mouths."

"Smoke? But no alarm is going off," I stupidly told him.

"I'm pushing Patty. You're at my side. Do not stop. Not for anything or anyone. Ready?"

"Yes," Gran answered.

He didn't wait for my acceptance, he just moved,

pushing Gran at a near jog. Once we were in the hall, I could see smoke pouring out of a room at the end of the hall, near the lobby. Jackson went in the opposite direction toward the exit at the end of the corridor. When we passed by a red fire alarm, he broke the glass and pulled the alarm, but nothing happened.

"Fuck," he muttered.

Why weren't we telling people to get out?

"Shouldn't that have done something?"

"Yes," he clipped.

"Sweetness, I need you to take over. Get Gran outside, call 9-1-1, and move to the edge of the parking lot."

"Yeah, okay."

He stepped out of the way and let me grab hold of the handles. "Straight outside, baby. Please don't stop. And get away from the building."

The reality of what was happening hit me. He was getting me and Gran to safety, but he was staying in. And there was a fire. From the smoke now billowing, it was a big one.

Oh, shit.

Okay.

He started to turn when I grabbed his bicep and stopped him. "Let me get Gran outside and I'll come back in to help."

"Tuesday, the only way you can help me right now

is to get you and Gran out and safe. I can't do my job worried about you," he rushed out. "Now, go. Hurry."

"Please be careful," was the last thing I said to him before I practically jogged to the exit with Gran, not bothering to cover my mouth with the towel. But there was so much more I wanted to say. I wanted to tell him thank you for taking care of us. Thank him for making me feel safe—again. Beg him to come outside with us and not put himself in danger. I wanted to make him promise he'd be okay. However, there was no time for that, and even if there was, I wasn't sure I knew how to verbally express those things.

I turned around, pushed the lock release bar with my ass, and backed us out of the door so I could pull the wheelchair through. The door shut behind us and I continued to walk as fast as I could down the pathway that led around the building to the parking lot, stopping when I'd finally gotten us far enough away from the building.

I called 9-1-1, the dispatcher told me there were already crews on the way and asked for my location. The call was brief, and, thankfully, by the time I hung up residents and staff were pouring out of the nursing home. It was then the panic started to take root. Gran and I were standing, or I was, Gran was sitting, in the far corner of her nursing home's parking lot and it was on fire. Not only was there smoke coming out of the back of the building I could now see flames from the roof. Big, angry, red flames. And Jackson was inside. He'd stayed. Without hesitation. He'd taken care of us, then ran back down the hall. I wasn't sure why the sight of him going back toward the smoke was lingering in my mind, he was a firefighter, after all. But I couldn't stop thinking about it.

"I told you that man was smitten." Gran broke the silence.

"Not now, Gran."

"Now is the perfect time to remind you, while your man is in a burning building, that life is short. Anything can happen. You take what you're feeling right now and hold it close. Remember this when you get scared and want to hide away. Life is but a fleeting moment. Nothing is promised. Not people. Not time. Not love. You need to fight for it. Work at it. Hold on to it. But, most importantly, you need to give that man the opportunity to do all those things. If not, you'll learn a new meaning of regret. One that's far harder to swallow. Regret that you knew a man that had the capacity and desire to show you real love and you turned your back on it."

Her wise words were more than a punch to the gut, which they totally were, they hit me down deep in my soul, and I knew she was right. Then, again, she always was. But she was also wrong, now was not the time for me to be freaking about the fact that I thought I may've been falling in love with Jackson.

There was a fire. One my man had first made sure I was safe from and was now trying to fight. Despite what he'd said, I needed to help. I couldn't stand around selfishly thinking about the state of my love life when lives were in danger.

The area was filling up with patients and staff. I saw Emma, one of the daytime nurses, and called her name.

"Can you stay with Gran?"

"Absolutely," she told me. "But—"

"Be back."

I dashed off before Gran could scold me. I wasn't going to go back inside, but I could do something to help.

———

TWO HOURS LATER, there were still fire trucks, police, and ambulances surrounding Autumn Lakes. I'd seen Jackson briefly when the first engine pulled in and he'd rushed out covered in ash and soot. He'd gone straight to the truck, disappeared for a moment, before reappearing in turnout gear.

I'd watched as he scanned the area, his gaze hit Gran, his face went soft right before it went hard when he didn't see me. I think that was *the* moment I felt the first crack in the thick cement I'd poured around my heart. Seconds later, he'd found me, and with each step he'd taken in my direction, the crack had spider-webbed. By the time he'd made it to me, those tiny fractures were wide open holes. Jackson's lips touched mine, and the spark that touch created obliterated what was left. He was worried about me. Me and Gran. I'd never had that from anyone but my grandfather, and he was a hard act to follow. Jackson was proving he was up for the task.

Then he was gone, without a word, back into the burning building.

With a look and a soft kiss he'd done the impossible, broken down my every defense.

And I wasn't going to rebuild.

Now, I was standing next to my grandmother and her doctor, Laura Hudson, and Jackson was approaching. As soon as he was within reaching distance, he tagged me around the waist, pulled me to him, and kissed the top of my head. I didn't care the buckles of his gear were digging into my side, or that I'd probably never get the smell of smoke he was covered in out of my favorite shirt, I was happy to be in his arms.

"Are you doing all right, Patty?" he asked.

"Just fine, thanks to you." She beamed up at him. It

was good to know that even in a crisis Gran could still turn it on and lay it on thick.

"Any word on when we'll be able to go back in?" Dr. Hudson asked.

"Afraid not. The marshal has called in the arson investigators."

"Arson?" Laura's eyes rounded. "Damn. I better make some calls."

The doctor looked thoughtful for a moment before she turned to my grandmother. "If I don't see you before you leave, Patricia, good luck to you."

"Thank you, Dr. Hudson."

Before I could say my goodbyes, she'd turned and was lost in the sea of people. It was ordered chaos. Nurses and orderlies were helping load patients into ambulances and the nursing home had a fleet of passenger vans that were being utilized as well. I'd never seen so many first responders all in one place before.

"Gran's been discharged," I told Jackson.

"Well, that's good news seeing as she wouldn't be staying here any longer even if she hadn't been," he returned.

There was a harshness to his tone and an under-lying meaning. I wanted to ask what he meant, but I didn't. Not now, and not in front of Gran. He'd said the fire was possibly arson and knowing there's an on-going investigation into the nursing home didn't give me a warm, fuzzy feeling. But Jackson's swift answer told me he knew something I didn't. Therefore, I was happy Dr. Hudson had already been over to talk to Gran and given her proper discharge papers, because I was ready to get my grandmother away from Autumn Lakes. Today's incident was too close. I didn't want her anywhere near prescription drug fraud, overbilling, or anything else. Even if the fire had nothing to do with any of it, I was done.

"I see you've found yourself a bossy one." Gran smiled.

Jeez.

"Not bossy, Patty, just looking out for my girls."

His girls? Was he trying to give my grandmother heart palpations? I was never going to hear the end of that statement.

"Well, you're our ride, unless you want me to call Mercy to come get us," I told him, ignoring my contented sigh.

"Give me ten minutes and I'll be ready."

With another kiss to the top of my head, he let me go and wandered off into the crowd. He, however, didn't get lost in the crush of residents, family members, and staff. It was impossible for him to. Impossible for me to lose sight of him when my eyes were drawn to him like a moth to a flame.

"That man is smitten," Gran repeated.

"Not now, Gran."

"Hold on, sweet granddaughter. The man's playing for keeps." My heart skipped, and I sucked in a breath waiting for my grandmother to finish. "And when a man like Jackson, a man like your grandfather, decides they're playing the long game, which means they're not playing at all, they're just simply setting about winning. So, hold on and enjoy the ride. I hope it's a wild one."

A wild one?

It has been that.

I didn't want to think about how close Gran's observation fit with everything Jason had told me about Jackson. How close it was to everything I knew him to be.

No, instead, I was focusing on, *a man like Jackson, a man like your grandfather*. My grandfather had been the love of Gran's life, her everything, her soulmate. And she was comparing the two men, making them equals.

I wanted to hide

I wasn't going to.

I was going to hold on and enjoy the ride.

Tuesday hadn't been exaggerating even a little when she'd said The Manor was a southern mansion. If anything, she hadn't done it justice. The house was only ten minutes from my parents', in a part of the county where three-hundred-year-old oaks still stood. And, at first glance, I'd have guessed the majority of those trees lined the long driveway that led to a white, three-story, square, plantation style mansion. There were eight tall columns that were evenly spaced, from the ground to the roof of the third-floor balcony. I could only see two of the four sides of the house but the columns continued around.

The wealth could not be missed. However, the house itself looked warm and welcoming. Which, with a house that grand in size, should've been impossible.

The drive split, forming a teardrop driveway, either

side would lead you to the front of the house but only the right side branched off to a parking area by a very large outbuilding.

"In front okay?" I asked. It was a beautiful design that allowed you to drive right up to the large staircase, drop off, and continue around without having to turn around.

"Perfect," Tuesday answered.

It took us five minutes to get Patty into the house. I thought she'd protest when I scooped her out of the back seat of my truck, carried her up the stairs, and into the foyer. However, much like when I'd placed her in my truck when we'd left the nursing home, she just stared up at me and laughed.

"Well, if that wasn't a thrill, then I don't know what is," Patty remarked as Tuesday opened her wheelchair.

"Gran!" Tuesday's rebuke fell on deaf ears.

"My granddaughter needs to learn how to loosen up and have some fun. I'm hoping you're the man for the job."

"That I am," I told Patty and gently placed her in her chair.

"Thank you for the ride, now you two best be on your way," she shooed.

"Not a chance, Gran. I'm staying here with you," Tuesday told her.

"Nonsense—"

"Actually, we're both staying here with you this evening," I cut in. "I'm assuming there's no food in the house, and since I'm starved, I'm going to let you two get settled in and I'm heading to the grocery store."

Two sets of very pretty brown eyes swung my way. One gentle and soft with a multitude of wrinkles making them even softer. The other was no less beautiful and soft, and they were unguarded. Tuesday liked I was offering for both of us to stay and she wasn't hiding it.

Finally.

"Chicken parm okay for dinner?" Tuesday asked.

"If you're cooking, then yes."

Her face split into a wide smile and I had to force myself to stay upright.

"I'll write you a list."

Tuesday took off, leaving Patty and me in the foyer. "Would you like a tour while you wait?"

I glanced around the large, inviting space. To the right there was a gigantic room with floor-to-ceiling windows, a fireplace was the focal point of the room, and surrounding it was stunning antique furniture I'd be afraid to sit on. Dark wood accented throughout, and a piano stood in the corner. The other side of the room was almost identical, minus the piano and with the addition of an ornate bar. Directly in front of me was a huge staircase, with a landing that broke the stairs into two sections. A crystal chandelier, that I couldn't for the life of me figure out how you'd clean, hung down from the second story ceiling. I took it all in and realized, yet again, the wealth I was surrounded by.

"How long is her list? I'm thinking a tour might take the rest of the afternoon."

Patty smiled then she sobered. "Do you understand why?"

"Why?"

"All of this is too much for me. A house as beautiful as this isn't meant to be empty. It should be filled with love and lots of children running around."

"This house could never be empty. It's already filled with love. You and your husband did that. You filled it until it was overflowing, and you shared that with Tuesday. She loves this house because this was the only place she's ever felt it. This home is her safe place, you gave that to her. But, Patty, I want you to know, this old house isn't her only safe place, not anymore. And though she'll always want to be here, she won't need to be to know she's loved."

"I suspect you're right on all counts, Jackson." I didn't miss the wetness brimming before she sat tall and said, "Since I have a feeling that one day, and I'll say, I hope it's soon, you'll be sharing in the responsibilities of this old house, you should know the toilet off the dining room runs nonstop. And there's a sink on the second floor that no one can seem to stop from dripping. Both drive me crazy."

"Noted."

"The back porch screen door squeaks something fierce," she continued.

"I'll make sure I fix it."

"Don't let her hide from you," Patty whispered. "My Tuesday, she's a good girl. That mother of hers did a number on her and I can't bring myself to think of that Travis. She will love you until her dying breath, that's just her way, but you'll have to work—"

"I have no intentions of allowing your granddaughter to slip through my fingers. I know who she is, I've known from the moment I saw her."

"And who is she, Jackson?"

"She's my forever."

———

I'D MADE the grocery store run, helped Tuesday make dinner—we ate in the breakfast nook because Tuesday liked the view of the orchard—and we'd cleaned up. I was surprised when Emma, the nurse from Autumn Lakes, showed up, but neither of the women were. They'd forgotten to tell me she'd be over every day to help Gran. Not that she needed much. Luckily the fire hadn't impeded Patty's recovery. She'd only had two more days at the home to finish up her physical therapy before she was released anyway.

Patty had long ago converted what would be considered the live-in maid's quarters into her bedroom. She'd explained going up and down the stairs was tiresome. She'd also told me she couldn't remember the last time she'd been on the third floor. It was a shame. But Patty didn't seem the least bit sad about it. She laughed and smiled when, over dinner, she'd told stories about playing hide and seek with Tuesday when she was a child. One time, Tuesday was so well hidden neither grandparent could find her and even after they'd both called out that they'd given up and the game was over Tuesday still hadn't come out. It was hours before she came down with a smile of victory. Patty explained that was the day they knew Tuesday's competitive nature needed to be tamped down a bit.

———

EMMA AND PATTY had gone into her downstairs bedroom and Tuesday was giving me the tour. We were still on the first floor, and I'd learned the front room with the deep red walls and the bar was called the salon. That was where most of the entertaining had been done. To the side of the fully-stocked bar there was a hallway that led to the ballroom. The herringbone pattern, wooden floor was polished to a high gloss, a contrast to the flat finish of the bottom half of the cream-colored wall, before a chair rail divided the top, wallpapered half. That room opened to a formal dining room. And through there you could enter the kitchen and eating area.

The other room with the piano, which also had a harp in front of one of the large windows was the music room. Various instruments and old sheet music were exhibited. There was a hallway off the back of the room that led to the billiards room, everything was done in rich greens and velvet. The room smelled of cigar smoke, giving it a rich, earthy feel.

Through there you entered the library. There were so many books, floor-to-ceiling, neatly displayed in built-in cherry cases it would take you a lifetime and you still wouldn't get through half of them. High, wing-back chairs and side tables were positioned throughout the room. I wouldn't call them comfortable looking, but they were expensive.

It was huge.

It was also a lot to take in.

"That's the bottom floor." Tuesday finished her tour, ending back in the foyer.

"It's beautiful," I told her.

"It's stuffy, as Gran would call it. The bottom floor was always set up for entertaining. She called it the show-off floor. The second story was for living."

"And she's stuck on the first floor," I muttered.

"Exactly. She has a small sitting room in her bedroom. Whenever I come over that's where we go."

That was something, at least, but I now understood why Patty wanted something more manageable. Living alone in this house would be lonely. There'd be no getting away from it.

"Wanna go up?" she asked.

"How long we got before Emma leaves?"

Good God, the smile that broke free on Tuesday's face was nothing short of a marvel. I liked what the flirty grin said she'd thought I meant. Though, she was wrong, I wasn't taking us there again until we talked. And this conversation was likely to send her into a tailspin. But I wasn't budging, not this time. I shouldn't have the first time. The only good decision I'd made was that while I may've made love to her with my fingers and my mouth, my dick had stayed confined.

"At least an hour," she answered.

"That enough time?"

"I don't know, you tell me."

I pulled her into my arms hoping to soften the blow. "I'm not taking us there again—"

"Oh." Her smile faded.

"Let me finish." She nodded, but her face remained blank. "Until we get a few things straight."

"Like?"

"I've already laid it out for you. I didn't lie when I told you what I wanted. You agreed to give me twenty-four hours, that's slid into forty-eight, but, Sweetness, I'm not gonna renegotiate every day, asking for an extension. So, the conversation we're gonna have is to check where your head's at. Where *you're* at in all of this."

"I know where my head's at," she whispered.

"Yeah? You ready to get off that fence?"

She nodded, and a cautious hope started to bloom.

"Yeah? You ready to share?"

"Yes."

Caution fell away, and all I was left with was hope. My eyes drifted closed and in the darkness a weight lifted.

Thank fuck.

Jackson grabbed my hand and laced our fingers together. With a firm tug, he led me to the stairs and then up them. I waited for the nerves to hit, but they never came. This was it, I had to let it all hang out, let him in, and jump off the fence he'd rightly accused me of sitting on. Even though I'd let Jackson in the best I could, I needed to do better.

When we got to the top of the stairs, I told him, "You were right. I was on the fence. Or, actually, I wasn't even on it, I was hiding on the other side of it. I'm ready to get off now."

We walked the short distance to an old, worn, comfortable couch. This was the area we'd used as a family room when I was growing up. The second floor was what I considered home, my real home.

Jackson sat down and pulled me onto his lap.

"Sweetness, I need you to be sure." He held his hand up when I started to interrupt him. "Really sure, Tuesday. I haven't been holding back. Not emotionally. I've been letting this play out, but I'm all in. I can't explain how I know, but I do. You're it for me. I never believed in love at first sight until I saw you standing in Nick's living room. There's this glow about you. All it took was seeing you smile, and you awoke something in me. I've heard my dad and uncles talk about it, but I'd always thought they were blowing sunshine. I've listened to stories about how my uncles met my aunts and the struggles they went through, denying they felt what they'd felt. Hell, my dad let my mom move to Florida even though he knew he loved her. I am not stupid and I learned something important from them. I'm not going to hide from you, I'm not gonna play games, and I'm not gonna walk away. Not if I know you feel the same way I do. That's all I need, give me that honesty, and I won't let go."

My breath was coming out in ragged pants. I didn't know what to say. As a matter of fact, I wasn't sure I'd heard him correctly. I wanted to ask him to repeat the part about love at first sight.

Did he just say that?

"Jackson," I breathed. I couldn't find any other words.

"If we're doing this, we're all in," he told me.

"All in," I repeated.

"Tuesday, I swear if you try getting back on that fence, I'm burning the motherfucker down."

"Okay," I agreed.

Though I wouldn't need him to.

"So we're doing this?"

There was only one answer, so I told him, "Yes."

His eyes went from turbulent to cloudy. There was a storm brewing and it was seriously hot. So hot, in fact, I shivered. He'd looked at me a lot over the last few weeks. Sometimes his gaze was full of lust, sometimes it was soft and lazy, but no less passionate. But never like this. Never with a stare so penetrating I could feel it in my soul. Or maybe he had, but I'd been so blinded by stupidity I was too afraid to acknowledge it. But I didn't think that was the case. I wouldn't have been able to deny the stir that look was creating.

"You have no idea how badly I wanna take you back to your room and finally do all the things I've been fantasizing about."

Jackson's voice had gone deep and husky, and that made me shiver.

"Why don't you?"

I tried my best to wiggle my hips and grind my ass against his thick erection, but he easily halted my movements.

"Because we have more to talk about and your

grandmother is downstairs. This house is huge, Sweetness, but I plan on doing things to you that will make you scream."

"Oh, that's disappointing."

"What is, me making you scream, or you having to wait for it?"

"Waiting for it."

The storm had passed, and I got Jackson's lazy smile. Butterflies were dancing in my belly and a tingle of self-doubt was trying to creep in. I tamped it down the best I could. And because I'd promised him I was off the fence, I shared.

"I'm scared."

"Why are you scared?"

"I'm just afraid I'll give you everything and it still won't be enough for you."

His eyes fluttered closed, and he leaned forward, placing his forehead on mine.

"Thank you," he whispered. Something big swelled in my chest, he understood how hard that was for me. "But, straight up, Sweetness, not saying everything will always be easy, but I promise you it'll be perfect."

"You know that makes no sense, right?"

"We both have our work cut out for us," he explained. "You learning to open up and me keeping you in a place where you feel confident enough to share. But there's something you should know, I'll work my ass off for it. I'll give you everything I have and when you learn to take it and give yourself back in return, it will be perfect."

His words struck a chord. *Perfect.* I'd grown up around a perfect love. I'd watched how my grandfather had adored my grandmother. The kind of love my grandparents shared didn't just magically happen. They'd worked for it. They'd shared their lives, their thoughts, hopes, and dreams. My grandmother didn't hold my grandfather at a distance. She was brave and so much smarter than me. She'd known what she'd found in him and had pulled him close.

"I don't want perfect. I want us. I'm gonna work my ass off for you, too. I'm gonna make sure you know how much I appreciate you. I'm not gonna let you regret choosing me. I promise, Jackson, I'm all in. I won't lose you."

He was staring up at me with those cloudy eyes again. Ten minutes ago, his silence would've made me nervous now it simply settled around me. His hands on my hips were like two steel bands holding me steady. His presence was like a shroud of steadfast protection. He would keep my heart safe—I knew it.

"Kiss me, Sweetness."

This time when Jackson asked, I didn't hesitate. I placed my hands on his chest, and when he groaned, I felt my insides warm. Not with lust or need but with something wholly different, something I'd never in my life felt. Part feminine gratification that he liked my hands on him, but more of a contented happiness. I leaned forward and placed my lips on his. I waited for him to take over, but he didn't. Our kiss was gentle and light. This was not fueled by haste and lust, it was a slow exploration. Not exactly a getting to know you kiss, more of a welcome home, I'm glad you're here and want you to stay awhile kiss.

I liked this kind the most.

I wanted more of all the different ways Jackson could kiss me. But this felt like the beginning.

Jackson broke the kiss and whispered against my lips, "You know, I always thought your smile was full of hope and a promise of good things to come. But now I'm figuring out it's not just your smile. It's your kisses, too. It's in the way you look at me. It's everything about you."

"Jackson." I didn't know what to say. God, I'd been so dumb pushing this beautiful, strong, and thoughtful man away. "Thank you for not giving up on me."

"Never."

"Before you say something sweet again and make me cry, may I change the subject and ask you something?"

"Anything."

"Did someone really start the fire at Autumn Lakes?"

Since we'd been back at Gran's we'd avoided all talk of the fire. But now that we had a moment alone, I wanted to know what he knew.

"Yeah, Sweetness, someone did. And they tampered with the fire suppression system as well."

"Whoa."

"You know when I pulled the fire alarm and nothing happened?" I nodded. "That should've set off the alarm and the water mist system in that section of the building. It did neither. I don't know if the system hadn't been working and the home never repaired it, or if the person who started the fire figured out how to disengage the system."

"Could they do that?"

"If they knew where the control panel was, they could."

Holy shit, a control panel, that was it?

"Where was the fire started? Could you tell?"

"In the business office."

He was watching me closely, so he saw the moment I put it together. "The case?"

"That would be my guess, yes. No paper files made it. All of the electronics in the office are a complete loss. There were two backup servers in the room as well. Good news is, I would think being a medical facility they'd have some sort of offsite backup or cloud storage for the patient records and billing."

"Thank God, you were there."

"It's not—"

"It is. It *totally* is. Whatever you were going say "wasn't"—it was. It is a big deal. It was good luck. It worked out the way it did only because you were there. You got me and Gran out and went to work containing the fire until your buddies arrived, then you went back in with them. It could've been worse, and people could've been hurt, but they weren't. I'm proud of you."

"Thanks, Sweetness."

"You're welcome. Now do you want to see the upstairs or do you want to see if Gran's done with Emma so we can watch a movie with her?"

"Let's check on Gran."

My heart warmed some more.

———

MY EYES CAME open and the moment they did, I knew I was alone in bed. It took less than a heartbeat to admit I missed Jackson's presence.

Last night, after our conversation, we went down to Gran's room and watched a movie with her. I'd waited and waited for the panic to surface, but it never did. I'd watched him charm my grandmother, and her charm Jackson, and still nothing. No anxiety, no sinking feeling of dread, only calm contentment.

When the movie was over, I took him upstairs to my childhood bedroom, and we undressed like we'd done it a hundred times instead of never. I grabbed his discarded shirt, put it on, and crawled into bed. The second we hit the sheets he curved his body to my back and held me close. That was it. No hanky-panky, just him holding me, telling me to get some sleep.

Now I was alone in bed staring at the soft muted, sage green walls. Thinking about how much I liked Jackson holding me and wondering why the hell I'd fought him so hard. I was goddamned lucky he'd been patient or I would've missed out on something big.

Jackson Clark was not Travis. He was not my father. Jackson Clark was a man with integrity, morals, and a protective streak so wide I wasn't sure it ended. I had to trust he'd take care of my heart. On that thought, I rolled out of bed and went in search of my man.

It hadn't taken long to find Jackson. I heard them as soon as my feet touched the cool marble in the foyer.

Gran was laughing.

Jackson's deep, rumbling chuckle filled the house.

It was then it hit me, the one thing that had been missing from The Manor. Something that used to be a given when I was a child.

There was always love. Lots of it.

But somehow the laughter had faded.

Jackson gave it back to us.

I didn't move. I just stood in the grand entrance of the home that had never failed to surround me in love and enjoyed the sound of laughter.

I thought I'd known a great deal of happiness throughout my life. I had a great family, a job I loved, good friends, and a nice place to live. I'd been happy. But never like this. I'd never been filled to overflowing. With all I'd had in my life, I'd thought I had, but I'd been wrong.

My happiness had been brimming, but this morning seeing Tuesday in my tee, leaning against the counter in her grandmother's kitchen, holding a cup of coffee, smiling . . . that's when it overflowed.

She was bright and open and holding nothing back. Not her humor when she teased her grandmother, not her love when she spoke to Patty, and not her happiness when she smiled at me. It was a night and day change. Her walls had crumbled, and a blinding light shone through. Blinding. It was so bright it took every-thing in me not to turn away from it.

She was mine.

I would stop at nothing to keep it. What she gave me last night was precious. This morning's gift was beyond anything I could've imagined. She wasn't taking it back. No matter what, I was going to fight to keep Tuesday smiling and happy.

We were in my truck headed back to her place then to mine when my phone rang. I looked at the display on my dash and saw it was my dad. I hit the button on my steering wheel and the call connected.

"Hey, Dad."

"Where are you?"

His terse question had me on alert. I glanced at Tuesday as I rolled to a stop before making the left to hit her street. The happy vibe she'd been sporting was gone.

Dammit.

"Almost to Tuesday's."

"Brady caught something on the camera. He's there now checking it out. I'm five minutes out and Ethan is three."

"Fuck."

"Tuesday with you?"

"In the car, and you're on speaker."

"When you get there, straight into the house."

"Yep."

"Or turn around and go somewhere else."

"We're here," I told him as I pulled into Tuesday's driveway. Brady was out of his car and at Tuesday's mailbox.

"Right. See you soon."

Dad disconnected, and I turned to Tuesday. "Everything's gonna be okay, Sweetness."

"You keep sayin' that, Jackson, but every time I turn around something new happens to prove that's not the case."

"Look at me." I waited for her pretty brown eyes to connect with mine. All the happiness from the morning had fled. "Please—"

"I'm not gonna push you away," she told me. "I'm just . . . over this. All of it. My mom. Travis. The sick publicity stunt that just keeps on giving all these years later. My agent. Fires. Investigations. Lawsuits. I want it to be over."

"It will be. Soon. The only good news about what's happening right now is, hopefully, Brady caught something on the camera. Let's get inside and see what he found."

She nodded but didn't say anything else.

I jumped out of the truck, rounded the hood, not taking my eyes off Tuesday, helped her down, and moved her to the porch. Tuesday fished her keys out of her bag and handed them to me. Once the door was unlocked, I maneuvered her inside and waited for Brady to join us.

The storm door opened, and my dad and Brady both walked in. Dad was not five minutes out, or if he had been, he'd broken every traffic law to get to us.

"What'd you find?" I asked.

Today, Brady didn't look at Tuesday and me with the same longing I'd thought I'd noticed the last time he'd been in her house. Today, he looked pissed. Scarily pissed, and I knew why my dad and uncles had searched him out and offered him a job, it was because he had the capacity to harness the anger he was feeling right now. My guess was they'd poached him from their old unit at the Army base.

"Tuesday," my dad greeted her.

"Hi, Nolan."

"This morning I was watching the cameras." Brady jumped right in. "I saw a silver Nissan Sentra pull up to the mailbox, slip something in, and drive away. Problem is, both front and back license plates were removed. And the driver was wearing a ball cap pulled low, and black gloves. All I can verify from the video is the driver is ewhite. I'd guess a man due to the height and size, but I can't swear to it."

"So the driver was casing the house and saw you installing the cameras," Dad surmised.

"Absolutely."

"Wait. A Nissan Sentra? Old, beat up looking?"

Dad and Brady both went on alert. "You know the car?" Brady inquired.

"I've seen it. A few weeks ago, the morning after Tuesday got back from New York. I was leaving and wasn't paying attention as I backed out of the driveway. I almost hit the Sentra. They honked and swerved around me."

"Did you see the driver?" he continued.

"No. I was . . ."

I let my statement trail and before I could think of a better explanation Tuesday spoke.

"You were angry with me. It was the morning of flowers and payback. I heard the horn and went to the front window to see what it was, but you were already gone, and the street was empty."

Yes. She was correct. That was the morning of payback.

"Sweetness—"

"I'm fine Jackson. I don't know anyone with a silver Sentra. Or any color Sentra for that matter. And, before you ask, I've never seen it hanging around either."

"What was in the mailbox?" I asked.

Brady looked at my dad, waiting for his permission

before he handed it to me. A white sheet of paper had already been placed inside a Ziploc bag.

I warned you, bitch. Now you'll both pay.

I handed it back to Brady and looked down at Tuesday. She was pressed to my side, my arm over her shoulder, hers around my waist. She wouldn't be paying. Neither would I. However, no amount of reassurance would convince her of that.

There was a knock at the door and all of us turned, expecting to see Ethan. What none of us expected was to see an attractive woman, dressed in a business suit, step through uninvited. Further, I didn't expect Tuesday to tear from my arms and bear down on the woman.

Thankfully, Brady grabbed her around the waist and had her clean off her feet before she could clobber the woman.

"You cannot be believed!" Tuesday yelled. "You have some nerve coming to my house. But inviting yourself in—in-fucking-credible."

Brady set Tuesday aside, however, he didn't release her until I had an arm around her.

"We need to talk," the woman said.

"Who is this woman?" I asked Tuesday.

She turned her head to look me in the eye and if I thought she'd been hot around the collar when she was arguing with her mom, holy shit, that was nothing compared to the daggers she was throwing at the intruder.

"This *woman*, is Meredith."

"The fuck?" The growl that came forth had my dad stepping closer to me.

"Oh, good, I see you remember who she is." Tuesday's sarcastic remark had the woman standing a little taller.

"Could never forget the bitch who was behind the scheme that violated my woman."

Meredith's eyes got big before she whispered, "You know." Then louder. "Please, let me explain."

"Nothing to explain, Meredith. My mother told me everything. I think the only thing she left out is how you can sleep at night knowing what you did to me. And, now, you're trying to sue me."

"I can explain."

"No, you can't," I cut in. "There's not one single thing you can say to explain how you, a woman, no less, orchestrated a plan where a fellow woman was taken advantage of at her most vulnerable. Not one fucking thing. I don't know who's worse, you, her mother, or the piece of shit Travis. What I do know, is I'll be pushing for her to lock your ass up."

"She was blackmailing me," Meredith said.

"Who?" Tuesday asked.

"Your mother."

"Doesn't matter. Don't care what she was holding over your head. What you did, the part you played is so fucked, it doesn't begin to explain what you did," I continued.

"I know. That's why I'm here. I can't live with it anymore. She made me file the lawsuit, too."

"And why would she do that?" Tuesday asked.

"Because she's still blackmailing me. She gets the agency's cut of your bookings. When you wanted to slow down, I was relieved. I thought you were finally making your exit and the blackmail would end. But she caught wind and told me if I didn't force you to continue, she'd go public."

Tuesday was shaking in my arms. Goddamn, was there no end to all the ways Gladys made her daughter's life misery? Fucking bitch.

"So, what? You came here to lay this shit at Tuesday's feet to clear your conscience so you can sleep at night?" I asked Meredith.

"No. I came here to tell Tuesday, in person, how sorry I am. I was contacted by a Nick Clark from the FBI. He was asking questions about Travis Manning. I've already sent him all the correspondence between Gladys, Travis, and me, too. I've admitted the role I played, and he's made me aware Tuesday will be pressing charges. So, I just came to say I'm sorry in person."

Good to know my brother hadn't shared who I was. Or who he was to Tuesday.

"I hope you're not expecting forgiveness," Tuesday said.

"I'm not. I know what we did to you is unforgivable."

"You can leave now," she told Meredith.

"Okay. Well . . . I'm—"

"Save it. I don't care how sorry you are. I don't care why you did it. You think you understand what you've done to me, but you'll never fully understand until you see pictures of yourself out on the internet. You'll never know until you are emotionally raped. And make no mistake, that's what it was. I was forced against my will to see and read the most disturbing things about myself, all because you and my mother thought my career needed a boost.

"Forced. Do you understand that? I didn't ask for men to send me pictures and videos of themselves. I didn't ask to read death threats, which, by the way, have started again. All thanks to you and my mother and your greed. And don't get me started on Travis and what that pissant got out of it. So, you can take your apology and shove it up your ass. Nick was right, I am pressing charges. But, even then, you won't understand how badly you hurt me."

My arms gave an involuntary squeeze at Tuesday's

bravery. I was so proud of her for standing up for herself. Not that she'd given me any indication she wasn't the type of woman who would, but after the showdown with her mom and then the fire I knew she was worn down. But hearing her give it straight to Meredith proved how tough she was.

Brady was already at the storm door holding it open. When Meredith was slow to move, my dad stepped closer and without a word ushered her to the door. I stopped paying attention to them and turned Tuesday in my arms. I needed to see her face to gauge her reaction to this latest trauma. When her eyes met mine, I was surprised at what I found. Hurt and betrayal. The emotions weren't surprising, it was the fact she was showing them openly.

"I'm all right," she said.

"Yeah, you are. I'm proud of you."

"You are?" Her nose scrunched, and she looked at me in shock. "For what?"

"Sweetness, the past two days have been rough. Yet, here you stand, strong and tough. So damn proud of you."

She gave me a small smile before her forehead collided with my chest. I wrapped my arms around her and hugged her close.

"Now I just want the rest to be over so we can

move on and put this behind us," she said with her forehead still against me.

"Soon, Tuesday. Very soon," my dad told her.

"I hope so."

I looked over Tuesday's head at my father. When our gazes met, his slid from anger to determination. There were a lot of times in my life I was grateful to have such a good man in my corner, and each time I thought I couldn't be more thankful, I was proven wrong. I could. If my father said he was going to assist in making this end for Tuesday, he would.

Nolan Clark never made a promise he didn't intend to keep.

30

"Did you know you have a freckle behind your ear, next to your hairline?" Jackson asked.

We were lying in my bed after a very long and full day. He was down to his boxers, and I was in the tee he'd taken off and a pair of panties. I was also trying my hardest not to jump him. And he was trying to torture me by pointing out my freckles. He had to be close to done. There was no way I had so many in places I couldn't see, like behind my ear, next to my hairline.

I knew he was trying to lighten the day we'd had. After Meredith had left, Ethan had shown up. Then Nick was called, and he came over. Next Mercy had called about the fire, then she and Jason had shown up. The initial findings had come back; the fire had been purposefully set in the business office.

The good news was, there was off-site back-up for

the patient records and billing. The bad news, it had been manually turned off over thirty days ago. Mercy's case was going to take a hit, but she was confident the fire only helped prove guilt once they could narrow down the players involved.

Ethan's face had gone from furious to stone the more he learned what had transpired over the last two days. I think he was feeling it the most, what had happened to me and what was still happening. Not that Nolan wasn't a father, but he just had boys. And Nick's kids were still tiny bundles of baby goodness. But Ethan had a little girl whose tenth birthday was coming up, and he was a cop. He knew what kind of evil lurked on the streets, but what had happened to me was different, there was no stranger danger. The people who'd taken advantage of me and hurt me were people I trusted. One who was supposed to always protect me. One I'd stupidly thought loved me. And one I'd thought was a friend. So, Ethan was getting an unfortunate lesson, though I figured he already knew, on how vulnerable his beautiful daughter was. Which sucked.

After all that ruckus was over and everyone had left, we'd headed to Jackson's so he could pack a bag. Emma was staying with Gran, and he was staying with me.

I wasn't surprised to find Jackson lived in an

upscale condo complex. The buildings were nice, the landscaping immaculately kept. Jackson's unit was in the newest part of the community, nestled in the very back of the housing tract. His floorplan was open and the whole downstairs was one big open room with his kitchen and a bathroom off the left side of the living room. His furniture was modern and sleek. Upstairs there were two bedrooms, another bathroom, and a laundry room. His bedroom was huge with double French doors that led to a balcony. He'd told me he'd picked this condo because of the view. You could lie in his bed with the doors open and see nothing but trees.

"What has you thinking so hard, Sweetness?"

"I was just thinking about your place," I told him.

"What about it?"

"How sad it is that, with you being a man and all, your pad is decorated way more than mine is."

"I noticed that, too."

I turned in his arms so I was facing him. "When I moved in here, everything was so screwed up, I didn't have the will or energy to do anything to this place. The longer I lived here with bare walls and bland color, the more I got used to it. That's what's packed in the garage. All of my paintings, boxes of books, knick-knack shit, throw pillows, that kind of stuff."

"Now you won't have to live with bare walls and bland color. The Manor is far from boring."

"It's not boring," I agreed.

"Hey?" Jackson's hand stopped trailing up and down my arm and went under my chin, forcing me to look at him. "What's wrong?"

"It's a big house," I told him unnecessarily.

"Yeah."

"I don't think I'm going to move in right away."

"I can understand that. So, then, we'll unpack your garage and brighten this place up."

"You understand?"

"Sweetness, Gran's house could fit five of my parents' houses in there and still have room to spare. It's huge. It would get lonely. So, yeah, I understand. I also understood before I saw it why it meant so much to you, but after being there, seeing it myself, spending one morning in that kitchen with your grandmother smiling, all that morning sun spilling in making it all that much more beautiful—I really got it. You wanting to keep the house in the family is not selfish. You not wanting to move into it right away, isn't either. And your grandmother won't think it is either."

He got it.

Completely and totally understood how I felt. I would move in, I wanted to live there exclusively, but I needed to sort out the rest of my life first. I wouldn't move there, only to bring all the shit swirling around me to the place that has only ever known love.

"Thanks for taking care of everything today with your family," I told him.

His features softened, and his hand slid from my chin up and across my cheek before he tucked a hank of hair behind my ear.

"Don't have to thank me for that, Sweetness."

"Yet I did." His lips twitched in amusement, and I returned his grin.

"You have no idea what that pretty smile does to me." He used the pad of his thumb to trace the curve of my lips. "It's like magic."

His hand moved, down my neck, my shoulder, skimming its way over my arm, to my hip, and finally to the back of my thigh. He hitched my leg up and over his and let it rest but didn't let go. I was trying to stay focused, he looked like he wanted to say more, but all my concentration was on the thrill of his touch.

"Every time you aim one my way, Sweetness, it never fails to do two things."

His voice had deepened and that sent a thrill through me, too.

"What are those?" I managed to ask.

"Makes all my blood rush straight to my dick, and at the same time hits me in the heart." His hand dove into the back of my panties and he cupped my ass. It didn't take long for his fingertips to slide lower and find my already drenched slit. "Sweetness," he groaned.

This time, when he spoke, I didn't get the thrill, I got fireworks. That's because two very thick fingers drove deep. My back arched at the intrusion and my eyes drifted closed.

"Makes me want to fight for the rest of my life to be the one who gets to see it."

Did he just say, the rest of his life?

"Sweetness?"

"Huh?"

"I'm gonna fuck you now."

Bright lights were sparking behind my eyes and all I was seeing were flashes of purples and reds and blues. I lost his fingers but only so he could yank my panties down my legs, then rip his tee over my head. By the time I had my wits about me he was looming over me. Turbulent, lust filled, brown eyes stared down at me, but all I felt was adoration.

"Baby, you are so fucking beautiful, but it's what's beneath all that beauty I can't get enough of. I'll take the long way, the hard way, the shortcut, whichever way I have to go to keep it. I want it all, Tuesday. Whatever way I have to prove it, I will. I want your beauty, I want your smiles, I want what's underneath it all, and I promise to protect it."

"Kiss me, Jackson," I whispered, unable to take anymore of his sweet.

"That's my line," he protested.

"Well, it's mine right now." I smiled up at him and something sparked, I saw it. His face changed, and I knew blood was running south, and nervousness hit. Which was silly considering not only had I already had sex with him, but he'd kissed, licked, and nibbled every inch of me. What hadn't happened was, I hadn't had the chance to do the same. Smartly, I wasn't going to ask for the chance to return the favor. Not right now, when Jackson looked like he was getting ready to devour me.

"The pill?" he asked.

And even though it was hard to think when Jackson's hard body was pinning me to the bed, and I could see his pectoral muscles flexing as he held himself above me, I knew what he was asking, therefore, I answered, "Yes."

"Fuck."

That was the last thing he said before he drove his dick in deep.

My breath fled, and I'd swear on all things holy I'd never felt anything better.

Nothing better.

Not ever.

And he hadn't even kissed me yet.

"Mouth," he clipped.

I righted my head and gave him my mouth. Jackson went down on his elbows and both of his hands fisted my hair. I followed suit and plunged mine into his and gave it a tug, forcing his lips to press harder on mine.

I felt it. It was all around me, surrounding us. More than lust. Better. Bigger. Heavier. The profound realization that we were encased in love. Jackson was moving inside of me, his tongue was dancing with mine, our bodies connected in every way they could be, but it was more. I could feel his heart pounding and he was healing mine. I knew it, down to my soul, just him driving deep was knitting me back together.

His words had started it, his steadfast pursuit had further helped, and our bodies finally connected in a way that was honest had cemented it.

"Wrap those long legs around me, Sweetness."

He jerked my leg where he wanted and came up on his knees bringing me with him so I was sitting on his dick and he was back on his haunches.

"Lift one up, baby."

I looked down to see what he wanted. "One of these?" I asked, cupping both of my breasts, pushing them together but making sure I teased him by gliding my thumb over my nipples.

"Goddamn," he groaned, before he demanded, "Give me one, Sweetness."

"Ever heard of the word please, handsome?"

"Please," he growled. When I lifted a breast, he

didn't waste any time sucking my nipple into his mouth.

"Jackson," I panted as his tongue circled my nipple. "More."

I started unlocking my legs from around his back so I could plant my knees on the bed when he moved and I was again flat on my back, but Jackson was still upright.

"Hands above your head. Flat against the headboard."

My arms went over my head and when he started drilling hard, I understood the wisdom of his request. I was keeping myself steady and he was holding my ass up high with one hand, and the other was working my clit.

"Good Christ, I've never seen anything as sexy as my cock disappearing into your pussy. Dippin' in and coming out covered in your cream." His gaze lifted from our connection, lingered on my breasts moving with the rhythm of his thrusts. I felt that everywhere, like a physical touch. There was no hiding he liked what he saw, even if he hadn't just told me he did. I wished I could see what he was seeing because it sounded hot as fuck. "Yeah, I'm burning that fucking fence down and anything else you try to hide behind. You're mine. All mine, Tuesday. No matter what, I'm keeping you."

My insides spasmed, and his eyes flared. "Take it, baby."

His thumb on my clit worked faster, and I couldn't hold back, not my hips reaching up to meet his thrusts, not the shout of pleasure that tore from my throat.

"Hell, yeah, Sweetness. There it is."

Sweet, *sweet* bliss.

———

IT WAS SOMETIME after we were done, after we'd both cleaned up, and he'd gathered me in his arms. Jackson kissed the top of my head while his arms were holding me close and he murmured into my hair, "The beauty that is beneath is so much more than I imagined. It's everything."

Jackson fell asleep.

I did not.

I was wide awake thinking of all the ways I'd almost fucked up.

But I hadn't.

I was happy. And, if I'd let him, Jackson would work to make us happier.

31

"Knock, knock." I opened Mercy and Jason's front door and yelled.

"Why do you always announce your arrival?" Jason asked as he shoved his phone and wallet in his pocket while standing close enough to the front door he might need to get his hearing checked from my announcement.

"Um. Because I don't want to walk in on the two of you playing hide the sausage."

Same excuse I always gave. I had a key but I didn't use it unless they knew I was coming over. And I still yelled when I opened the door. One part for their benefit, the other part to save my eyes from seeing things they couldn't unsee.

"Stop calling my dick a sausage," Jason demanded.

Mercy joined us in her entryway and, obviously,

found his outburst funny because she laughed before she told me, "You know he gets rather offended when you insult his manhood."

"I didn't say what kind of sausage. And for the record, I wasn't referencing those little cocktail wieners. I was thinking more along the lines of a Bratwurst."

"Seriously, Mercy. Make her stop."

She didn't make me stop. She was almost bent double and cracking up when she added, "Luckily for me, you are correct."

"Christ," Jason mumbled.

He was full of shit and I knew it. Not only were his lips curving up, but we'd been through this skit a hundred times. I asked if they were playing hide the sausage and he complained I'd called his penis a sausage.

"Just wait until I get to knock on your door and ask Jackson where his sausage is," Mercy proudly said.

"Babe, you are not asking my cousin where his dick is. Not ever. Not even as a joke."

"Come again?" Jackson asked from behind me.

Shit, I really wished Jackson had stayed in the car and hadn't heard our embarrassing exchange. He'd driven me over so he could pick up Jason. They were headed to the batting cages, while the girls all met at Mercy's to go over wedding plans.

"Nothing," Mercy and I said at the same time.

"Oh, hell no. Finally, I'm not outnumbered. Cousin, please tell these two it is not cool to call a man's dick a sausage."

Mercy and I both stood with our arms crossed over our chests, brows raised, and waited. The longer Jackson took to answer, the larger my smile became. When his eyes started dancing, I knew I'd won.

"I don't know, Jay, I'm telling you right now, Tuesday wants to play hide the sausage, I'm game. She can call it pretty much anything she wants except junk, because *it* is not that."

I busted out laughing, and Mercy soon followed. By the time I was done I had to wipe a tear from my eye.

"Fuckin' perfect," Jason grouched.

"I was thinkin' the same thing," Jackson said.

My hilarity died when I saw the look Jackson was giving me. I knew that look well, and it never failed to dampen my panties. Luckily, Mercy knocked my shoulder with hers, pulling me from my sex-fueled thoughts.

"Well, you two better hit the road," Mercy said.

With a quick kiss as he passed Mercy, Jason made his way to the door.

"What are you waiting for Jack?" I asked when he didn't follow Jason.

"For my woman to get her ass over here and give me a kiss."

Well, okay then, I guess we'd moved to public displays of affection. I took the three steps needed to get to Jackson, leaned my head back, and gave him a soft but firm kiss.

"See ya', Sweetness."

"Yeah. See ya'."

The guys left and Mercy turned on me, grabbed my hand, and yanked me into her dining room. Once we were there, she ordered me to spill.

While we were putting out the spread of lunch meats and cheeses, along with three different kinds of breads, fixings, and condiments I spilled. I told her about the conversation Jackson and I'd had at Gran's, the next morning, and what had happened last night after she'd left my house.

Through it all, I got a bunch of "wows" and "I knew its" but other than that she didn't interrupt. I was finishing up filling her in as we were arranging the last of the food.

"Well, don't you look happy." Mercy smirked.

"Don't be smug."

"I'm your best friend, I'm allowed to be smug," she informed me. "Besides, you're in my house. I'm the boss. If we were at your house, you could be the boss."

"I'm happy," I confirmed.

She brushed a non-existent piece of something off the skirt of her dress and looked at me sweetly. "I'm happy, too."

I knew she was. Mercy soon-to-be-Walker was the best friend anyone could ever ask for.

Her face split into a huge smile before she said. "We have like two minutes before everyone gets here so there's no time for details. Besides, you've been smiling since you arrived, so I can guess that he's good in the *energetic* kinda way." That comment was complete with her brow wagging up and down. "Right?"

"I can confirm he's better than good in the "energetic" kinda way."

"Please, sweet baby Jesus, don't be talking about Jackson." Mercy and I both peered around the corner to see Quinn Walker standing there holding a huge salad bowl.

"Would you prefer we were talking about your brother?" Mercy asked her soon-to-be-sister-in-law with a smile.

"Hell, no," Delaney answered for her, coming to a stop next to her sister.

"Are the twins coming?" Mercy asked, thankfully changing the subject.

I knew Delaney pretty well. We were buds. She'd

come to my place a few times to hang out. At first, we only got together when Mercy had time, but then it slowly morphed into the two of us forging our own friendship. I knew there were things about the time she and Mercy were kidnapped that still plagued her. Delaney had never opened up to me about her demons, and I didn't push. All I knew was whatever happened cut her deep.

I didn't know Delaney before it happened, and the only comment Mercy had ever made to me was that she was afraid Delaney would never heal. Not because she couldn't, but because she didn't want to. I'd never wished my best friend to be so wrong before. And it wasn't lost on anybody the way Jason and his dad stared at her anytime they were around.

"Yeah, they stopped by Aunt Reagan's first. They'll be around," Delaney told her.

Quinn made her way to the dining room and turned to Mercy, "Wow. All of this looks great."

"Thanks."

I loved that my best friend was beaming. For so long it was just the two of us. Now she had Jason's sisters, too. All four of them had welcomed her into the fold. Actually, all of them had, the whole family. Not that I found it surprising because Mercy was a likable person.

"Drinks?" Mercy asked.

"Yeah, I'll go with you." Delaney followed, leaving Quinn and me in front of the mammoth spread of food.

"Before they come back, I just wanted to say thanks for making Jackson happy." Quinn smiled at me.

"Have you talked to him?"

My stomach suddenly felt like there was a swarm of butterflies circling. Quinn was Jackson's best friend, of course he'd talked to her.

"I don't have to talk to him to know. Your smile says everything. If you're smiling and happy, then he's happy. So, thank you."

I didn't know what to say, and, thankfully, I didn't have to. Mercy poked her head around the corner and called for us to come into the kitchen.

We spent the rest of the day laughing, drinking, eating, and most importantly putting the final touches on Mercy and Jason's wedding plans.

———

"DID YOU HAVE FUN?" Jackson asked.

"I did. Did you and Jason?"

We were in Jackson's truck on the way back to my place. My stomach was full, and the six of us had polished off three bottles of wine. With Mercy and I being the only two not driving, we drank the lion's share, so I was a little tipsy, too.

"We did. Hit a few balls, then headed to the clubhouse and had a few beers," he told me then asked, "Did you guys finish everything up?"

"I don't understand how the men got out of wedding prep. I thought everyone was supposed to participate," I grumbled. "There was a lot to finish, but, yeah, it's done. We even wrote out the place cards."

"Place cards?" Jackson chuckled. "It's just family. I think we can all manage to find our seats without name cards."

"That's not the point. Mercy wanted pretty monogrammed cards on the tables. And so what if it's just family? It's a wedding. It's supposed to be fancy."

Jackson pulled to a stop at a red light and looked over at me.

"Is that what you want?"

"It's not my day; it doesn't matter what I want. Mercy gets whatever she wants."

"No." He shook his head. "Your wedding. Do you want a big, fancy church wedding, or a small, fancy, backyard, family wedding?"

"Um . . ."

Unlike many young girls, I'd never fantasized about my future wedding. I had no idea where or what kind of celebration I'd want. And the longer I thought about it, the more I wondered why that was. Why hadn't I ever allowed myself to dream about the day I'd walk down the aisle?

I was thinking how weird that was when Jackson's next words rocked my world.

"You should start thinking about it, Sweetness."

"What?"

Was he serious?

"Where do you think this is headed?"

He *was* serious.

I couldn't breathe. My lungs were burning from the lack of air moving in and out of them.

"Babe, I told you I was all in. So, I'll ask again, where did you think this was going?"

"It's only been like a hot minute," I told him when I was finally able to suck in some oxygen.

"And?"

Was he nuts?

"That's just crazy," I told him.

"Probably."

"You can't know after only a hot minute."

"Sweetness, I told you I knew the second I saw your smile from across the room. Knew it then, know it now. Another day, another week, another year, doesn't matter, I don't need time, because I already know what I know."

He was crazy. But damn if I didn't like the way he thought.

"Something small. At The Manor. There's a clearing in the orchard, it's beautiful. I don't want anything big. I don't even think I want a big, traditional dress. Something simple and elegant. Maybe even a sundress depending on what time of year it is. I don't want anyone to be stressed. Just a celebration and good memories."

Huh. It seems I *could* be that woman, I just needed the right man by my side.

32

I had a new favorite way to wake up.

Not that I'd had one in the past, but this, right here, with Tuesday's bare ass snug against my morning wood, with my arms wrapped tight—nothing better.

This was how I wanted to wake up for the rest of my life. I'd learned a long time ago not to question my instincts. And every instinct I had, told me Tuesday Knowls would be my wife. She was the woman who would give me babies. She'd be the one walking through life with me, and if I went before her, she'd be the one I waited for on the other side.

That morning, unlike the others, I didn't prepare for the fallout. I didn't brace as I waited for her to open her eyes. I simply enjoyed the feel of her, because I could and I wanted to.

Last night when we got into her bed, she attacked.

There was no other way to describe it. Tuesday was the aggressor, and I learned those pretty, full lips could do something else besides steal my breath when they curved up into a smile.

She'd tasted every inch of my chest and stomach. She was torturously slow in her exploration. By the time she'd made her way to my dick and fisted it, fluid was freely leaking. Upon seeing what she'd created she promptly lapped it up before she sucked me deep and commenced giving me the best blowjob I'd ever had.

She was talented, but it was her excitement that made it out of this world. She moaned and mewed around my cock as she glided up and down. It was wet and sloppy with lots of tongue. I was begging for her to pull off so I didn't blow in her mouth. By the time she climbed on top of me and rode my cock, I was counting backward from one hundred to stop myself from climaxing.

I didn't have to tell her to keep her eyes on me, she was watching, memorizing my every reaction and when she saw something she thought I liked she did it again. She fucked me senseless and when she finally came, in screaming, wild abandon, *I* watched. Seconds after she was done and she smiled down at me, I blew. That was all it took for me. Her perched on my lap, my dick deep inside of her, neither of us moving. Her smile took me there.

"Morning." Her husky voice pulled me from my memory.

I tightened my arms around her and shoved my face in her neck. "Morning," I mumbled.

"Mmm." Tuesday wiggled her ass against my hard-on.

"Sweetness," I warned.

"Jackson," she returned and pushed back again.

"Last warning, Tuesday."

She didn't heed my warning. Her hand found mine resting on her stomach and she started moving it between her legs. We hit the soft curls between her thighs, and she pushed my middle finger in with hers.

"Jesus."

I shoved mine deeper and our fingers tangled together in her pussy.

"You like fingering yourself for me, Sweetness?"

"Yes," she hissed.

Together we brought her to the edge. I yanked our fingers free and fisted my cock. Keeping us on our sides, I lined myself up from behind and slid home.

"Jackson!"

Fuck I loved hearing her moan my name.

"Yeah, Sweetness."

"Harder."

Damn, I loved that, too.

I drove in, and at the same time, Tuesday shoved her ass back to meet my thrusts.

"Touch yourself, Tuesday."

I felt her fingertips brushing my shaft every time I pulled out. Sexy as fuck. Knowing she was rubbing her clit while my dick was working her tight, sleek pussy was too much.

I jerked her leg up higher, going deeper and harder with my thrusts.

"Faster, Sweetness. I'm gonna blow."

"Almost."

My balls were drawing up, heat had started to spread, and I was seconds from losing it.

"Come on, baby, come with me."

"Jack. Don't stop."

There it was, her pussy clamped down, and I planted deep, letting her climax detonate mine.

The words "I love you" were on the tip of my tongue as hot jets of come spilled into her. I held them back, not because I didn't mean them, but because when I first said those words to her we'd be face-to-face so I could see her smile and know she'd felt them.

———

"ARE you coming with me to see Gran today?"

I glanced over my shoulder to see Tuesday pouring

her second cup of coffee, her wet hair wrapped up in a towel, face free of makeup, and toned, tanned legs on display.

She was beautiful.

"Yeah. Brady will be over this afternoon to install your alarm. We don't have to be here when he's working. I thought we could hit Tommy's for lunch."

"Tommy's Burgers?" she questioned.

"Yeah, you been?"

"Um, hello, they only have the best chili fries known to man. Though, I limit them to once a year."

"Once a year? Babe, that's a travesty."

Her hip hit the counter and she leaned to the side with her elbow resting on the granite top. She stared off into nothing for a second before she blinked and refocused on me.

"You know, you're right. Depriving myself of the things I like *is* a travesty. For years I couldn't wait to break free of my mother's bullshit. Yet, when I'd had the chance, I didn't. Her shit was so ingrained, she didn't even need to be around for me to follow her rules. No more. No more limits. No more rules. I want to be happy and if that means I eat five donuts, or five Tommy's burgers, I'm gonna do it. If that means I never step foot in front of another camera, that's what it means. And, Jackson, I don't want to."

"Then don't."

"Then don't," she repeated. Shrugging her shoulders she added, "Guess it really is that easy, isn't it?"

"It is. If you don't want to model, don't. If you want five Tommy's burgers, I'll get them for you. If you want to unpack your garage and breathe some life into this house, then that's what I'll help you do. Whatever you need to be happy, I'll get for you."

"And if I told you all I needed was you in my kitchen making awesome coffee and handing out advice over breakfast?"

Christ, that felt good.

"Then, I'd say it's my lucky day. Because, Sweetness, that's a given."

"And what do you need to be happy?"

That didn't just feel good, that felt like a shot of whiskey straight to my veins. Warm as it slid down until it burned all over.

"You. Just you. Any way you'll let me have you. Standing in your kitchen, lying with you in your bed, sharing our day, out on the town, watchin' a movie, across from you at dinner, under you, over you, any goddamn way I can have you. As long as, at the end of every day, I get that pretty smile. I'm ecstatic knowing I'm the man who's going to have it for a lifetime."

"I know it hasn't been too long, but I need you to know, even when I was pushing you away, I was the happiest I've ever been. Even then, I knew the best part of my day was going to be when you showed up unannounced and scared the hell out of me."

Fuck, fuck, fuck. She was killing me.

"You totally left your door unlocked for me."

When that slow smile hit her face, I wasn't prepared, therefore, when I saw it, the intensity of it, I jerked in surprise.

"I totally did," she admitted.

"Bedroom," I growled as I stalked toward her.

"Bedroom? What about Tommy's?"

"Lunch is gonna have to wait, Sweetness."

"But, what about my five burgers?" Damn, but I loved Tuesday's playful side.

"We're gonna help you work up an appetite."

Her arms wrapped around me as soon as I stopped in front of her. "Does that mean I get to be on top again?"

"Whatever you want, Tuesday. But we're finishing with you on your knees."

Her smile slipped, and her eyes turned hazy. "Whatever you want, handsome."

Goddamn, I liked that, too.

33

I didn't eat five burgers yesterday, and it wasn't because of my lack of appetite. When Jackson had said he was going to help me work one up, he'd meant it. Not only did he mean it, he delivered. He let me climb on top but then cut my fun short when he proclaimed, I was "done fucking around" and placed me on my hands and knees, showing me another way he could bring us to the edge of insanity before he provided bliss.

Thinking of all the ways I'd almost screwed this up had me wanting to go back in time and duct tape my mouth shut. God, I'd been so stupid. So stupid. I needed to think of ways to make it up to Jackson. He'd tell me it wasn't necessary. I knew he'd say, as long as I was smiling that was all he needed. But I had to give him more. He'd worked his ass off proving to me I was safe to be who I wanted to be, and he was a safe place for me to land.

Jackson left for work, starting his twenty-four-hour shift. I knew the only reason he hadn't called in and changed his schedule was because Brady had finished installing the alarm. He was also monitoring the cameras. Thankfully, no more letters had been left. No flowers, no calls, no emails. I was hoping it was over.

My mother had also scurried her lying ass back to Hawaii. I only knew this because my father had called my grandmother to inform her his wife would no longer be an issue. He was right, because as much as some people may've thought it made me a horrible daughter, I was going to press charges against my mother for the role she'd played in my humiliation.

Nick assured me, with Meredith's confession and the evidence they had, it was an open and shut case. He also told me, he wouldn't be surprised if all three of them tried to make a plea deal. Which meant I wouldn't have to testify, so a plea deal sounded good to me.

Yesterday, Jackson had checked the mail, declaring I was going nowhere near the mailbox, even though no one had been caught on camera. He tore open a letter from my attorney before handing it to me after he'd read it. The dismissal of Meredith's stupid, unwinnable lawsuit had finally come. It was a relief, and one less thing I had to deal with. Some would think his alpha tendencies were purely bossy, but I appreciated them for what they were—him taking care of me. Yet another reason I needed to step up my game and show Jackson how much I appreciated him.

Jackson had also sat by my side when I'd called my manager, Lambert, and told him I'd be retiring from modeling, effective immediately. Lambert wasn't surprised. He'd known how much I hated it and said he'd seen the writing on the wall years ago. He also told me he was thrilled to hear I was finally putting my happiness first and he'd be ready to help me in the future if I needed it. I knew he meant those words, he'd been a good friend to me over the years.

Mercy had also called right after Jackson had left to tell me about Autumn Lakes. The nursing home would be shut down for quite a while with all the damage to the residential side, not to mention, the business office was a complete loss.

She shared what little she could and explained they had a suspect, part of the reason was because of what I'd found in Gran's statements. The person had been careful, but the investigation had revealed a pattern. The prescriptions had only been written on certain days of the week.

Mercy was able to cross reference some of the other patients' records and found their bogus prescriptions had been written on the same days of the week. It seemed, whomever they were looking for only worked Monday, Wednesday, and Friday. The schedule confirmed there was one full-time office person and two part-timers. Only one of the three people worked the right shift. Mercy was confident she'd have an arrest by the end of the day.

Thank sweet Jesus, Gran was out of there. Clearing up the billing with the insurance company was going to be a nightmare, but nothing compared to the fire. We were lucky Jackson was there. I hadn't smelled a damn thing, and with the fire alarm disconnected it was anyone's guess how out of control the flames would've been by the time someone had noticed.

But Jackson was there. And, once again, he saved the day.

I was cleaning up after lunch, listening to my country jam on my Bluetooth speakers, at a low volume, per Jackson and his father's instructions, when there was a knock on my door. Mercy, Jackson, and Jason were all at work, so was Delaney, and Gran couldn't drive. I was going to ignore the intrusion, not wanting to buy cookies and not needing to find Jesus, when the doorbell rang.

I checked out the peephole to see a woman in a swanky business suit, hair perfectly coiled in a severe bun, with what looked to be dirt or grease on her hands. I'd never seen the woman before.

I unarmed the alarm and opened the door. Before I could say anything, the woman started. "Oh, thank God someone's home. My car was making this horrible sound. I pulled over and turned it off and now it won't start. I forgot my cell at the office; I didn't go back and get it because I was only going to grab a quick lunch. God, sorry, I'm babbling. May I use your phone?"

"Sure." I stepped aside and she entered, the storm door whispering closed behind her. "Follow me, I left my cell in the dining room."

I hadn't taken more than two steps when I felt a pinch to my neck and jerked in surprise. My hand didn't even make it to swat away whatever had bitten me. Without warning, everything became too heavy to move. Too fuzzy to walk. My ass hit the floor, and through a hazy fog I stared up at a woman I didn't know, and she smiled down at me.

"You couldn't fucking listen, could you?"

Everything went dark.

———

"YOU SAID you weren't going to hurt her." A man's voice pulled me from my daze.

"Really, Dolph?"

Dolph?

I tried to move my arms, but they wouldn't budge, neither would my legs. I was bound. Trapped. I couldn't move. When I was five and had fallen into a pool and almost drowned, I'd thought I'd been scared. And when I started to get death threats and I'd shake in fear, I'd thought I'd known the meaning of terror. Nothing, not anything I'd ever felt before, had been close to how petrified I was in that moment.

I was slowly coming back to my senses, and the first thing that hit me was the smell of gasoline, so pungent I gagged.

"Hurry up," the woman ordered.

I was violently jerked up by my bicep, pain sliced through me as my joints strained and bent unnaturally behind my back. Before I could process what was happening, I was on my feet then I wasn't. Randolph roughly swung me up and into his arms, and without my hands free I had no way to stop my face from slamming against Randolph's shoulder. My cheek felt like it'd been slit open I'd hit so hard, and I cried out in agony.

"Shut up." He held me tighter, wrenching my tied arms to the point I thought they'd come out of socket.

Everything was foggy, and even though my eyes were now open they wouldn't focus, not on anything.

Bright light and blurry silhouettes were all I could make out.

"Please don't do this," I begged, barely able to get out a whisper.

"I warned you," he hissed, his beard rubbing my cheek as he spoke. "I told you to leave it alone."

I had no idea what he was talking about, but I couldn't ask. My stomach revolted as my body shook with each step he took. The light dimmed, before it brightened, then dimmed again. With a violent shake he got my attention. "This is your fault."

"Please don't. My grandmother. I'm all she has." I still couldn't get more than a murmur out.

"You should've thought about that. I could've kept you safe. All you had to do was say thank you for the flowers, let me take you out. I *wanted* to keep you clear of this."

Flowers? Randolph had sent the flowers?

I was unceremoniously dropped into my bathtub, the door was slammed shut, and I was left in the dark.

I hadn't screamed. I hadn't fought. I was paralyzed from fear, and if the gasoline smell was anything to go by, I'd just allowed Randolph to lock me in my tomb.

I opened my mouth to belatedly call for help but no sound came out.

I should've been panicking. I should've been screaming my house down, but I couldn't. I was too disoriented to move and the only sound I made was a croak.

This was wrong. All wrong.

Please, Lord above, don't let Jackson be the one to find me.

So much had been left unsaid.

34

"So you finally broke her down," Brice said as he tossed a slice of apple into his mouth and continued to talk while crunching. "'Bout damn time."

"She's worth it," I told him, finishing up the last of my lunch.

It wasn't often the firehouse was quiet but with inspection looming, most of the squad was in the bay cleaning gear or making sure it was in good working order, giving Brice and me a rare moment of privacy.

"I hear that. The good ones are."

"Speaking of good ones, you still talking to Liza with a Z?"

No lie, that was how the woman introduced herself. She'd walked straight up to Brice, bold as brass, and said, "Hi I'm Liza with a Z." I knew Brice, therefore I knew he wasn't serious about her, he never was. He'd been telling me for years, until "the one" knocked him on his ass, he was playing the field. Considering his field was open, he tapped a lot of ass; he just never got serious.

"Nope. She asked how many kids I wanted. We finished dinner, I took her home, gently explained why I wouldn't be callin' again, and went on my merry way."

"Damn, that was quick," I noted.

"I reckon it was a record, for sure."

The piercing sound of the paging alarm cut off our conversation and we waited to hear the details of our first call out of the day.

"Engine forty-two. Truck eight. Ambulance thirty-one. Report of a house fire three one six Willow Drive."

We were both out of our seats and jogging to the bays when the page repeated the call.

I kicked off my sneakers, stepped into my boots, and was jerking my pants up by my belt when Brice turned to me and asked, "So, you thinkin' of keeping this one, or what?"

Hell, yes, I was keeping her.

Warmth slid down my chest, something I was finding happened a lot when I was thinking about Tuesday.

Tuesday.

The warmth turned to ice.

"What was that address?" I asked, yanking my coat over my tee.

"Three sixteen Willow Drive," Brice answered as he finished with his gear.

"Fuck! That's Tuesday's house!"

"Shit." I saw him looking around the bay before his gaze stopped and he yelled, "Chief! Job's at Clark's woman's house."

I was prepared to disobey an order and roll out with my squad even if he told me to stay behind when chief bellowed, "Get a move on!"

I slammed my hand twice over the Station 57 insignia proudly displayed on the red paint of the engine and climbed into the jump seat. Brice followed suit, and behind him, Louis, Mark, Pete, and Joanne followed, with Mike driving, and Captain Casey in the front seat. Mike did not delay flipping on the lights and pulling out. We cleared the building and he hit the sirens and we were off.

"She's fine, brother. You know she's probably the one that called it in."

"Yeah," I answered Brice.

She was fine, she had to be. We'd pull up, it'd be nothing, and she'd be out front waiting.

Except her motherfucking house was on fire.

"Request squad two." Came through the radio. "Engine twenty-nine, Truck five. Fire jumped. Second structure involved."

What the fuck? I stared out the window trying to remember how close Tuesday's neighbors were. They weren't, there was at least twenty-five feet of space between the two homes. There was no wind. Tuesday's house had to be fully engulfed for the fire to have jumped so quickly.

Mike turned the corner and my heart stopped.

None of the normal adrenaline that spiked right before a job was present. Nothing but ice-cold fear. So much fucking terror I was choking on it.

"She's not in there," Brice quickly said. "Slow down, brother. Breathe. Focus. This is what we do. Just like every job, slow, steady, easy. We got this."

I didn't answer, and I didn't wait until he moved. I simply climbed over him, jumped down, and took a moment to scan the area.

No Tuesday.

Nowhere.

I yanked an air pack from the compartment and belatedly noticed Brady's pickup truck was half on the curb in front of Tuesday's house.

"Fifty-seven, be ready with a hose line!" I heard Chief yell. "Aerial in place. Squad three, check the back."

For the first time since I'd become a firefighter, I was frozen. All I could do was stare at the flames as they danced, watch as the vinyl siding of Tuesday's house melted and fell away. The front windows had already exploded, red and orange flames swirled together. Thick black smoke billowed. The fire had roared to life; popping and crackling of burning wood was all I could hear. I was motionless, mesmerized by what I'd once thought was the most beautiful sight. The colors as they mixed before they were extinguished. Now, I understood the devastation.

Brice thumped me on the shoulder, pulling me from my stupor.

I ran full sprint between Tuesday's house and the nonburning one, finding Mark and Louis already surveying entry points. Joanne was using a fire rescue chainsaw to cut the impact resistant glass pane out of the sliding door frame.

Please, Sweetness, do not be in there.

"Only way in is here." Mark pointed to the kitchen window. "Maybe a four-minute pocket."

We had three minutes before we'd need to pull back. I checked Joanne's progress, there wasn't enough time to wait for her to finish with the slider. I needed to get through the kitchen window.

"Help me up."

"Whoa!" Brice yelled over the crackling, grabbing my sleeve.

"I know this house. If we only have four minutes, I'm going in."

Understanding I was right, he let go of my sleeve and hoisted me through the window. My boot went into Tuesday's kitchen sink, and I easily jumped off the counter and started to yell out, though between my mask and the roaring of the fire it would be damn near impossible for her to hear me.

"Tuesday, call out if you're in here."

The kitchen was clear. The dining room was clear. Through the thick haze of smoke, I cleared the living room and headed for the hall.

"Tuesday! Call out, baby, if you can hear me!"

"Jackson!" a male yelled.

I made it to the end of the hallway, which, thankfully, wasn't fully engulfed. I found Brady dragging Tuesday out of the bathroom.

To say my world tilted was an understatement. Her arms and legs were bound, and Brady was struggling. Without the help of oxygen, he'd never make it, and I couldn't carry them both out.

"Get that ambo ready. Two vics." I radioed in.

"Here." I yanked off my mask and placed it over Brady's head even though he was shaking his. "Don't argue with me. We have to get out of here, and I can't get you both."

"Clark, locate egress. Now." Chief's angry voice filled the room.

"Copy that. Securing victim." I shrugged off the air pack, and Brady swung it over his shoulder.

I scooped up Tuesday, trying my best to ignore her bindings, and told Brady not to stray from my back. Between holding Tuesday, the lack of oxygen, and the sweltering heat, all I could manage was a semi-fast clip, retracing my steps.

"Exit!" Chief barked, and when we made it into the dining room, I understood the urgency. The kitchen was fully engulfed, and we were surrounded. The flames crawled up the walls and covered the ceiling.

"We have one shot," I told Brady over the raging inferno. "You go first. On the other side of those flames is the sliding glass door. It's gone. You haul ass through it and when you're outside you drop and roll. They'll be ready for you.

"We're coming through the slider," I radioed in. "Is it clear?"

"Clear," Joanne answered.

"Do not—" Chief started but I ignored him.

"Only way. In three, two . . . Go! Go! Go!"

Brady took off in a full run, and I prayed I hadn't

just signed the death warrant for the man who'd risked his life for my woman's.

"Here we go, Sweetness," I told a comatose Tuesday, and with what was left of my strength I rushed through the fire.

35

"You're goddamn crazy." I heard Jason say.

"It wasn't that bad."

"That's not the way Brady tells it."

I closed my eyes and fought back the tears. It had been two weeks since a man I barely knew had endangered his own life to save mine. Fourteen days since Jackson had rescued me from the fire. Brady and me.

I don't remember any of it. At least not the part where Jackson had literally walked through fire to save me. Randolph and his crazy sister had given me a shot of diazepam and the heavy tranquilizer had knocked me out. I was lucky I hadn't died from that alone.

When I woke up in the hospital to see Jackson next to my bed, still covered in black soot and smelling like a campfire I'd been confused. I didn't even remember opening my door and letting the crazy woman into my house. It had taken nearly twenty-four hours for the memories to flood my brain, and, when they had, I'd wished I could go back to being clueless.

I didn't remember Brady breaking down the bathroom door, which, apparently, Randolph had oh-so-nicely locked on his way out. I also didn't remember Jackson coming in and saving us both.

When the memories came back, the last thing I did remember was lying in my bathtub with my hands and feet tied, thinking I was going to die. I was looking back over my life with regret. But it was right before I'd passed out, after the room had filled with smoke, I'd found peace. Even though I'd never told Jackson I'd fallen in love with him, and he wouldn't get his lifetime with me, I'd had mine with him. I'd end my life loving him. I'd started my day in bed with him, seeing him happy, and my day was ending knowing my last thoughts were about how happy he'd made me.

Thankfully, that was not where our story had ended. However, I'd been as prepared as a person could be.

"Sweetness?" Jackson called my name.

I opened my eyes and focused on the man, who I now had my third chance at finding happiness with, and smiled.

"For one day, can no one mention the fire? Mercy and Jason are getting married today. All I want to do is enjoy the day and not think about ash and flames."

"Damn, you look beautiful," he said.

"Is that your answer?"

"Tuesday, you look so damn sexy in that bridesmaid's dress, I can't even remember your question."

Nolan, Jason, Nick, Ethan, Levi, and Lenox all chuckled. I looked around Nolan's study, which I'd been told used to be a playroom for Jackson until he was too old for toys, and then Nolan had taken it over, and I was taken aback by the hotness that surrounded me. Mercy was in Nolan and Reagan's master bedroom with the women getting ready for her big day and she'd sent me down to talk to her groom.

"Sweetness," he growled.

"Sorry. Sorry." I waved a hand in front of my face. "I just don't think I've ever seen so many good-looking men in the same room."

"Tuesday," he warned.

"I mean, I've been backstage during fashion shows. And those can get pretty wild. Men in all stages of undress while they change into their next outfit. But a room full of fully dressed men? Hands down, never seen a hotter bunch."

"Why are you here?" he clipped.

"To annoy you?" I smiled.

"Now you're being cute."

"As much as this is fun and all, I need you to take something to Mercy for me," Jason cut in.

"Actually, that's why I'm here." I stepped farther into the room and held out a small box and card in Jason's direction.

"Damn," Jason murmured, overcome with emotion and handed me an envelope.

"She looks beautiful," I whispered.

"I have no doubt; she's beautiful every day."

"She can't wait to be your wife," I told him. "Thank you."

"No, thank you, Tuesday, for taking care of her until I found her."

I pinched my lips together and willed myself not to cry. God, I totally loved Jason Walker.

"Come on, Sweetness, I'll walk you back."

Jackson tucked me close and kissed the top of my head. Something I will never, *ever*, take for granted again.

"I love you, Tuesday."

I stopped midstride and looked up at him. "Uh, duh. I love you, too, Jack."

"Only you would be a smartass when I'm telling you I love you for the first time."

"It's not the first time."

"Sweetness, I've never said those words. Not to you or anybody."

"I didn't need the words. You told me when you didn't give up on me. You told me when you held me in your arms when I cried. You told me when you took my back with my mom, and by how you treat Gran. And when you carried me through a blazing fire. But, mostly, you tell me every time you look at me like I'm something special. I never need the words, Jack. I just need you."

"Fuck," he growled. "Never gonna be able to top that, babe. Never in my life will I ever be able to give you back anything close to what you just said."

———

I WATCHED Jasper Walker walk my best friend down the aisle to marry the man of her dreams. There wasn't a dry eye as we surrounded the couple while they said their vows. There was no wedding party, or maybe there were no guests and only wedding attendants because we'd all participated in their ceremony.

Mercy had everything she wanted. And Jason Walker looked like he was floating on sunshine and rainbows he was so happy. His sweet mom had cried before, during, and especially after Jason and Mercy were pronounced Mr. and Mrs. Walker. It was then she pulled Mercy into a hug and told her she was the answer to their prayers.

No one wanted to bring Kayla, Jason's first wife, into the day, but I knew something no one else did. Mercy had visited Kayla's grave first thing this morning. She also had an old gold locket that had belonged to her tucked into her flowers. Mercy's something borrowed. No one else may've agreed, but Mercy wanted Kayla there. Jason and Kayla may've been ending their marriage before she'd passed away, but they were best friends and that hadn't changed throughout their marriage, their separation, or her death. One day, I was sure she'd tell Jason. Just not today.

"What are you thinking about?" Jackson asked when he sat next to me.

It was the first time I'd sat down all day and I was exhausted.

"How beautiful the day turned out," I told him.

"It was perfect," he agreed.

Almost perfect, but there was something seriously wrong with Delaney, though I wouldn't tell Jackson that and thankfully everyone was having such a great time no one seemed to notice. Except for Jasper, he was keeping a close eye on his daughter. The only time his gaze seemed to veer off her was when they landed on Carter Lenox. He'd barely made the wedding by the skin of his teeth. He'd rushed in with less than five minutes to spare. Rushed may've been an over exaggeration, it was more like he'd limped in, but he'd done it quickly.

"Carter was eyeing Delaney, too. I wasn't oblivious to the fact something was going on between the two of them, I just didn't know what that *something* was. But Carter's patience looked to be wearing thin as Delaney had avoided him all day.

"So, I was thinking. Gran's finished movin' out of The Manor and since everything I owned is now gone, I was wondering . . ." I paused and looked around the makeshift dance floor in front of us. Honor Lenox was spinning Carson around, Honor's tiny baby bump evident in her form-fitted bridesmaid's dress. "Would you like to move into The Manor with me? I know it's soon," I rushed out. "But these last two weeks I've been living with you at your condo and, honestly, I don't want that to end."

I slid my eyes from the dance floor and chanced looking at Jackson. I wasn't sure what I thought I'd find, but his blinding smile calmed my racing heart.

———

Jackson

TUESDAY WAS FULL OF SURPRISES.

Each day she opened up more and it was a thing of beauty.

But I was hoping this conversation could have been put off for a while. Not because I wasn't ready, I was. However, I wanted a few things to happen before we moved into The Manor together. Or at least one thing.

As Tuesday liked to say, we'd only been together a hot minute, but like any member of my family would remind her, I'm a man who knows what he wants. And when I find it, I go for it.

The first chords of Dan+Shay's "Speechless" started playing, and Mercy and Jason walked to the dance floor for their first dance. The song was perfect. Both for them, and for Tuesday and me. Every time I saw Tuesday's beautiful smile light up a room I was, indeed, *speechless*. She took my breath and, in its place, left something so warm and content I could survive on that feeling alone.

I turned and scooted my chair around so I was directly facing her. Our knees were touching, and I gathered both of her hands in mine.

"I didn't want to have this conversation here," I started. Her smile faltered, but that was okay. "I wanted this to be special. I figured I'd take you out to your orchard and listen to you tell me stories of your childhood, surrounded by all the goodness and love your grandparents gave you. But, maybe now is better, surrounded by all the people who love us." I transferred both of her hands into one of mine and reached into my pocket. "Yes, I want to move into The Manor with you, on one condition. That house is more than a house, it's where we will start and grow our family. It's the place where we'll take what your grandparents started and continue the tradition of filling it with so much love it overflows." I pulled the ring I'd been carrying around since the day it was finished from my pocket and held it out for her to see. "Gran's diamonds from her engagement set and my mother's emeralds from her anniversary band make up this ring. I'll move in with you, but only after you're my wife."

"Are you—"

"Yes, Sweetness. I'm asking you if you'll marry me."

Tuesday's eyes hadn't left my trembling hand, and I started to doubt my timing. Today was supposed to be about Jason and Mercy. Their wedding day. Maybe she wanted her own day, her own special time to remember.

Shit.

"Yes." She spoke so softly I wasn't sure I'd heard her correctly.

"Yes?"

"Yes, Jackson. One condition."

"What's that, Sweetness?"

There it was, her smile. The one that'd changed my life. My weakness. My future. The smile she'd pass down to my children, and I'd get to see for the rest of my life.

"I don't want to wait. When I was in that bathtub waiting for my life to end, I realized something. I've wasted too much time. I had so many regrets. And when I thought I was going to die, my biggest regret was you and the time we'd never have. So, yes, I want to marry you, but I want to do it soon. I want to start our life, our family. You're sure, I'm sure, and there is no need to postpone getting married."

"We can absolutely not wait," I told her and slipped the ring on her finger.

Mercy and Jason were dancing off to the side, lost in their moment and everyone was watching them as they finished their first dance. All but three, that was. My mom, Gran, and my dad had their eyes set on us. All three smiling. Two of them wiping tears of joy. My dad gave me a lift of his chin, my mom a shaky, but no less happy, smile, and Gran looked over the moon her beloved granddaughter was getting her happy ever after.

"I love you, Jackson."

"Love you, Sweetness."

And finally, she leaned closer and kissed me.

————

Delaney

THE DAY HAD BEEN BEAUTIFUL, exactly as my new sister-in-law, Mercy, had intended. My dad had walked her down the cream runner that had been laid over the grass and had given her to my brother. She'd told me she'd married the man of her dreams. And by the way she looked at my brother, I believed her. I couldn't have been happier for the pair. There was so much love in the air it was contagious. Lucky for me I was no longer susceptible to the affliction.

Once upon a time, I'd thought we'd have all of this. A happy ending to our rocky start.

Carter Lenox.

My one and only.

The only man I'd ever loved. A sweet and innocent love that had grown over the years until it had consumed me. Every part of my life had revolved around when I'd see him next, when he'd call, when he'd email me. I couldn't remember a time I didn't love him.

Then it ended.

Not the love, the innocence of it. All that was left was pain and misery. Tainted love and shattered dreams. I couldn't forgive him, and he'd never forgive me if he knew what I'd done.

What I'd lost.

So, I was doing the only thing I could do, I was trying to move on. From the memories, from love, from Carter. It was time—well beyond time. Our story wouldn't end with a happily ever after.

I'd thought I was moving toward my new normal, settling into a life that no longer included Carter, when he barged back in. Just like he'd always done.

He was home from whatever mission he'd been sent on, a mission he'd never tell me about, a part of his life he'd gone to great pains to keep me away from. I knew Carter Lenox the man, not Lenox the deadly Navy SEAL. I'd never known that part of him and I never would.

I didn't know his friends, never seen where he lived in Virginia. He had stuff at my house and what wasn't hanging in my closet was still at his parents'.

So, now he was here, he'd made the trip to see Jason and Mercy get married. Carter, the man I've been trying to avoid all night, was standing across the dance floor from me talking to my dad and brother, but his eyes were on me. For as long as I could remember I'd dreamt about the next time I'd have his attention. And when I had Carter, I had all of him. Nothing in the world felt as good as being in his arms, having all his focus solely on me. But then he'd leave and I'd have nothing.

Now it didn't feel good—it felt like a dagger.

Carter broke away from my brother and started toward me. His steps were deliberate, and he had a look full of fierce determination. I glanced over Carter's shoulder to see Mercy grab Jason's bicep, halting his progress. Damn her. I didn't want to do this here. Why couldn't Carter leave it alone? Everyone would know. The secret we'd kept all these years would be for naught.

Without warning or permission, he grabbed my hand, threaded our fingers together, and pulled me smack in the middle of the dance floor. And with our families watching, he tucked me close and started to sway.

I started to pull back to leave an acceptable distance between us when he spoke. "No more."

"No more?"

"That shit is done," he growled.

"What are you talking about?"

"Me giving you space."

"Space? All you've ever given me is space, Carter."

"And that shit is done, too."

"I agree. It's done. We're done."

"We are never done, Laney."

This was not going to happen here.

"Let go of me," I hissed.

"That's never going to happen either."

"You're unbelievable. You say you love me, but you don't care how badly this is hurting me."

"I love you, with every fiber of my soul. It started the day I understood what the emotion was, and it will be true until the day I die," he told me.

I'd heard that for years, and it was always followed by a "but."

But I'm not good enough for you, Laney.

But I can't have you, Laney.

But you deserve better, Laney.

I waited for the pain to slice through me and when it did, I used it.

I cut Carter Lenox straight through and I hated every second of it.

"You're too late, Carter. We're done. I'm sorry, I just don't love you anymore." I jerked out of his arms, my eyes met his furious ones, and I used the anguish that caused, too. "Take care of yourself."

He didn't come after me.

No one did.

I made it home from Mercy and Jason's perfect day, and once and for all, I mourned the loss of young, innocent love.

The weight of it was astounding.

And I'd never be the same.

Find out if Carter can win Delaney back in Adoring Delaney

Redeeming Violet

Recovering Ivy

Rescuing Erin

The Gold Team - Susan Stoker Universe

Brooks

Thaddeus

Kyle

Maximus

Declan

Blue Team - Susan Stoker Universe

Owen

Gabe

Myles

Kevin

Cooper

Garrett

The 707 Freedom Series

Free

Freeing Jasper

Finally Free

Freedom

The Next Generation (707 spinoff)

Saving Meadow

Chasing Honor

Finding Mercy

Claiming Tuesday

Adoring Delaney

Keeping Quinn

Taking Liberty

Triple Canopy

Damaged

Flawed

Imperfect

Tarnished

Tainted

Conquered

Shattered

Fractured

The Collective

Unbroken

Trust

Standalones

Romancing Rayne

Falling for the Delta Co-written with Susan Stoker

BE A REBEL

Riley Edwards is a USA Today and WSJ bestselling author, wife, and military mom. Riley was born and raised in Los Angeles but now resides on the east coast with her fantastic husband and children.

Riley writes heart-stopping romance with sexy alpha heroes and even stronger heroines. Riley's favorite genres to write are romantic suspense and military romance.

Don't forget to sign up for Riley's newsletter and never miss another release, sale, or exclusive bonus material.

Rebels Newsletter

Facebook Fan Group

www.rileyedwardsromance.com

facebook.com/Novelist.Riley.Edwards

instagram.com/rileyedwardsromance

bookbub.com/authors/riley-edwards

amazon.com/author/rileyedwards